The DIVA Hosts a Murderer

Kensington books by Krista Davis:

The Domestic Diva Mysteries:

The Diva Cooks Up a Storm

The Diva Sweetens the Pie

The Diva Spices It Up

The Diva Serves Forbidden Fruit

The Diva Says Cheesecake!

The Diva Delivers on a Promise

The Diva Goes Overboard

The Diva Poaches a Bad Egg

The Diva Hosts a Murderer

The Pen & Ink Mysteries:

Color Me Murder

The Coloring Crook

Murder Outside the Lines

A Colorful Scheme

The DIVA Hosts a Murderer

KRISTA DAVIS

Kensington Publishing Corp.
www.kensingtonbooks.com

KENSINGTON BOOKS are published by

Kensington Publishing Corp.
900 Third Avenue
New York, NY 10022

All Kensington titles, imprints and distributed lines are available at special quantity discounts for bulk purchases for sales promotion, premiums, fund-raising, educational or institutional use. Special book excerpts or customized printings can also be created to fit specific needs. For details, write or phone the office of the Kensington Special Sales Manager: Kensington Publishing Corp., 900 Third Avenue, New York, NY, 10022. Attn. Special Sales Department. Phone: 1-800-221-2647.

KENSINGTON and the KENSINGTON COZIES teapot logo Reg. US Pat. & TM Off.

Library of Congress Control Number: 2026931878

ISBN-13: 978-1-4967-4348-0

First Kensington Hardcover Edition: June 2026

ISBN: 978-1-4967-4350-3 (e-book)

10 9 8 7 6 5 4 3 2 1

Printed in the United States of America

The authorized representative in the EU for product safety and compliance
is eucomply OU, Parnu mnt 139b-14, Apt 123
Tallinn, Berlin 11317, hello@eucompliancepartner.com

To my parents
with love and gratitude

Acknowledgments

Like many of you, I am a first generation American. I am so grateful that my parents immigrated to the United States. Both of them had been through rough times in their countries of origin, so I grew up hearing their tales of woe and caution. It was a genuine pleasure to research details about the Declaration of Independence for this book.

When I started this series in 2007, I certainly didn't have July 4th in mind. But when I went back and looked at THE DIVA RUNS OUT OF THYME to confirm Aunt Melly's name, I found that the plaque on Sophie's house designating it as a historic building was dated 1825! Never in my wildest dreams did I ever imagine that I would be writing this series eighteen years later, when her house would be two hundred years old!

As always, thanks to my writing group, Ginger Bolton, Allison Brook, Laurie Cass, Peg Cochran, Kaye George, and Daryl Wood Gerber. Daryl gets credit for Natasha's questionable contribution to the 4th of July party menu! Thanks also to my friends, Susan Smith Erba, Betsy Strickland, and Amy Wheeler who bring me back to reality.

The Divas wouldn't exist without my editor, Wendy McCurdy, who is so kind and patient, and publicist Larissa Ackerman, who doesn't get nearly enough credit for her hard work.

Last, but most important, thanks to my agent Jessica Faust, who always steers me in the right direction.

Happy July 4th!

Cast of Characters

Sophie Winston

Daisy, her mixed hound dog

Mochie, her Ocicat

Houseguests:

Paul and Inga Bauer, Sophie's parents

Hannah Bauer, Sophie's sister

Aunt Melly Eberle, Sophie's aunt

Gus Eberle, Aunt Melly's new husband

Stan Cox, Gus's friend

Roscoe O'Brien, a family friend

Cyril Chevalier, a family friend

Neighbors:

Dollie Peabody

Georgy, Dollie's cat

Joanna Kowalski, Dollie's neighbor

Julian Kowalski, Joanna's son

Tony Fontana, tour guide

Sophie's friends:

Nina Reid Norwood

Bernie Frei

Mars Winston, Sophie's ex-husband

Humphrey Brown

Natasha, domestic diva

Wanda Smith, Natasha's mother

***Police*:**

Sergeant Wolf Fleischman

Officer Wong

Sergeant Morales

Chapter 1

Dear Sophie,
Our daughter has moved to an exciting town. My husband and I would love to take a weeklong vacation to visit and explore. Hubby says we should stay with her the whole time and buy her something significant for her apartment with the money we would spend on an expensive hotel room. I'm afraid we'll be cramping her style. What do you think?

Worried Mom in Boring, Oregon

Dear Worried Mom,
Benjamin Franklin allegedly said, "Guests, like fish, begin to smell after three days." You know your daughter better than anyone. Would you be in the way? Is there a guest room? A roommate? If you think your daughter would enjoy your company overnight, stay with her for three days. Then check into a hotel for the remainder of your stay.

Sophie

It had only been two days, and I already smelled trouble. Several members of my family as well as their friends were staying at my house for the grand July Fourth celebration and it was quickly turning into a very long visit. A few minor squabbles had erupted that made me feel as though I had been dropped into a Fourth of July *Vacation* movie where the entire family began to fuss.

It didn't help things that a stranger was with us.

My father's sister, Melly, had been married for forty years to a kind and humorous man whom we all loved. He had passed away two years ago, leaving Melly lonely and depressed. When Gus Eberle came along and suggested Melly join him in a seniors-only trip to Las Vegas, even my parents thought it would be a fun getaway for Melly. But Gus and Melly shocked everyone when they returned to Melly's big country farmhouse as husband and wife.

They had all arrived in Old Town on June 30. I had enough bedrooms to accommodate most of them, although as one of the youngest, Roscoe O'Brien was sleeping on the foldout bed in my little den. To his credit, he hadn't complained. Stan Cox, Gus's friend, had driven up with Gus and Melly, but was staying elsewhere.

I had rented a tour bus outfitted with tables and, most important, a bathroom. A scrumptious tea with sandwiches and cookies was served each day throughout the tours. Our guide and driver, Tony Fontana, knew everything about Washington, DC, and the Declaration of Independence. He enjoyed sharing racy stories about American history that may or may not have been true but were fun even if a few people were turning in their graves.

One day we ate lunch in the Dirksen Dining Room where Senators are like movie stars. My guests were still talking about that experience. Because the Fourth would be very busy, I had planned a free day for July 3 so everyone could do what they wanted. No rising early, no rushing, no having to be anywhere on time except for a fancy dinner hosted by our friend Natasha. Unfortunately, relaxing did not apply to me.

The first worrisome surprise came when I found my front door unlocked in the morning when I left the house. Not only did I check to be sure it was secure every night before I went to bed, but I recalled locking it the night before. Maybe one of my guests needed something from their car. That thought made me feel better though I wasn't convinced it was the case. Or maybe my sister, Hannah, had opened the door and failed to lock it. She was coming in very late each night.

I ambled along behind Daisy, my hound mix, as she followed her nose across the street to the home of my best friend, Nina Reid Norwood, who yawned as she waited with Muppet, her little white fluffball of a dog.

"Remind me why we're up so early," groused Nina.

"So we can walk the dogs before it gets too hot and so I can buy fresh breakfast breads for my houseguests."

"Are you sure they're worth it? You have a toaster. I'm told they sell perfectly good sliced bread at the grocery store."

"You would be the first to complain if I didn't serve something special. And the toaster doesn't walk Daisy."

At the mention of her name, Daisy stopped and looked back at me.

"You're a very good girl."

Assured that all was well, she sniffed a spot that intrigued Muppet.

The first rays of the rising sun glowed in the sky as Daisy and Muppet rounded the corner, passing homes that were decked out in red, white, and blue for the holiday.

We crossed to the next block and Daisy steered us into

an alley just in time for us to hear a gate unlatch and see my Aunt Melly's new husband, Gus, step out of someone's backyard!

I pulled Nina and Daisy back in a hurry lest Gus spot us. When I peeked around the corner, he was dashing along the alley away from us.

"Was that Gus?" asked Nina.

"Ohh, this is not good."

"I'll say! Poor Melly! Do you think he saw us or was he running so he could get back to your house before Melly wakes up and realizes he's gone?"

We heard the latch snap closed on a dark red gate with a rounded top.

"I hope he didn't see us. That's Dollie Peabody's house. Now exactly what would Gus be doing at Dollie Peabody's house?"

Chapter 2

Dear Sophie,
I am proud to be an American. But all those red, white, and blue banners and flags and adorable plates and napkins add up! How can I express my spirit for less?

Penniless Redhead in Blue Bayou, Arkansas

Dear Penniless Redhead,
Look around your home. You can use a white or blue tablecloth or place mats. You might have a red lantern or a blue vase. How about baskets? Or throw pillows? You could tie red, white, or blue ribbons on them. Grab the napkins for next year when they go on sale.

Sophie

Nina shot me a horrified look. "At this hour? I think there's only one possibility. We just saw the male version of a run of shame."

"They've only been married a month!"

"Are you going to tell her?"

"I think I have to! What would you do?"

"She has to know."

"I wondered why my front door was unlocked. He doesn't have a key. That explains it. Maybe he'll wake Melly up when he gets to my house and crawls into bed with her. Then she'll ask where he's been and find out."

Nina snorted. "Oh right. Men always immediately confess to being with another woman. Yeah, that happens all the time—not!"

We walked on. "Gus told us he'd never been to Old Town before. Of course, his wording didn't exclude the possibility that he knew someone who lived here. And Dollie is about his age."

"You know what they say about her. She has a 'way with men.' "

"In simpler terms, she seduces them? She's been widowed three times and divorced once. And she's no spring chicken anymore. Surely she's not still, you know."

"Why does she walk around with her right hand up and her fingers curled as if she were carrying a handbag?"

"I have no idea. It's kind of funny. I have a feeling she's quite a character."

"How well do you know her?" asked Nina.

"Not well. She goes to a lot of the charity events I handle. She's always very friendly, as if she knows me. At one time, she was remarkably beautiful. Have you seen the portrait of her that hangs over her living room fireplace?"

"You've been inside her house?" asked Nina. "Where was I?"

"It must have been a meeting about organizing a charity event. The painting is stunning. Long blond hair cascades onto her shoulders. She's wearing a white satin wedding dress with long white gloves. Sapphire earrings bring out the vivid blue of her eyes. She could have been a movie star."

"Well, I am sorry to say that she doesn't look like that

anymore. I know we all want to look young, but the excessive amount of makeup she uses in an effort to appear younger only ages her more. I suspect she would be a stunning older woman if she didn't try so hard to look young. It must be difficult to embrace the ravages of age having been so gorgeous."

"Dollie hails from a long line of Old Town residents. She told me about her great-great-great-grandfather who was a surgeon during the Civil War. She still has his surgical kit."

"Cool! What did it look like? My husband and I would love to see it."

"The mere thought of the suffering people went through when they'd had amputations back then makes me very queasy. Thank heaven we have anesthesia today. I declined her kind offer to show me the surgical kit."

Nina waited outside with the dogs while I entered Big Daddy's Bakery, still wondering what Gus's connection to Dollie might be. Gus had been very knowledgeable on the tours we took over the previous two days. We all noted how well read he must be about the country's history. Maybe he had run into Dollie somewhere and taken her up on an offer to see that surgical kit? Although—it was an odd time of day for that kind of visit. And why wouldn't he use her front door?

I selected croissants in plain, ham, and chocolate. And for those who didn't care for croissants, blueberry muffins, carrot muffins, and cinnamon rolls.

Forty-five minutes later, I was still thinking about Gus and his early-morning foray as Nina and I set up breakfast in the backyard on my covered porch. The skies were a gorgeous blue with not a cloud to be seen. Nina had set up coffee and tea outside and they were ready for everyone to help themselves. I brought the waffle maker outdoors along with ripe, red strawberries, plump blueberries, and whipped cream for those who didn't care for maple syrup. A long basket of the breakfast breads graced the center of the table.

In anticipation of my family visiting for the big July Fourth celebration, I'd kept my eye on blue and white Johnson Brothers Historic America plates with old images of the Capitol, Boston, ferryboats, farmhouses, and colonial homes. I'd gotten lucky with a huge set at a yard sale. I couldn't believe that no one in that family wanted them. Slowly, I gathered enough to accommodate everyone this weekend and even added a few in red and white for fun.

Red, white, and blue bunting draped my fence. Blue hydrangeas bloomed in profusion as though I had planned it that way. I had debated about napkins. Cotton ones were always best, but with seven houseguests plus friends dropping by, I did not want to waste time in the basement laundering them. Caspari's elegant Flags and Hydrangeas paper napkins were just the ticket.

My parents and Dad's sister Melly were the first ones up. Nina and I caught them tiptoeing down the stairs so as not to disturb anyone else.

"I didn't have the heart to wake Gus," said Melly. "I hope his snoring didn't keep you up."

Nina and I exchanged a glance. I wasn't quite sure what to say but thought it best to omit any mention of Dollie Peabody. At least for the time being.

Dad smiled at his sister before turning to me. "Something smells delicious."

I led them out to the porch.

Mom poured coffee for everyone. "I see Gus isn't the only one sleeping in."

I hustled into the kitchen to whip up omelets for those who might prefer a savory breakfast. When I brought them to the porch, my guests were relaxing over coffee, discussing what they might do that day.

No sign of Roscoe or Cyril yet. My sister, Hannah, who was staying on a blow-up mattress in the main bedroom with me, had crept into bed at four in the morning. Daisy, had nudged me awake to let me know.

"Good morning." Stan Cox appeared in the backyard. He wasn't a big man, but slim, as if he were a runner. He had a medium brown mustache and wore his beard in the current short fashion that looked like he'd forgotten to shave for a couple of days. He had hitched a ride with Aunt Melly and Gus. Melly had introduced him as Gus's friend. He wasn't staying with us but appeared each day to hang out with us. Pleasant and polite, he wasn't an objectionable person by far but curious nonetheless. He claimed to live in Berrysville, but my parents thought it odd that they had never met him. Berrysville was a very small town and news about newcomers spread fast. I had asked him what he did for a living. He told me he was a freelance graphic designer. It sounded like a great job. He could travel wherever he felt like going and still get his work done.

We welcomed him, and he helped himself to breakfast.

I relaxed with everyone for a few minutes, enjoying their company. It didn't matter what they were talking about. It had been too long since I'd seen them and just being with my parents and Aunt Melly was a wonderful gift to me.

Nina phoned her husband. We all heard her say, "Hi honey. They're having a super breakfast across the street at Sophie's house. Beats the toast and jam we were going to have."

He agreed to join us.

I thought I heard people stirring inside the house and popped back to the kitchen to whip up more ham and cheese omelets. I could hear footsteps on my creaking stairs just before Cyril Chevalier entered the kitchen.

"I hope walking up and down from the third floor isn't

too hard on you." Cyril was a friend of my father's and in the same age group as Melly and my parents. I felt as if I had known him forever.

"Not at all. I'm thoroughly enjoying the third-floor room. You did a wonderful job renovating it. I can feel the age of the house there. The windows that begin at floor level for starters. Especially at night, I love looking down on the lights and people who are walking by. I can imagine the many things this house has seen. Life in the 1800s must have been so different. Old Town was something of a hub during the Civil War. I like to imagine the spies who probably walked by this house or may have even hidden here." He smiled at me. "What are you cooking?"

Cyril struck me as a gentleman. He was always neatly dressed and clean shaven. A professor emeritus of engineering, he wore rectangular metal-rimmed glasses which gave him a slightly bookish appearance that suited his personality. As far as I knew, he had never married.

"We're eating al fresco this morning. I thought I'd take some omelets outside."

"Perhaps I could help you with that. Are they ready?"

Just as Cyril was carrying omelets to the porch, Aunt Melly's brand-new husband, Gus, entered the kitchen and looked around. "I thought I smelled coffee, but I don't see any."

Unlike Cyril's neat attire, Gus wore a ratty brown bathrobe that had parted enough for me to see turquoise boxers imprinted with yellow rubber duckies.

"Good morning! Coffee and breakfast are outside on the covered porch."

"Wonderful. I'm famished!"

Of course he was. He'd been out visiting local widows instead of sleeping.

He followed me as I carried a large bowl of fruit salad through the dining room to the French doors in the living room, where a covered walkway connected the house to the porch and breakfast. I glanced around to see if we needed more of anything, but everyone appeared to be having a good time and there was plenty of food.

"Mornin', folks," said Gus.

Everyone chimed in, "Good morning!"

In the meantime, Nina's husband had arrived and taken a seat next to her. His dark brown hair was shot through with silver. While it should have made him look older, it brought out the vibrant blue of his eyes. Two deep horizontal furrows crossed his forehead, probably from worry, and there was a dent in the bridge of his nose from wearing reading glasses. "Hello, Sophie. Thanks for including us. I feel like family."

"And we think of Nina as one of our girls," said Mom. "It's so nice that you're home and can join us."

Gus piled food onto a plate and slid into an empty seat next to Melly. But before he ate, he leaned over and gave her a sweet peck on the cheek.

Nina and I exchanged a glance. How dare he? What nerve!

Melly seemed pleased, though. She must not have noticed that he left the house while she was sleeping. Or maybe he was a habitual early riser, so it had seemed normal to her.

I poured myself a mug of tea with a bit of milk, but as I settled at the table, I could hear my phone ringing inside. I intended to ignore it, but Mom said, "Shouldn't you get that?"

"No. I'd rather be out here with you."

"Sophie! It could be important. Is that what you do when I call from home? Where is Hannah? What if she needs us?"

"Mom, she's upstairs, fast asleep."

"I can't stand it." Mom left and returned with my phone.

I had no choice. I excused myself and walked into my living room with the phone to my ear. Carol Harrison was calling to find out what we were wearing to Natasha's party that night.

Natasha had sent out elaborate invitations made to look as if they had been handwritten in the 1800s on yellowed stationery.

Natasha requests the favor of M. Sophie Winston to dine with her
on Friday, July the third, at half after six.
The favor of an answer is requested.
Attire: Appropriate for the year 1826.

It was, remarkably, the most coveted event of the year. Even more so than the charity balls! Local costumers had soon run out of men's jackets cut short in the front with two long tails in the back. Waistcoats and neckwear had also been in demand. Apparently, the fashion for men in the 1820s was to have padding inside jackets designed to give them a large chest and small waist, which prompted several amusing articles as it had when they were the fashion.

Women's dresses were a bit easier but local seamstresses found themselves in high demand. Silks and cottons in bright colors were easy to come by. The sleeves were enormous puffs. It was an era of romanticism in fashion, with pearls and ribbons in high demand. The hats, as it turned out, would have given today's fascinators a run for their money.

No one had expected the dinner to have become the talk of the town, but it led to other, lesser dinners of the same nature and propelled Natasha into the spotlight, which was exactly where she wanted to be.

Natasha and I had competed at everything as children.

Everything except the beauty pageants she loved. These days we each had an advice column answering questions about the domestic life. She even pursued my ex-husband, Mars. But he had broken off their relationship and as far as I could tell, never wanted to go through that relationship again despite her efforts to reconcile.

Sometimes I felt as if she still meant to compete with me. In general, while I always wanted to do my best, I wasn't big on competition. But Natasha thrived on it. When possible, I tried to give her the impression she had won. After all, it was so important to her, and I didn't care.

When Natasha was seven years old, her father abandoned her and her mother. Years later, genetic testing turned up a half sister and a second wife to the very same man who had disappeared from Natasha's life. He had abandoned his new family in the same manner. He walked out one day and never came back. He had a type, though. The second wife was remarkably like Natasha's mother, Wanda, and the two wives now co-owned a new age store in Old Town.

My parents were convinced that the abrupt departure of Natasha's father had spurred her to excel. She longed to be the Martha of the South and already had her own local TV show. Maybe my parents were correct about her father's absence driving her ambitions. Natasha could be highly annoying, yet on occasion, she was surprisingly thoughtful. We all had our strengths and drawbacks.

When I returned to the table, everyone quit talking as if they expected me to report about the phone call. I had to laugh. What if it had been a client? I took my seat at the table to indulge in a chocolate croissant and told them that I pitied those invited to Natasha's party who hadn't made arrangements for their attire in advance.

I noticed that Mom was watching Aunt Melly and Gus carefully. "Melly and I thought we would do some shopping today. We can't wait to browse through the antique fair in town. We'll grab lunch in one of the cute restaurants." She smiled at me, and I knew that was a suggestion to everyone for my benefit so I wouldn't have to prepare lunch.

"That suits me." Dad selected a ham croissant from the basket of breads. "I know the rest of you are burned out on tours, but I'd like to visit the George Washington Masonic Memorial and time permitting, the Apothecary Museum."

Gus stopped eating. "Me too! I'll go with you."

Nina gazed at her husband questioningly.

"Having been to those places, I pass. I have a rare long weekend at home and golf is on my agenda."

Roscoe O'Brien, with whom I had gone to high school, finally dragged himself to breakfast. I was surprised how quickly he joined in the plans. Hannah brought up the rear. Wearing an oversize T-shirt and shorts, she walked onto the porch barefooted, followed by none other than Dollie Peabody!

Chapter 3

Dear Sophie,
I chose to live in a very popular place where a lot of people want to go on vacation. I love my friends and relatives but some of them seem to think my house is a B&B. Aside from the cleaning, I'm tired of staying up late and entertaining them. I invent excuses but am afraid I'll get caught and that's more stress! How do I stop this?

Not a B&B in Las Vegas, Nevada

Dear Not a B&B,
You don't have to make up excuses. Tell them you are sorry that you cannot accommodate them, but you would enjoy meeting them for dinner or a drink. The end. You are not under any obligation to entertain or provide a bed for everyone who visits your town.

Sophie

I sucked in a deep breath and looked over at Melly and Gus. Dollie's eyes were ringed in black eyeliner, reminiscent of a raccoon. She had used a generous hand with foundation and a bright pink lipstick. "Good morning. My, but it smells good. Sometimes I wish I knew how to cook but it's just too much work and makes such a mess."

"Everyone, this is Dollie Peabody. One of my neighbors."

My mother promptly invited Dollie to join us.

"I'm so sorry," she drawled. "I didn't mean to interrupt your breakfast, but I desperately need to speak with Sophie."

I tried my best not to show my horror. I looked from her to Gus and back. My heart pounded. I hoped there wouldn't be an ugly scene. Poor Melly!

Dollie ignored Gus as if they were strangers and he did a fantastic job of showing more interest in his waffle. I introduced everyone.

"You have to tell me where you shop," said Melly. "I love that outfit. Did you buy it in Old Town?"

Dollie plucked at the silky pink fabric of her dress, which showed off her sun-bronzed décolleté. "This old thing? I think it's Dior. I love their clothes because they're so elegant."

I breathed a little easier when Mom said, "Shall we meet in the kitchen in half an hour, Melly?" She rose and carried dishes into the house, followed by my dad, Melly, Gus, and Cyril.

Nina's husband thanked me and excused himself. "My tee-off time is in an hour. I'll see you back at the house, Nina?"

Nina nodded, barely able to take her eyes off Dollie.

When only Hannah, Roscoe, Nina, and I were left, I asked, "Would you care for some breakfast, Dollie?"

"I really shouldn't. Maybe just a bite?"

I rose and poured coffee for her, then prepared a dish of breakfast foods and set it in front of her.

She thanked me and ate every last bite before leaning on

her elbows. She knit her bony fingers together. Two rings with huge stones which I suspected were amethyst and citrine flashed in the sun. "Sophie, I need your help."

Oh no! Was this about Gus? He hadn't acted uncomfortable around her. Were the two of them good enough actors to hide their relationship? I forced a smile at her hoping she wanted me to arrange a benefit ball of some sort.

"I found a dead man in my house this morning."

Roscoe's eyes widened as if he were watching a horror movie.

Hannah's coffee cup clattered onto the saucer spilling the contents.

Nina's mouth dropped open.

I tried to remain calm. Surely Dollie couldn't mean what she had actually said. "You saw a ghost?"

She flicked her hand around. "I don't know how that works. Are you automatically a ghost when you die?"

In some ways, I guessed that was a legitimate query. But it didn't answer my question. "So you saw a ghost in your house?"

"No, darlin'. I saw a dead man."

"Who is it?"

"I have no idea. I've never seen him before."

Roscoe's gaze flicked to me. His complexion had turned pasty.

"Did you call the police?" I asked.

"I thought I should speak with you first. I've never found a dead man, except for one of my husbands. They always took care of things like this when they were alive."

"Your husbands took care of dead men in the house?" asked Roscoe.

Dollie waved her right hand. "Not per se. They handled things that happened. You know, spiders or a mouse in the house or a leaking pipe."

I gulped my tea. "Are you saying that a dead man is in your house right now and you have not called the police?"

"Yes. That's it, exactly. I didn't know what to do. And the police are always so grumpy with me when I call them."

Shivers ran through me. We had to get over there. "Hannah, you see everyone off to their destinations. Make sure Daisy and Mochie are inside and that my doors are locked. I'll go over to Dollie's house with her."

"Watch Muppet for me, too, Hannah," said Nina.

Roscoe fidgeted with his fork.

I didn't have time to soothe his nerves. Hannah would have to do that. "Come on, Dollie."

She and Nina followed me out the front door. Instead of chatting with her, I phoned the police station and asked if Officer Wong was working. Ordinarily, I would have phoned 911, but Dollie's explanation struck me as peculiar. Of course, Dollie *was* a bit unusual. Who wouldn't have called 911 right away? Who would walk a couple of blocks to ask someone what she should do and then eat breakfast before mentioning the dead man? Maybe that was exactly what an elderly lady who wasn't thinking straight anymore would do. I glanced at her while I waited to be connected to Wong.

When she answered, I asked her to meet us at Dollie's address.

Wong repeated the address in a dull tone, then asked, "Dollie Peabody's house? Are you kidding me?"

"Yes, Dollie's house. No, I'm not kidding. I'm on my way there."

"Good grief. What is it now?"

I was glad I hadn't called 911. Wong must have responded to Dollie's home before. "A dead man."

"Uh-huh. Are you on speaker?"

"No."

I could hear Wong suck in a deep breath of air. "She

imagines things. Ever since her last husband passed away or left her. I get them confused. But I'm on my way." She disconnected the call.

"Officer Wong will be joining us."

Dollie smacked my arm. "Why did you go and call *her*? She treats me like I'm deranged."

That didn't sound like Wong. She was always polite and thoughtful.

"I'm sure you're mistaken. Wong has always been terrific to work with," said Nina.

Dollie didn't walk fast, but she wore high heels that were beautiful, if treacherous, on the brick sidewalk. "Aren't you afraid of falling in those shoes?" I asked.

"Honey, I've been running on these sidewalks in heels since I was a baby. You're single, aren't you? You really ought to wear heels. They do so much for your legs."

We had reached her house. A creamy color with a dark red front door, a gray roof, and shutters, it stood three stories high and abutted the house next door on the left. Stately and elegant, it appeared to have tiny basement windows aboveground that were blocked from the interior.

Dollie ran her fingers over the top of the doorframe for the key and unlocked the door.

She didn't need me lecturing her on proper places to hide keys. Maybe Wong would do that.

As if she could read my mind, she said, "I leave the key where it's easy for the police to find in case they have to come in."

"I gather you've called them before?"

"Many times. But I don't like to. You know, they treat me like I'm crazy. That's why I went to you for help today. You're sensible. You follow clues and things. They never do that. They leave and I never hear from them again. I don't think they do anything."

A picture was beginning to form. Poor Dollie. I wondered if she was getting confused and needed someone around to help her. I stepped inside her foyer. A large, gilded mirror reflected light from the tall windows of the living room. A demilune table inlaid with a beautiful leaf motif stood beneath the mirror and held a tall crystal vase.

I knew instantly that the living room must have been two rooms originally. Few of us had a parlor that large in a historic home unless it had been renovated. Sometimes it was an addition, and sometimes two rooms had been merged. Fringed swag valances hung over long gold drapes. The huge portrait of a much younger Dollie hung over the marble fireplace mantel. "Where is the dead man?"

"This way." We followed her through the small foyer, passing her dining room, which was stunning. An inlaid Regency-style dining table gleamed. The sideboard held a large oval centerpiece with graceful flowers around the edge of the bowl as well as around the bottom of the foot. It had to be sterling.

I braced myself for what was to come. We turned right and walked past the stairs toward the rear of the house into a large kitchen by Old Town standards. It was spotless with white cabinets, white marble countertops with a gray vein, hardwood floors, and a charming breakfast nook that overlooked the backyard. Her kitchen looked like a TV set with large white stoneware salt-and-pepper cellars marked 1920. A tall pitcher hand painted with a blue rabbit and blue flowers held faux blue and white hydrangea. A large, aged cutting board hung on the wall, adorned with a grapevine wreath and a white ribbon. An ancient fireplace remained, possibly from the original house. A huge copper bowl with brass handles sat on the hearth. The scent of bleach lingered in the air.

One thing was missing, though. A body. I gazed around the kitchen.

"He's gone!" Dollie seemed surprised.

"Where were you when you saw the body?"

"Right here where we're standing."

"Where exactly did he lay? Show me where his head was."

She pointed with her long and beautifully polished index finger. "He lay on his back with his head here and his feet toward the fireplace."

The floor looked clean to me. There was a tall door nearby. Holding my breath, I opened it slowly lest a corpse fall on me. Inside, a narrow back stairway led up to the second floor, but there was no sign of a man, dead or alive. A second door led to the basement.

As I closed it, we heard the door knocker in the foyer. "I'll get it."

I opened the front door to Wong. Her name was misleading because she wasn't Asian. She had kept her husband's last name after their divorce and told me she preferred it that way. She'd let her hair grow out and pulled it back into a neat bun at the nape of her neck. Her police uniform tugged tight around her waist. Like me, she had never met a cupcake she didn't like. Unfortunately, police uniforms didn't take that into consideration. I was always relieved when Wong showed up because she was observant and smart.

"Hi, Sophie."

"She's back here."

Wong followed me and said politely, "Hello, Mrs. Peabody. What do we have today?"

"Dollie was just telling us that the dead man lay on his back with his feet toward the fireplace," Nina said.

"Uh-huh. And where is he now?" asked Wong.

"I have no idea. He was a nice-looking man. A full oval face and a bit of a tummy. I always like that in a man. Means they're well fed and generous."

"This is where he was when you left for my house?" I asked.

"Exactly."

Wong roamed the kitchen. "Is anyone staying with you, Mrs. Peabody?"

Dollie shook her head. "I'm afraid it's just me these days."

"Did you have any visitors last night?" Wong crouched on the floor, eyeing the spot where the dead man had allegedly been.

"No."

Nina and I exchanged a look.

"When did you see him?"

"This morning."

"Did you hear any odd sounds last night?"

"Not a thing."

"Why does it smell of bleach in here?"

"My housekeeper was here yesterday. It always smells like this for a couple of days after she leaves."

"Your bedroom is still on the second floor, right?" Wong looked up at the ceiling.

"Yes."

"Could you tell how he died?" I asked.

"No. He just lay there bleeding. But to be honest, I didn't try to move him or touch him or anything."

"How did you know he was dead?" asked Wong.

"He was bleeding, his eyes were closed, and he didn't move."

Wong studied Dollie. Her eyes narrowed. "Let me get this straight. You got up this morning and found a man in your kitchen on the floor, bleeding."

"Yes. That's correct."

"And then you called Sophie instead of nine-one-one?"

"I went over to her house, actually."

Wong cocked her head. "Did you check his pulse? Maybe he was alive."

Dollie leaned against the wall and placed a hand on her throat. "Thank heaven! I guess he *was* alive or he would still be here. But what was he doing in my house?"

"Why didn't you call nine-one-one?" Wong demanded.

Dollie met Wong's gaze holding her chin high with determination. "Because all of you make fun of me when I call. You treat me like I'm a doddering old fool who imagines things." She shook her bony forefinger at Wong. "Did you think my daughter wouldn't tell me that you called her and said I should be placed in a home for the insane?"

Wong winced. "It wasn't for the insane, it was for the elderly. And you have to admit that you call us a lot and when we get here, there's nothing wrong. There aren't voices. There aren't ghosts. There's no one lurking in your house. And now there isn't a body."

Dollie's lips wrinkled as she pursed her mouth, angry. "Why do you always bring up ghosts? Because I told you my psychic thinks I have ghosts? I will grant you that this house has seen a lot of people come and go. Many of my own relatives died here. A lot of them! Folks didn't always have funeral homes, you know. They died at home and then they were buried. But that doesn't mean I'm seeing ghosts or things that aren't there."

I broke in quickly to cut off the argument. "Did the man look familiar to you at all?"

"No. I never saw him before."

I was afraid to wink at her lest she misinterpret it as jollying her, but I shot her a little grin. "So it couldn't have been one of your dead relatives because you would have recognized them."

Dollie's mouth fell open. "Oh, Sophie! You are exactly right. And he was dressed in modern clothes, not something from the 1800s." She squinted at Wong, then turned to Nina. "My first husband died in Vietnam, the second one died outside of the house in the street, so he could be a ghost here, the third one died in a plane crash, and I divorced the last one. I have never seen any of them hanging around. If I could see ghosts, don't you think I would be seeing my husbands?"

"Do you want me to look around for this missing man?" asked Wong.

"You might as well since you're here," I said.

Dollie seemed annoyed and walked to the front door.

Nina waited with Dollie, but I accompanied Wong on her search of the house. Dollie's bedroom was huge with three tall windows overlooking the street. The walls were papered with a light blue print that coordinated with the curtains and the scalloped canopy of a four-poster bed. Ornate wood side tables embellished with gold bore white marble tops and flanked the bed. The other furniture in the room carried out the same theme. I wasn't a pro but my short time as an antique store owner told me these were expensive when they were purchased and probably worth a lot more now.

I peeked into what had probably been children's rooms. With the exception of a gilded antique cradle, the furniture and décor were overwhelmingly modern in comparison to the main bedroom. They were sweet but didn't have the designer touch or valuable antiques. Paintings in ornate gilded frames covered the walls in the hallway. The third floor had been finished. But the rooms were packed with boxes and toys and clearly used for storage. We returned to the foyer. On the stairs and the rooms on the first floor, large family portraits hung everywhere, except the kitchen. Wong peeked half-heartedly at the basement. I had a feeling she didn't go all the way down the stairs.

"All clear," said Wong.

Dollie opened the door and raised her chin again. "Thank you for visiting." The terse manner in which she uttered those words conveyed her resentment toward Wong.

"Have a good day, ladies." Wong walked out.

Dollie closed the door behind Wong and leaned against it. "Well! Now do you see why I don't call nine-one-one? They never believe me. They want to put me away."

"Have you ever found a dead person in your house before?" I gazed around, half expecting to see a ghost.

"No. I hear noises. They sound like someone is in the house. It's usually footsteps or a voice. I've heard someone clearing their throat. Once I heard a sneeze! I've talked with a lot of people who hear similar sounds and they think they're ghosts. But I don't really believe in ghosts and even if they existed, why would they sneeze? Who ever heard of a ghost with allergies? Honestly, Sophie, if I didn't love this old house so much, I would move! But I have lived here almost my whole life. There are so many memories. Like the big holiday celebrations that my mother always threw. Relatives came from all over. She was the queen of an elegant Christmas table. I tried to do the same for my children. And I'd like to be able to pass the house on to my daughter one day."

"Won't your sons resent that?"

"They might but their wives won't. They have lovely homes. And they have lives elsewhere. I think my daughter might move back if she inherited the house."

"Where does she live now?" asked Nina.

Dollie flicked her hand through the air. "North Dakota. Their house is hours from anything. Do you *know* how cold it is there?"

"Did you hear any throat clearing or footsteps this morning or last night?" asked Nina.

Dollie toyed with a gold rope necklace while she spoke. "I heard footsteps before I drifted off to sleep. So many of my friends can't sleep well anymore. But I have been blessed in that regard. I know they say your brain won't work right if you sleep with a TV or a light on in the room. I think that's hogwash. I love sleeping with the curtains open. A little bit of city light filters into my bedroom and I like that. I like hearing the sounds and knowing people are on their way somewhere. Plus, I keep the TV on. It helps me doze off. My friends say that doesn't make any sense because it would keep them awake. Well, not me. I fall asleep and wake bright and fresh with the sun shining into my bedroom. I say 'do what works' and that does it for me."

I tried to steer her back on track. "Okay. But what happened last night?"

"That's what I'm telling you. I don't know! I was asleep."

"Really? You didn't hear voices? Thumping on the floor? A dead man falling to the floor would certainly make noise. I know my stairs creak. Don't yours?"

She smiled at me. "You see? If you slept with the TV on, you wouldn't notice those spooky nighttime sounds. I don't hear the wind or traffic. Even when the windows are open. All that is just nighttime background. You know, people who live in New York City get so used to all the city sounds at night that they can't sleep out in the country where it's quiet. I guess I'm kind of like that. All those sounds from the TV have become ambient to me. They help me sleep and shut out everything else. You understand, don't you? The police would never believe I could have slept through someone being murdered in my home."

I was no lawyer, but I could see how she might have trouble convincing people of that. Especially a jury of tired people who weren't getting enough sleep. "I guess the good news is that he must not have been dead." The bad news was that a strange man had been in her house. Playing dead, maybe? The whole situation was very odd. "When did you first notice something awry?"

Dollie placed a fist under her chin and looked up at the ceiling. "Well, my alarm goes off every morning at seven thirty. Ever since my last husband left, I don't bother getting dressed and putting on makeup right away. I usually just brush my teeth and come downstairs wearing my nightgown. In the winter or if the air-conditioning is on, I might put on a robe." She shrugged. "There's no one here, so I can do whatever I like. I come downstairs to the kitchen and start coffee. I am useless without coffee. It's the only thing I cook. I put one of those little cups into the machine and it comes out perfect every time. I had planned to enjoy my coffee right here overlooking the garden. But then I saw the body. It was hard to miss. So I went over to your house."

I strode to the back door, which had a window in it, and gazed out at the yard. "There's a cat in your garden."

Chapter 4

Dear Sophie,
My friends and I are going to a B&B for a girls' weekend. I have never stayed in a B&B before. Should I make my bed every morning?
On the Road in Traveler's Rest, South Carolina

Dear On the Road,
While your very good manners are appreciated, you do not need to make the bed in a B&B. In that instance, you may treat it as a hotel and expect to return later in the day to a nicely made bed.
Sophie

"What?" Dollie rushed toward me.

Nina opened the door.

I noted that it wasn't locked.

"That's my Georgy! She's a house cat!" In her high heels, Dollie hurried outside, navigated the garden, and picked up Georgy. She cuddled her as she carried her back to the house. "I never let her out to roam, not even in the backyard. There's too much danger for cats to wander about. Not to mention all the lilies my neighbor, Joanna Kowalski, grows. One bite of those and poor Georgy would be a goner." She held Georgy up and spoke to the cat's face. "How did you get out there, sweetie?" Georgy mewed at her. Dollie snuggled her close. "I named her Georgy after that song 'Georgy Girl.'" Do you remember it? I loved that name!"

I tried locking the door from inside. It worked just fine. "The door wasn't locked. Did you leave through this door when you came to my house?"

Dollie's eyes widened in horror. "No. I must have overlooked locking it the night before. So foolish of me but it happens sometimes." She hurried into the kitchen, opened a can of cat food, and spooned it into a bowl. Georgy settled to eat.

Dollie turned toward me and leaned against the counter. "That proves the man who wasn't dead *was* in the house. I might have forgotten to lock the door, but I *never* would have let Georgy out."

I wasn't sure what to think. Wong wasn't a fool. She could be right about Dollie. And that meant Dollie might have unintentionally let Georgy out. "Well, I'm glad she's safely inside now." But I was becoming more and more worried about having seen Gus emerge from Dollie's garden.

Nina opened her eyes wide and raised her eyebrows as if she was prompting me.

"Dollie, do you know Gus Eberle?"

She thought for a moment. "I don't believe so. Gus . . . The name sounds familiar." She waved her hand. "I'm thinking of Gus Blackstone. You know, the baker? He makes those wonderful bialys."

She was right about the bialys. I tried a different way. "Did you recognize anyone at my house this morning?"

"Oh! Was one of those people Gus? I'm such a dunce

about names. Always have been. They go right out of my head." Her tone soft, almost fearful, Dollie asked, "You do believe me about the man, don't you?"

I believed that she thought she had seen something. I wasn't sure what it might have been or whether it had been real or imaginary. For a moment, I wondered if she drank alcohol to excess or took medicine that might make her imagine things. Thinking it would comfort her, I said firmly, "Yes. Yes, I do."

Dollie threw her arms around me. "Thank you! Oh, my heavens, thank you so much. The police always make me feel like an incompetent ninny."

I patted her back. "I'm throwing a barbecue for my family and friends tomorrow at my house. Would you like to join us?"

"I would love to! I haven't done anything fun for July Fourth in years. This year is special. I love to dress up and tonight I'm going to Natasha's 1800s party. Will you be there?"

"Nina and I are both going. We're looking forward to it."

She eyed me. "You're single, aren't you? I have just the man for you. He's quite the catch. Wear something seductive tonight. Should I do your hair and makeup for you?"

Perish the thought! "That's a very nice offer but I think I can handle it." Lest she protest, I hastily added, "My sister will want to help me with that."

Dollie scowled at me. "The one who wore a big old T-shirt to breakfast?"

"She was out late last night. I imagine she wanted to grab some breakfast before we put everything away."

"Ohhh. Well, I admit I can understand that! I've had a few of those mornings myself. Thank you both for coming over here and for believing me."

I left the house wishing I knew what had happened. I

was glad she thought I believed her even though that wasn't quite true.

"Do you think there was a dead man?" asked Nina as we walked home.

"I don't know. It doesn't make much sense. The one thing that really disturbs me is the smell of bleach in the kitchen. It backs up her story about the bleeding dead man. But if there was a dead man bleeding on her floor, then why would she clean up the blood and hide the body before reporting it? And to me of all people?"

"She said it always smells that way after her housekeeper cleans the kitchen. I can relate to that. My kitchen and bathrooms reek of bleach after the housekeeper has been there."

"She got up at seven thirty," I mused. "And she showed up at my house around nine thirty. Even if she had very reasonably changed out of her nightclothes before leaving the house, she obviously also took the time to do her hair and makeup."

"I wondered about that, too. If I had found a body in my house, I would have called nine-one-one and put on a bathrobe, never mind the bedhead hair or lack of makeup. And who doesn't call the police? That sounds off to me, too."

"If Wong really called Dollie's daughter to recommend moving her to a retirement home, I can understand why she might forgo calling the police. But she didn't phone me to save time. She chose to dress and do her makeup and hair first and then she walked over."

"There's something wrong with the whole picture. Do you think she wanted to impress Gus?"

My home was blissfully quiet when we entered. Daisy, Mochie, and Muppet greeted us at the door. After pets and hugs, Nina and Muppet went home. "See you tonight!"

I made myself a strong mug of tea with milk and doled

out treats to Daisy and Mochie. Someone, probably my mom, had taken the time to wrap up the leftovers and clean the kitchen. As I drank my tea, I heard the rumble and squealing brakes of a large truck on the street. I looked out the window. I'd forgotten all about the seating I had rented for the barbecue tomorrow!

I rushed outside, glad that they hadn't arrived while I was at Dollie's house. I opened the gate for them and watched as they unloaded long tables and chairs. On a snowy day in February, I had calculated the number I would need and reserved them. Now I could only hope that I'd gotten it right. I'd learned from experience to order a few more because there were invariably some people who were added to the guest list at the very last moment. And others brought a friend along because of the informal nature of barbecues.

They set up the tables and chairs on the lawn in no time and were off to their next delivery.

I returned to the empty, quiet house and felt like a maid in a B&B as I wandered through making beds and tidying up.

I should have been thinking about my guests, my plans for the rest of the day, and tomorrow's big festivities, but Dollie dominated my thoughts. I tried to imagine what had happened. She claimed she saw a dead man in her kitchen, but there was no sign of a corpse. I couldn't imagine a scenario in which a corpse disappeared so quickly. There were a few possibilities. Either there had never been a corpse, and it had only been in Dollie's imagination. Or there had been a person on the floor who wasn't dead and got up and left. Or there had been a dead person, who was removed by the killer, which would mean there were at least two people in Dollie's house that night. While Dollie could probably murder someone, I couldn't imagine that she had the strength to remove a body. Dead weight was heavy.

The notion that someone else besides the dead man had been in her house frightened me the most because I had seen Gus leaving Dollie's backyard. Surely, he couldn't be a killer! My initial thought that he and Dollie might be involved in a romantic way was terrible, but murder was far, far worse.

Maybe Gus murdered the man, then Dollie saw the corpse lying on the kitchen floor. If she was having an affair with Gus, that would explain why she didn't call the police. A definite possibility! But why involve me? She could have simply gone about her business as if nothing happened and waited for Gus to clean up. Unless she was being vindictive. Had her visit to my house been her way of meeting Aunt Melly and issuing a subtle threat to Gus?

Or what if Dollie killed the man, and it was Gus who moved him and cleaned up the blood while Dollie dressed and primped? They hadn't acted awkward when Dollie arrived at my house in the morning. If they knew each other, they had done an admirable job of pretending they hadn't met. Of course, there was the outside chance that Dollie knew Gus under a different name. But wouldn't she have recognized him? Oy! What a mess.

One other little thing bothered me. If they truly did not know each other, would Gus have wandered inside her gate? That seemed unlikely. Who would do something like that? Or had he confused her gate with that of someone else? That was a possibility. But it begged the question—who was he looking for at that hour?

And what about the unlocked back door and Georgy being out in the yard? That was probably the most persuasive thing in favor of Wong's belief that Dollie wasn't thinking straight anymore. Of course, I hadn't spent a lot of time with Dollie, but she didn't strike me as needing to be in a retirement home yet. I hadn't seen any other signs that would lead me to that conclusion.

I fluffed up the pillows on Hannah's bed and moved on. Mom and Aunt Melly had made their beds and left their rooms neat, which wasn't surprising. My mom couldn't stand an unmade bed.

While I knew it was wrong of me, I did snoop just a hair in Aunt Melly and Gus's room. It was justified, after all, by his unorthodox conduct. I peeked under the mattress to see if anything had been stashed there and kneeled on the floor to look underneath the bed. I stopped myself from peering inside their luggage. I eyed it, though. But if I were hiding something, especially from Aunt Melly, I would be more clever than simply stashing it with my folded clothes. Besides, searching luggage was going too far, even for me. Still, I worried about Gus's expedition to Dollie's house. I did take a minute to page through the papers on top of the drop-down desk in the secretary. They were mostly brochures and leaflets about American history and the various museums in Washington, DC. I shook my head. I was being ridiculous. It's not as if Gus would leave a love letter from Dollie where Aunt Melly could see it.

I gave up and went to Cyril's room on the third floor. He had made his bed and left his clothes neatly stashed away in the closet. Even the small bathroom looked pristine. Too bad Aunt Melly hadn't married him!

Done upstairs, I headed down to the den where Roscoe slept. What a difference! Clothes were strewn about. A damp towel lay on the floor and his sheets indicated a restless night. I felt awful. The sofa bed probably wasn't very comfortable. There wasn't much I could do about that, though. I straightened the sheets and blanket, and left the bed open in case he wanted to nap or lounge a bit when he returned.

Shortly after one, I took Daisy out. I thought she would want to return to the house quickly because of the heat, but she pawed at the gate. I slipped her harness over her head and took her for a brief walk.

On our return, I squeezed fresh lemonade in two pitchers and set out tall glasses and a bucket of ice on the island so everyone could help themselves. I added a board of cheeses, crackers, briny olives, pistachios, and fresh purple grapes for my company to nibble on when they came home.

Dad and Cyril were the first to return. They couldn't stop talking about the Masonic Temple and the Apothecary Museum.

"Where are Roscoe and Gus?" I asked in what I hoped was a very innocent tone.

"They left us after lunch," said Dad. He didn't sound concerned, rather matter-of-fact, actually.

"Together?"

Cyril shook his head. "I don't think so. Gus isn't here? I thought he was coming straight back."

"He's so knowledgeable about history," said Dad. "I bet he got sidetracked somewhere. I thought we would never get him out of the Masonic Temple."

Eventually, everyone returned. Some of them headed to their respective rooms for naps or to freshen up.

Gus babbled with enthusiasm about Old Town. "1825! I cannot believe I am staying in a house that was built two hundred years ago. Sophie, this is a true once-in-a-lifetime treat." He turned to Aunt Melly. "How about we sell your old farmhouse and buy us a place like this in Old Town?"

Mom stared at him in shock for a moment before zeroing in on Melly. Mom's lips tightened. A look I knew all too well. She was not pleased.

Melly stammered slightly when she said, "S-sell my h-home?"

"Yes! Wouldn't you like to live here and be part of history? Look at this fireplace. Can you imagine how many people sat here in this very kitchen eating their dinner warmed by the fire? Candles flickering on the table, the sound of hoofbeats outside."

Cyril Chevalier watched from the doorway and appeared as distressed as my mom. "I believe we're part of history no matter where we live, Gus."

Aunt Melly sagged and rubbed her forehead.

"I often feel that way when I travel." I smiled at Aunt Melly. "Especially in exotic places. I like to imagine what life would be like there. I love Old Town and my house, but no matter where you live, eventually you get used to it and the day-to-day matters of life take over."

Dad smiled at me. "You're so right, Sophie. Melly, maybe the two of you should consider an annual vacation to Old Town. You could stay in one of those rental houses they have now. It would be like living here but then you could return to the comforts of home."

Aunt Melly nodded. "That's a great idea! I'd enjoy coming up here to visit Sophie more often."

Gus's mouth skewed to the side. "If you'll excuse me, I believe I'll head upstairs to change for dinner."

I guessed he didn't like the turn the conversation had taken. Silence fell over us. We could hear Gus's footsteps on the stairs.

Aunt Melly sighed. "He was never like that before. I think the heat is getting to him."

"It wasn't hot in Las Vegas?" Mom asked dryly.

Dad winced, as if he couldn't believe Mom's nasty quip about the heat in Vegas, but he quickly focused on Aunt Melly. "As long as he makes you happy, Melly. That's all that matters."

"So true. If only we could find nice men for Sophie and

Hannah." Mom grinned and winked at me. "C'mon, Melly, let's rest up and change for dinner."

A few hours later Aunt Melly moseyed into the kitchen dressed for Natasha's fancy 1820s dinner in a blue silk dress with short sleeves so puffy that they were round. In the square neckline, she wore an elaborate sapphire and diamond necklace, which suited the dress perfectly. She wore her hair swept up with a matching ribbon embellished with white feathers. And on her wrist she wore a corsage of flowers in various blues and a white rose in the middle.

"Oh, Aunt Melly! What a beautiful dress!"

If she heard me, she didn't react. She stared out the bay window. "What do you think of Gus?"

I handed her a glass of lemonade. I couldn't tell her that I thought he was sneaking around early in the morning with another woman and may or may not have been involved in the murder of a man who may or may not exist. "He seems nice." There. That was neutral.

"Things were so much easier with my first husband. He was a bit of a bore sometimes, preferring to stay home when I'd have liked to come up here for a visit, but he never raised his voice, or slammed a door, or had a fit of anger. Never. I know he was upset sometimes. Everyone is. But he was a peaceful man, inclined to forget about his own needs and put others first."

"You miss him, don't you?"

"It wouldn't be fair of me to compare other men to him. None of us are exactly alike. And we had been together so long that we were used to each other's ways and habits. We accepted each other for who we were. Life was peaceful. I admit, I got testy with him sometimes when he tried to get out of traveling or going to an event, but he usually came through in the end with a smile. Gus has me so upset, but he gave me this necklace and then surprised me with this lovely wrist corsage, something that would never have occurred to my first husband."

"He was a very special man in many other ways." I tried to sound casual when I asked, "Does Gus know anyone who lives in Old Town?"

She shook her head and continued looking out the window at the street.

I pushed a little more. "Given his interest in American history, you'd think he would have visited Washington before this."

Cyril appeared in the doorway. He looked quite fit in the classic combination of navy-blue tailcoat with black trousers. A cream vest peeked out underneath the short front of the tailcoat. A cream cravat had been wrapped around his neck and tied with a fancy bow in the front.

"Cyril!" I exclaimed. "You're so chic!"

He grinned and turned in a circle. "It's not as hard as one might think to obtain men's clothes appropriate for the 1800s. Very formal clothing hasn't changed all that much. I'm told this is the sort of attire one wears today when meeting the King of England." He paused. "I know Natasha is a bit of a celebrity with her TV show and all, but do you suppose any royals will be in attendance?"

I laughed. "I seriously doubt it. But there could be a congressperson or two. Lemonade?" I asked.

"Yes, thank you." He accepted a glass from me. "My, you look lovely, Melly. That blue brings out your beautiful eyes. Are you looking forward to the dinner?"

"More like lamenting my spur-of-the-moment decision to marry Gus."

Chapter 5

Dear Natasha,
My son's new wife is never ready on time. He claims he has explained to her that we are punctual in our family. I don't care what they do on their own, but I feel she should have the courtesy of showing up on time when we have reservations or are attending a performance. Causing a commotion by sneaking in after the show or dinner has begun is simply terrible manners. How do I handle this?

Distraught Mom in Time, Illinois

Dear Distraught Mom,
You have two choices. You can tell them the dinner begins an hour earlier in the hope they will be on time. Or you can accept them as they are. If they arrive late for a meal, they can have dessert with you. But in any event, stop inviting them to performances.

Natasha

"Oh? Melly, I'm sorry to hear that," said Cyril.

"What was I thinking? Seriously, who finds love again at our age? It's so rare. I should have realized that we hadn't known each other long enough. I was positively giddy. I felt like a young girl again in Las Vegas. He never told me he didn't want to live in Berrysville or that he thought I should sell my house. Those are such major changes!"

"It sounds like you didn't know each other long enough," Cyril commiserated.

At that moment, my parents and Roscoe O'Brien joined us in their costumes. Mom wore a bright red dress that featured silk roses all around the hemline.

I quickly fed Daisy and Mochie an early dinner and hurried upstairs to change clothes.

Hannah was using the curling iron. Her blush-colored puffy-sleeved dress featured a neckline deep enough to guarantee a raised eyebrow from our mom even though we were long past the age where such reprisals were necessary or even a good idea. And I had a feeling that such necklines had been appropriate in the 1800s.

"You look stunning."

She looked at my reflection in the mirror. "Thank you. Let's hope Mom agrees with you."

"I think we're old enough to choose our own clothes." The two of us burst into giggles.

I scooted onto the bench next to her. "It's nice having you around."

She placed the hot curling iron on the vanity, swung an arm around me, and squeezed gently. "I've missed you, too."

I rose to get dressed. I tried not to sound nosey when I asked from my walk-in closet, "Did you get in touch with the cop you used to date?"

"Heavens no. I haven't seen or heard from him in forever."

She must have been with *someone* last night. She wouldn't just barhop by herself. Or would she? Even if she had, last call in Old Town was at two in the morning.

I slid into my own emerald-green gown with the obligatory puffed sleeves. I pinned my hair up in a bun and donned a ferronnière, a circle of faux diamonds and emeralds that I draped across the very top of my forehead and hooked into my hair on both sides. A matching necklace featuring a giant faux teardrop emerald surrounded by fake diamonds hung on a chain that clasped at the back of my neck.

When I emerged, Hannah had left the room, but Daisy waited for me and accompanied me down the stairs.

I cleaned up the cheese board that I had left in the kitchen and placed the used glasses in the dishwasher.

Roscoe, whom I had known as long as I could remember, walked into the kitchen looking worried. "So what happened at Dollie's house this morning? Was there a dead guy?"

"It was completely anticlimactic. A police friend met us there. There were no dead bodies anywhere. No blood, no evidence whatsoever."

"You're kidding!" Roscoe blinked at me as if I was the confused one.

"I'm afraid not. I don't know what to think."

"Really? That's incredible. Where is it that she lives exactly?"

"We're going to pass her house on our way to the restaurant. I'll try to remember to point it out to you. I think we should get going," I said cheerfully.

Everyone filed out the front door. I locked it behind us and joined my big crew on the sidewalk.

Nina and her husband joined us and greeted everyone.

We raved about Nina's amethyst slightly off the shoulder dress with long puffy sleeves.

She curtsied. "Who knew these dresses would be such fun?"

Aunt Melly gave her a big hug. "I have heard so much about you over the years that I feel like we're already fast friends!"

Dad and Nina's husband led our group toward the dinner venue. Cars passing us slowed so occupants could take pictures. Nina and I brought up the end of the group.

"Who is Hannah trying to impress?" she whispered. "The cute guy with the curly hair?"

"Roscoe?" I murmured. "I hadn't thought of that. She *was* out most of last night." I giggled. "It would be funny if she was downstairs with Roscoe the whole time! But that would explain why she was out well beyond last call."

"Who is he?"

"He went to school with Natasha and me. We've known him forever. He started a brewery in Berrysville."

"He's very good-looking. I love those loose curls. Not married, hmm?"

I shot her an amused glance. "Please don't try to fix me up with him. Divorced. His wife ran off with someone else. He claims she literally walked right by him carrying a suitcase and never returned."

"Ouch! That's brutal!"

"No kidding. I don't know what was at the root of their problems. He's been very pleasant."

We stopped at Dollie's house to pick her up. I pointed her house out to Roscoe, who studied it.

Dollie wore a low-cut dress that I suspected was silk. Giant flowers in pink and gold adorned the neckline and hem. I could not have managed her gold high heels but they were adorable with little flowers that matched her gown.

Melly whispered to Mom, "Isn't she about our age? I feel like a frump."

Dollie's hair had been teased and sprayed in place to stand up in a 1960s style. Not even a tornado would move it. Her earrings nearly touched her shoulders.

A man who looked to be about my age was with her. His short light brown hair appeared sun-kissed with tinges of blond.

"Sophie!" cried Dollie. "You must meet my favorite man. I love him to bits. If he were just a little bit older, I would have snatched him up by now. This is Julian Kowalski. His mother, Joanna, is my next-door neighbor."

Julian reached out to shake my hand. "I've heard a lot about you." Long dimples down the sides of his face enhanced his good looks. His eyes slanted downward ever so slightly toward the outer edges.

"Don't believe half of it," I joked.

Nina leaned in. "Nina Reid Norwood, I think I've seen you somewhere."

He smiled at her and tilted his head. "Tennis courts, maybe?"

"Yes! That's it." They continued chatting while I led the others toward our destination, an easy ten-minute walk.

Natasha had reserved a ballroom known for its delicious food.

Musicians played classical music softly in the background. A quick glance around the guests told me she had invited everyone she knew in Old Town who had a connection to our hometown of Berrysville, Virginia.

The tables had been arranged with a large space in the center of the room, probably to accommodate dancing after dinner. A waiter approached me with red, white, and blue cocktails. Nina and I each took one and sipped.

"Do you think Julian is really Dollie's boyfriend?" asked Nina, watching them mingle. "I don't know whether I'm jealous or want to be like her when I'm that age."

"I honestly don't know. She has to be twenty or thirty years his senior."

Mom and Dad sidled up to us.

"Your mother tells me I'm too old for Dollie," Dad chuckled.

Mom leaned toward us. "Do you think they're really a couple?"

Everyone was wondering that! "It happens," I said, "but she told me she knew the perfect guy for me, and I think she meant him."

"Wasn't that sweet of her!" Mom didn't try to hide her stare. "I believe I'll have a little chat with him."

"For pity's sake, Inga," Dad said dryly, "leave Sophie alone. She did very well with Mars."

"Yes. And look how that turned out."

I groaned. "Don't be so quick to dismiss the gold-digger possibility between them. Did you see the beautiful pin on his cravat with a hunting dog on it?"

"What's all this stuff hanging around the walls?" asked Nina.

Drinks in hand, we strolled by period attire from the 1880s. Women's silk dresses elaborately decorated with fabric flowers and ribbons hung on the wall. We passed similar gowns in children's sizes. Men's formal wear, much like what they were wearing for the event, also hung on display.

"Oh my gosh!" cried Nina. "They have price tags on them. Do you see these prices?"

Mom coughed. "Good heavens! We paid less than a fourth of that for both of our outfits."

Nina held up her empty drink glass. "Mmm. These are

delicious. I have to speak with the bartender about how he made them."

"I'm sure whatever you bring to tomorrow night's barbecue will be just as tasty," I assured her.

"I always find it helpful to chat with the professionals. They often have clever tricks if I can coax them into sharing their secrets." Nina wandered off straight toward Julian, who was not a bartender, at least not as far as I knew.

Not too far from me, Gus appeared to have cornered my father, who didn't look at all happy about it. I sidled toward them and overheard part of the conversation.

"Look," said Gus in an angry tone, "I don't need you trying to make me look like a dream husband. It's embarrassing."

Dad cocked his head. "I have no idea what you're talking about."

"I'm telling you to stop giving Melly flowers and stuff. Like that corsage on her wrist. Maybe you meant well and maybe I should have thought of it myself, but I felt like an idiot when she thanked me for it."

Dad's eyes narrowed. "It wasn't me. If I had bought something like that for my sister, don't you think I would have given them to my wife and daughters, too?"

Gus paused and eyed Dad. "No. I think you're trying to come between us. You don't think I'm good enough for your sister."

"I hardly know you. I would like to think that I'm the kind of man who doesn't jump to premature conclusions about people. Although I will admit that marrying Melly on a spur-of-the-moment trip to Las Vegas when you barely knew each other was a bit premature. But it's up to Melly to choose a husband. She must have seen something in you that appealed to her. I had hoped to get to know you better this week. Accusing me of trying to embarrass you isn't exactly a good start."

"Then who gave her that thing for her wrist? It must have been one of you trying to shame me."

"Did it occur to you that maybe Melly bought it for herself to make you look good?" Dad walked away from him and over to me.

"Sophie!" Humphrey Brown, who had attended grade school and high school with me, waved to me from across the room. He made his way over, smiled, and opened his arms for a hug. His waistcoat outfit looked debonaire on him. I hadn't seen him in over a year. He had put on a little weight, which was becoming. His hair was still the lightest, almost white, blond I had ever seen. With his pale complexion, he had always appeared wan, but today he seemed a little bit bronzed. As an undertaker, he didn't get out in the sun very much, but whatever the reason, Humphrey looked well and happy.

He greeted my parents enthusiastically. "I hoped Mom might come to visit this week. I know she would have enjoyed seeing you."

I doubted that. His mother thought she was the Queen of Berrysville and the rest of the population were her subjects. "What a shame," I fibbed.

"I'm so glad Natasha arranged this. There's Melly! I heard she got married. Maybe there's hope for me yet! Which one is her husband?"

"I'll introduce you." We walked toward him. "Gus? I'd like you to meet Humphrey Brown, also from Berrysville. You may have met his mother."

"Brown? Is your mother a tall woman? Very elegant?"

Their topic of conversation quickly changed to Old Town during the Civil War, which was admittedly rather interesting because it had been commandeered by the North but was surrounded by the South. Quite the land of espionage at the time. But while they talked, I was wondering how I could find out what Gus was doing at Dollie's house this morning.

He was so engaging with Humphrey that I began to think I was being too hard on him. But it was difficult to overlook the fact that he was visiting Dollie. I chided myself. It could have been something completely innocent. For all I knew, maybe Dollie was an old friend whom he hadn't seen in a very long time. A pretty close friend if he left her home from the backyard instead of the front door.

Maybe investigating murders had made me too cynical. Not everything was suspicious. In fact, most things were completely aboveboard and had perfectly reasonable explanations. But really, were there any truly good reasons to be visiting someone before dawn?

Natasha sailed to the center of the room where a microphone stood at the ready. "Hello, everyone!" she called out over the din.

Chapter 6

Dear Natasha,
My husband and I are staying with his sister for a week. On our fourth morning here, I couldn't sleep, so at three o'clock, I went out on their porch, which set off an alarm that could have awakened the dead! Then phones started ringing because the alarm company was calling. I took care to be quiet but now everyone is angry with me! I have apologized profusely but it appears all will not be forgiven. I think it's his sister's fault for not telling us that opening a door would set off an alarm. Dear hubby is siding with his sister. Who was at fault here?
They Should Have Told Me in Wake Village, Texas

Dear They Should Have Told Me,
You are at fault. A guest remains quietly in the bedroom until the host can be heard stirring.
Natasha

Natasha had informed me she was having a dress worn by Queen Victoria recreated. The silvery white gown set off her black hair beautifully. Like most of the dresses, it featured an off-the-shoulder neckline and puffed sleeves, but it was embroidered with roses and petals all the way around the skirt.

Her mother, Wanda, was an earth mother type, the exact opposite of Natasha. I spotted her standing nearby in a much simpler pale green gown.

Suddenly, the lights went down. One by one, spotlights flicked on, highlighting dresses and other attire of the 1800s that hung on the walls of the room. At the end, a spotlight shone on Natasha, who stood on a podium in the center of the room.

After welcoming us, Natasha announced, "Encouraged by the amazing number of inquiries about this party and the constant chatter in the news cycle, I have decided to add antique reproduction clothing to my new Americana store, which I hope you will visit. As you move about this room, you will see gowns, children's clothes, and menswear, all authentically replicated and available for purchase. Staying with our 1820s theme, tonight's dinner is based on recipes from the 1800s. Enjoy!"

Aha. I knew Natasha too well. Her big public splashes always had a business purpose behind them.

My ex-husband, Mars Winston, snuck up beside me, took my hand, and bowed to kiss it. Unfortunately, he caught me quite by surprise, which caused me to shriek. Bernie Frei, who had been the best man at our wedding, shook his head. "Never sneak up on Sophie!"

The two of them lived on the next block over from me. Mars and I had long gotten over the discomfort of our divorce and were friends now. He was a handy babysitter for Daisy when I needed to go out of town or had a particularly busy week. When we split up, neither of us could bear to give up Daisy, so we shared custody of her, swapping her every other week. I didn't mind if he wanted to run with her early in the morning and he was fine with me stopping by to pick her up for a walk during the week when she stayed with him.

"You're very jumpy. Was someone murdered?" Mars still held my hand, which I was certain my mother would notice.

I hoped Mom would also notice that Bernie kissed me on the cheek, thus nullifying any romantic intent. Born in England, Bernie had a wonderful British accent that made him sound knowledgeable about everything. Much to our surprise, footloose Bernie had opened a restaurant in Old Town and made it quite successful. We never expected him to remain, but then he bought a house and settled in.

"Who's the guy with Dollie?" asked Mars.

"That's Joanna Kowalski's son. He comes to the restaurant quite frequently," said Bernie. "Sometimes with his mom, other times with Dollie, and once in a while with both. He's divorced. And a very good son. He moved in with his mother before her knee surgeries so he could help out. I'm surprised you haven't met him, Mars. He's quite the history buff."

"I suppose there's no truth to the rumor that Dollie killed someone?" asked Mars.

A waiter offered us smoked salmon bruschetta and tiny tomato tarts.

"Killed someone?" I had dismissed the idea that Dollie could have murdered someone and removed the body. I didn't think she had the strength for that. But it might explain a few things, like why she came to my house instead of calling the police. Did she think that would somehow cover up what she had done? I had been feeling sorry for her and thought she was confused. Could she really be using that as a cover to get away with murder? I looked at her across the room. She was talking with my father and

Roscoe. From a distance, she looked elegant and rational. Not that you could tell a rational person from a confused person by looking at them. Or could you?

"Sophie?" Mars prodded my arm. "Are you okay?"

"What do you know about Dollie Peabody?" I asked.

Mars shrugged. "I've seen her around. Don't know beans about her, though."

"She reminds me of my mother," said Bernie.

I gazed at him in shock. I had never met his mother. I only knew that she had married more men than Elizabeth Taylor and had lived all over the world. If memory served, her current home was in Shanghai.

Bernie nodded. "Always well dressed in the latest fashion. Mum would rather be dead than caught in jeans and an ill-fitting top. Heaven forbid that anyone expect her to don a T-shirt. I would be surprised if she owned any jeans, actually. Dollie likes men. Better than women, I think. I'm not sure that she has many women friends. She flirts quite a bit, which wives tend to find annoying."

Bernie was not only astute about people and their quirks, but he had the opportunity to observe their behavior in his restaurant. So far in my experience, he had been dead-on about his customers and their character.

"She claimed she saw a dead man in her house," I said. "But there wasn't one when Nina and I went over there with her."

Mars cocked his head and snickered. "Oh right. How does that happen? Was anyone else there?"

"Not when we arrived. She's still sticking to her story." I looked around in search of Julian. Was he big enough to have removed a man for Dollie? Most people underestimated the weight of a corpse. Perhaps more important, would he have removed a dead man for Dollie and kept it quiet?

Bernie ran his hand through thick sandy hair, leaving it unruly. "That doesn't make any sense. Either she saw someone or she didn't."

"One would think that, but Wong went through the house and reported it clear. I honestly didn't see any signs of blood or disarray. The only odd thing was that the kitchen door to the backyard was unlocked, and her cat was outside. Dollie doesn't let her cat outside. But she did say that she sometimes forgets to lock the door."

"Did she say who the alleged dead man was?" asked Mars.

"She didn't recognize him."

Bernie snorted. "That's curious. So probably a burglar then? Interesting that I didn't hear any scuttlebutt about this at the restaurant today. I wonder why."

"Probably because the police don't take her seriously. She calls them regularly but there's never anything to see."

Humphrey spied us and ambled over. "What a fun evening. I'm glad we're eating inside, though. The humidity is awful. With the shirt, vest, jacket, and cravat, I think I would melt outside." He stopped abruptly. "I'm sorry. I obviously interrupted something here."

"Not at all," I assured him. "We were just dispelling silly rumors. It's good to see you!"

Guests were taking their seats. The four of us were sitting at the same table, along with Hannah, and Roscoe. A menu lay on top of a napkin before each seat.

Welcome to Dinner in 1826
Some liberties have been taken, but most recipes follow an authentic 1800s recipe.
Vermicelli Soup
Buttery Shrimp Pie
Baked Salmon Cutlets with Oregano

Roast Venison Medallions with Rye Rolls
Mustard and Shallot Pork Chops with Roasted Potatoes
Strawberry Ice Cream
Raspberry Tarts
Blackberry Cordials

"Wow!" Mars held a menu card in his hand. "Do you think they really ate this much food at one sitting?"

Bernie laughed. "Lots of courses have been served at fancy dinners for centuries. The portions are probably on the small side for most of them."

We thoroughly enjoyed the dinner and decided the soup, buttery shrimp, and pork chops were worth trying to replicate at home.

After dinner, my mom and dad were the first ones waltzing on the dance floor.

Nina sidled up to me and whispered, "Either Hannah isn't particularly interested in Roscoe or they made a pact not to be seen together in public."

I gazed around and spotted Hannah dancing with Humphrey.

Aunt Melly smiled as she danced with Gus. Evidently, those second thoughts she was having had vanished and all was well again in their marriage—except for his visit to Dollie, which only Nina and I knew about. I was still on the fence about telling Aunt Melly.

Ever the gentleman, Cyril danced with Dollie. They made quite the chic, if somewhat curious, pair.

Julian Kowalski made his way over to me and held out his hand. "Would you care to dance?"

"I would love to."

"I must warn you. My mother insisted that I attend social dancing lessons as a child. But I spent most of that time shooting spitballs at the other boys."

At least he had a good sense of humor. It turned out he was being modest and the dancing lessons had paid off.

"It's a relief to finally meet some people my age. Between taking care of my mom and Dollie, sometimes I have to remind myself that not everyone eats dinner at four p.m. and is in bed by eight."

"You're very kind to look out for Dollie. I'm sure she told you about the dead man she thought she saw in her house?"

" 'Thought she saw' would be the operative phrase there."

"Does she do that a lot? See things that aren't there?"

"Periodically. I haven't decided yet whether she makes things up to get attention or really believes that they are there."

"So she has seen dead men in her house before?"

"This may be the first dead man. More often it's voices or footsteps. The police are quite grumpy about it."

"I noticed that. What do you do for a living?"

"I'm a data analyst by day but an avid history buff in my spare time so I love living in Old Town."

"Dollie relies on you heavily. Thank you for looking out for her."

Julian shrugged. "I'm next door. It's no big deal. And she knows so many interesting people. She's always taking me to parties and events I wouldn't have even known about, much less been invited to. Like this one!"

"I'm sure she told you that the police think she's confused."

He nodded.

"Do you think she's confused?"

We danced out to the deck and stopped. "Confused is not the word I would use. Some people have abilities that I don't have or fully understand. Like people who communicate with the dead. I can't say whether they do or not. I know *I* can't do that but then, I can't play the saxophone, either. That doesn't mean no one else can."

I smiled at him. I liked his attitude.

"Sometimes I wonder if she's just an active dreamer," he said. "That would explain the dead guy she claimed she saw but clearly, there was no one there."

"Has she seen anyone else?"

Julian nearly choked. "No. I think I would know about that."

"Did you ever meet her last husband?" I was beginning to feel as if I was interrogating him. I needed to be careful and back off a little bit.

"No. I never did. Heard stories about him though, so I feel like I know him.

Mars sidled up to us, took my hand, and we waltzed away from Julian. I danced the evening away with Bernie, Humphrey, and best of all, my dad. As we departed, each person received a twenty-three-inch by twenty-nine-inch copy of the Declaration of Independence rolled up and tied with red, white, and blue ribbon.

"Is one of these an original copy?" asked Mars.

Dad laughed. "Wouldn't that be something? Somehow, I don't see Natasha giving away anything worth four million dollars."

Mom groaned. "Isn't it amazing that only twenty-six of the original two hundred copies have survived? I bet there are still some others stashed away somewhere. I know I won't be quite as quick to throw out old papers anymore."

British Bernie immediately quipped, "Two hundred years ago, you'd have locked me up as the enemy."

"Aha! A spy among us," I joked.

I thought the evening had gone well. Natasha pulled off a very fun and different event. Something I should keep in mind for my clients. Everyone seemed happy and chatty, if a little tired on our way out.

Our group split up as we departed. Hannah, Humphrey, Julian, and a number of the others weren't ready to call it a night and headed to the bar at The Laughing Hound.

Julian jogged over to me, a bit breathless. "Since you're walking the elder group home, I'm going to join the younger crowd. Do you mind making sure Dollie gets home okay?"

"Not a bit. Go ahead and have a good time."

My parents and those in the group around their age were ready to return home. It had been a long day. We ambled up King Street where store windows glowed in the night showing off their wares. We turned and strolled through a residential section, enjoying the flickering gaslighted lanterns on buildings. They occasionally shone on porches that had been decorated in honor of the Fourth of July festivities.

We were close to Dollie's home when the flashing light of police cars alarmed us. I heard someone shriek. Probably Dollie.

I hurried ahead, with Dad right behind me.

As we drew closer, I realized that the focus wasn't on Dollie's house, but just past it. Dad and I continued toward the police cars. We wedged between onlookers and saw that someone lay in the alley behind Dollie's home.

Chapter 7

Dear Sophie,
When staying with us, in the middle of the night my father-in-law had the audacity to make himself a drink and snack on cookies I had baked for the next day. Hubby insists that I not make a fuss, but I think that's just plain poor manners. What kind of guest raids the kitchen?

Exhausted in Midnight, Mississippi

Dear Exhausted,
Your father-in-law may view your house as a place where he can make himself at home. To avoid such surprises, prepare a little tray with bottled water and a selection of his favorite snacks, and leave it in his room so he won't have to raid the kitchen for a midnight snack.

Sophie

All the lights were off in Dollie's house, except for one on the main floor but it didn't aid us in seeing any better. The streetlight helped a little bit. I hoped it wasn't anything serious. Maybe the person had too much to drink and had passed out.

Neighbors clustered as close as the police allowed. One young police officer had been positioned at the back gate to Dollie's house to shoo people away.

I spied Dollie's neighbor, Joanna Kowalski, and sidled up to her. "What happened?"

"Oh, Sophie! We don't know." Joanna clutched my elbow. "Someone said the medical examiner has been called! I'm just distraught over it. Poor Dollie! I hope she's all right. She insists on wearing those spiky heels. At her age! I have told her time and again that she should wear sneakers like the rest of us. It's just not worth tripping at our age. My son, Julian, is out with her tonight. But wouldn't they have used the front door? What would they be doing in the alley?"

"They're fine. They were with us this evening." I turned to look for Dollie in the crowd that was growing bigger by the moment.

"What? Where are they?" asked Joanna.

A high-pitched scream came from behind us as a long-haired white cat fled across the alley. "Georgy!"

I ran toward her instinctively. The people and flashing lights must have scared and confused her because Georgy paused just long enough for me to scoop her up in my arms. I headed toward Dollie's gate, hoping they would allow me to put Georgy in the house.

Dollie broke through the crowd like she was swimming the breaststroke and half ran toward me.

"Ladies, you have to step back," said the young police officer.

"Excuse me, young man, but I live here!" Dollie wasn't shy. "This is my home, and I would appreciate it if *you* would step aside."

I handed Georgy to Dollie, who held her tight and buried her face in the white fur.

Joanna edged toward us. "I'm so relieved to see that you're all right, Dollie."

"Thank you, Joanna. Poor Georgy. She must be scared to death."

"What's going on?" I whispered to the officer.

"Some man died in the alley. Now, I'm sorry, but you have to back away."

Joanna screamed. "Where's Julian? Didn't he go out with the two of you?"

"He's fine," Dollie assured her. "He went out for a drink with the younger crowd."

"Some man? Who is it?" I asked.

"Ma'am, I can't tell you anything more."

Well, at least Dollie and Georgy seemed fine. What an odd thing to happen. Someone just dropped dead in the alley behind her house? In spite of the July heat, chills skittered across my arms as I watched the police. As far as I could tell from where I stood, he lay on his back. Hit by a car in the alley perhaps? I was so focused that I blocked out the crowd and inched closer.

"Hello, Sophie. It didn't take you long to get involved."

I knew that voice all too well. Deep and calm, as if there wasn't a dead man in the alley. I tuned to see Detective Wolf Fleishman of the Alexandria, Virginia Police. He must have noticed me in the crowd. I had dated him for a couple of years after my divorce, but we split up. Things were definitely awkward at first, but as time went on, we worked that out and managed to solve a few murders together. I noted, though, that he still tried to avoid being alone together. That was probably just as well. Even if nothing happened, people could draw incorrect conclusions. He was a good guy, even if he didn't always tell me murder details that I wanted to know.

"Nice to see you," he said. "Please tell me that you have no involvement with this man."

"I don't know a thing about it. We were just walking home from dinner."

Wolf smiled at me as if he thought I was making up an excuse to have happened to be there at that moment. "Nice dress."

The presence of a body had pushed all thoughts of my 1800-style attire out of my head. "It's all the rage," I quipped.

Dad joined us and shook Wolf's hand. "It has been quite a while since I saw you, Wolf. I hope everything is okay here?"

"Good to see you, Paul." Wolf asked us, "Do either of you know Dollie Peabody?"

Dollie smiled and cocked her head coyly as if she were flirting with Wolf. "Why, I'm Dollie Peabody, sugar!"

I was more amused than surprised. I had always found Wolf attractive and apparently Dollie did, too. In the lights the police had set up, the silver hair creeping in just above his ears seemed to stand out against his tanned skin. I hoped that meant he'd had some time off for golf.

Wolf flashed his badge at her. "Wolf Fleishman of the Alexandria Police. Could you step over here with me to see if you can identify this man?"

Dollie handed Georgy to me and took Wolf's arm as if she was a debutante. "Of course. Anything you need. I thought I knew all the handsome men in Old Town."

It was a good thing their backs were to me, and they couldn't see me rolling my eyes.

It wasn't any of my business, but I trailed along behind them. Dad followed me.

I gasped when I saw a dark stain on the corpse's clothing near his waist. It had to be blood.

Surprisingly, Dollie kept her cool when she peered at the corpse. "I'm sorry. I don't know who he is. He's a nice-looking man, though. What a pity."

Dad stepped past me for a better look. "Good heavens! That's Tony Fontana, our tour guide."

I edged closer. Dad was right. I looked at Wolf. "I hired Tony to drive my family and guests on a two-day tour of Washington, DC."

"Does he live around here?" asked Wolf.

I nodded. "On South Columbus, I believe."

"When is the last time you saw him?"

"Yesterday when he brought us home around four in the afternoon."

Wolf's face never showed what he was thinking. It drove me nuts when we dated because I could never deduce his reactions to anything. I certainly wouldn't ever play poker with him. His impassive expression usually led me to blather more. I always suspected he thought I would blindly proffer useful information. But I was onto him.

"Williams!" called Wolf. "Send some of the new recruits to look for a bus." He turned to me. "What did it look like?"

"It was the size of a school bus—"

Dad interrupted me. "It actually was a school bus once. He bought it at auction, painted it red, white, and blue for tourists, and retrofitted the interior."

Wolf nodded. "You get that?" he asked Williams. "Have them look for it around here."

"He could have walked," I pointed out.

Wolf nodded. "Do you know his home address?"

I looked it up on my phone contacts and read it to him.

At that point, the medical examiner arrived and everyone except Wolf was shooed away.

"We should go home. I'm sure our crew is tired of standing around."

Dad nodded. We wished Dollie a good night and located the rest of our group.

"Finally!" Mom let out a big sigh. "We were beginning to think you would never come back."

I didn't point out that they could have gone on to my house. I held my tongue because I knew they were as curious as the rest of us. I counted noses and encouraged them to come with us. Word that the corpse's identity was Tony Fontana put an immediate damper on our spirits.

Minutes later, we arrived at my house. While the others settled in, I took Daisy out for her evening walk. I couldn't help it that Daisy steered me back to the commotion.

Most of the onlookers were dispersing. Tony's body was in the ambulance. For transport to the morgue, I supposed. No lights blinked on police cars anymore. A handful of people examined the alley with flashlights in hand murmuring respectfully as if Tony still lay there.

One man muttered to no one in particular, "There's no blood."

Daisy walked along the alley, her nose to the ground. I looked up at Dollie's house, wondering how Georgy had managed to slip out again. Had she let Georgy out and forgotten about her while we went to dinner? If I had mistakenly let Mochie out, I would have been hypervigilant about it for quite a while.

The lights were on upstairs on the second floor. Dollie was probably changing out of her fancy gown. I made a mental note to ask some of her dancing partners if she had seemed forgetful or said anything odd or inconsistent with the conversation.

Daisy drew toward the middle of the alley. I turned on the flashlight in my phone. Assuming we were in the correct place, the man had been right. There were no signs of blood. I didn't know what to make of that. It made no sense that blood would be on his clothing but wouldn't have dripped onto the ground.

The Tony I knew was a nice guy. What could he have done to prompt someone to stab or shoot him? And why was he there anyway? I couldn't help wondering if there was some connection to Gus being there early in the morning, almost in the same location.

That was ridiculous. I relaxed a little. If Gus had harmed someone, wouldn't he have had blood on his clothing? Besides, when Nina and I saw Gus, there was no sign of Tony. I couldn't explain why Tony was in the alleyway behind Dollie's house, but he had every right to be there. I cut through alleys all the time. Everyone did. Why walk all the way around a block to get where you were going?

I steered Daisy in the direction of home. When we entered the house, I could hear Mom, Dad, Aunt Melly, Gus, and Cyril in the kitchen.

I removed Daisy's harness, and she trotted toward our company wagging her tail.

"I thought you would be outside on the porch," I said, hanging up the harness.

"Tomorrow," said Mom. "I made everyone warm milk with turmeric and bananas. We're so upset about poor Tony that I don't think any of us will be able sleep."

I preheated the oven to 350, removed homemade chocolate chip cookie dough from the freezer, cut it into thick slices, divided them into triangles and placed them, pointing upward, on a cookie sheet, and slid it into the oven.

"Such a nice man." Aunt Melly clutched a mug in both of her hands. "What a wonderful sense of humor he had. I never knew they buried dead politicians in unmarked graves so they wouldn't be dug up by their enemies."

Gus patted her arm. "And then they couldn't locate them after the war to send them home for a proper burial!"

Cyril watched the two of them. "He certainly knew his history. I've never heard anyone talk about it in such detail. Like the spying during the Civil War. Fascinating. I will never look at a laundry line the same way again. From here on out, I shall assume that all laundry drying in the sun is a spy message to someone! The world has lost a truly interesting man. Such a pity that he died."

"Did Wolf tell you how he died?" Mom held her cup out to me for a refill.

"No. But Daisy walked over that way. There's no blood visible on the alley." I pulled the cookies out of the oven and piled them on a platter. "Which is weird because I thought I saw a good size bloodstain on his clothes."

"Do you think Wolf will tell you what the autopsy shows?" asked Dad.

I placed the platter of cookies on the table. "It's hard to say. But if he doesn't, Humphrey often gets the scuttlebutt from the medical examiner's office."

"Is it my imagination, or did Humphrey look particularly handsome tonight?" Mom bit into a cookie.

"Didn't he, though?" Melly finally smiled. "I remember him as such a thin, pale little boy. Like a ghost!"

Dad laughed. "He had such a crush on Sophie, and she plain ignored him."

Mom grinned at me. "I think he must have worn out the tires on that bicycle he rode by our house every afternoon. Is he seeing anyone now? Wouldn't he make a wonderful son-in-law? Did you invite him for dinner tomorrow night?"

She gave me a hopeful look that screamed, *You're both single!*

Fortunately, Aunt Melly seemed oblivious to Mom's encouragement. "If you ask me, you dodged a bullet, Sophie. You would have had the witchiest mother-in-law on the planet. Nothing you ever did would have been right."

I should have been appalled that Aunt Melly spoke as if I had ever even considered a relationship with Humphrey. The truth was that I didn't even remember him when my mother had the nerve to set me up with him by inviting him to dinner at my house at few years ago. He was a kind person. Sometimes a little awkward but well meaning.

"Melly!" exclaimed Mom as if Aunt Melly had said something incredibly rude.

"I never have liked that woman. She's such a snob. I don't care for people who think they're better than everyone else." Melly pointed her forefinger at me. "There isn't a woman on this green earth good enough for her son. You did well to let that one slide on by."

I really needed to stop that line of conversation. "Have another cookie, Mom." I promptly changed the subject to Gus. "So where are you from, Gus?"

"We moved around a lot when I was kid. New Jersey, Maryland, Arizona."

"Are you retired?" I asked, knowing full well what the answer would be.

"Yup. Loving every moment of it!"

I paused, hoping someone at the table would ask him the logical next question. But no one did. "What line of work were you in?"

"Oh! Well now, I owned a pawnshop. Met a lot of people. Heard so many down-on-their-luck stories and dreams of making fortunes. I'd like to think I helped some of them over their financial troubles, at least for a little while."

Aunt Melly smiled at him. "He still does some buying and selling when he smells a good deal."

"It's not as much fun when you don't meet the people

involved. You know what I mean. It tugs at your heart when a college kid pawns a fancy camera, a gift from Dad, to pay her bills, or a mom is looking for a bike she can afford for her kid's birthday."

"Did those things really happen?" asked Mom.

"Oh, sure. I gotta tell you, you'd be surprised by how many people brought in their engagement rings. Now that was always tragic."

"Divorce?" asked Cyril.

"Sometimes. But more often than not they needed money and that diamond landed in my showcase until they could get back on their feet. Sometimes it had sold by the time they returned looking for it and I always felt awful bad about that."

Aunt Melly held out her hand and gazed at her ring, which held a sizeable diamond. According to her it was three carats. "Was my ring pawned by someone?"

Gus chuckled. "Would that matter?"

"Maybe. I guess it would depend on the situation. I don't think I would want to wear the ring of a murdered woman. That would be creepy."

Uh-oh. I could see where this was going. I needed to change the subject in a big hurry. "Poor Tony," I said. "I guess they've informed his wife by now."

Whew! The conversation switched back to our deceased bus driver. After that, everyone slowly drifted off to bed.

I cleaned up the kitchen and headed upstairs to my own bed, exhausted.

Daisy woke me, whimpering.

I opened one eye and looked at the clock. Midnight. What was that saying? *Nothing good happens after midnight.*

The stairs creaked as someone walked downstairs. I

was too tired to get up. Someone probably wanted a glass of water. I rolled over but I couldn't quite get comfortable on my pillow. Something was crunching under my ear. I reached inside the pillowcase and discovered a piece of paper.

I flicked the light on to read it.

Gus murdered Tony.

Chapter 8

Dear Sophie,
One of my husband's best college buddies came to visit with his wife, whom we met for ten minutes at their wedding. I discovered her in our bedroom one morning pawing through a drawer! She was clearly snooping. I politely asked if I could help her. She claimed to be looking for a pen. Really? In my underwear drawer? They departed rather suddenly thereafter and now her husband won't take my husband's calls. It's a big mess. Hubby is furious with me! What was I supposed to do?
None of Her Business in Dresser, Wisconsin

Dear None of Her Business,
I think you handled it well. If she didn't feel guilty, they wouldn't have left so abruptly. The ball is in their court to apologize. In the future, you might suggest they stay at a local hotel or B&B.
Sophie

My breath caught in my throat. I grabbed for the water on my nightstand and gulped it, hoping I wouldn't have a coughing fit and wake everyone. My heart pounding, I examined the note.

The first thought that came to me was that we didn't know for sure that Tony had been murdered, although the blood I saw on his clothing certainly suggested that was the case. Whoever wrote this thought so, as well. That was very interesting. How could the author of the note know that? I stared at the note in horror. It had been handwritten in awkward block letters as if someone was trying to disguise his or her handwriting. I flipped it over. It appeared to have been torn off a larger sheet of ordinary white paper. Had it been card stock or linen, I might have been able to locate the source, but this was simple printer paper. At least that was how it looked to me. Any of my guests would have had access to printer paper in my home office. It sat out in the open in the paper feeder of my printer.

My second thought was concern for Aunt Melly. She lay beside Gus in bed right now, not realizing that he could be a murderer. She had looked so content as she danced with him only a few hours ago.

I took deep breaths to calm my nerves. Maybe this person was wrong. And how would *anyone* know anyway? We didn't know for sure how Tony had died. There was still the slight possibility that he had expired from natural causes or an accident. I didn't know anything about his health. Maybe he had some underlying condition that he didn't talk about. He hadn't been the most physically fit person.

Unless—I felt sick to even imagine it—unless the person who wrote this note had been present and seen Gus murder Tony. I couldn't imagine any other way that the author of the note could be so certain.

It didn't help that I had spied Gus yesterday morning in almost exactly the same place where Tony's body had been found tonight. Gus had definitely been inside Dollie's backyard in the morning. But why? There was no question in my mind that most people didn't open the gate to a stranger's backyard and simply walk in. Did he know Dollie? He hadn't shown any recognition when she showed up at my house. Nor had she.

Was he scoping the area out because he planned to murder Tony? Was he looking for Tony? Had he arranged to meet Tony there?

I shook my head as if that might help me get rid of the ugly thoughts. There couldn't be a connection between the dead man Dollie saw in her home and Tony. Could there? If Gus had murdered Tony early in the morning just before I saw him leaving Dollie's backyard, where would Tony's body have been all day? Plus, Dollie said she didn't know Tony, so it wasn't as if Tony had been hanging around her house. The pieces just didn't fit for that.

I rose and carefully slid the note into a copy of Agatha Christie's *And Then There Were None*. It was silly of me to hide it, but I didn't know what to make of it yet. I didn't think it was true, but then why write the note? And I certainly didn't want to throw everyone into a panic, especially if it was a hoax of some sort.

What worried me most was that it could be accurate. The timing wasn't right, though. After all, Gus had been with us all evening at the party. I remembered him dancing with Aunt Melly. He hadn't been out murdering anyone.

I felt comforted by that thought. But if that was true, why would someone point a finger at Gus? To deflect attention from himself? It would certainly do that!

I crawled back between the cool sheets but I sat up in bed thinking. For the longest time I couldn't sleep. Hannah rolled in at four fifteen in the morning.

"Did you lock the front door behind you?" I asked.

"Oh! I woke you. I'm sorry."

"No problem. I couldn't sleep. The door—are you certain you locked it?"

"Yes, Miss Worrywart."

Only then did it dawn on me that she might not know Tony had died. Since the bars closed at two, where had she been all this time anyway? I would sound cranky if I questioned her. She was an adult, not a kid who needed someone looking out for her. It was possible that she had gone home with Mars and Bernie for a last drink and they had gotten involved in some kind of fun game. But Mars wasn't much into late nights anymore. Not that I knew of anyway. Or, for all I knew, she might have been downstairs or out on the back porch flirting with Roscoe all this time.

I finally drifted off.

Morning arrived all too soon. My first thought was about my guests. When I remembered the note, what scared me the most wasn't that Gus might have murdered Tony, but that the person who wrote the note had to be one of my houseguests.

Chapter 9

Dear Natasha,
I enjoy having houseguests. I remember the days when staying with friends was all I could afford. But I'm not much of a cook, so breakfast is always a dilemma for me. I can manage coffee and juice, but that's about it. Is it rude to take my guests out to breakfast?

Only a B, Not a B&B in Bacon City, USA

Dear Only a B, Not a B&B,
It's not rude if you actually take them to breakfast somewhere. Tossing them out before coffee or tea, and at least a breakfast bread, screams, "and don't come back!"

Natasha

No one outside of my invited guests had been in my house the day before, except for Dollie and Stan. I had been with Dollie the entire time. But I couldn't recall whether Stan even entered the house. He may have departed after breakfast. And in any event, neither of them would know where *my* bedroom was or whether I was sleeping in it. It had been mildly chaotic with all the visitors, but none of my Old Town friends had been here. And as far as I knew, none of my guests invited anyone into the house.

On the other hand, Stan was the only one who hadn't been invited to Natasha's party. The invitations went out months ago, before we even knew that Stan Cox existed. He would have had the opportunity to leave Tony in the alley.

Mom and Dad would have told me in person of their concerns if they suspected Gus had murdered someone. It would have been a big stink. Do we tell Aunt Melly or not? Has she married a killer? Did we see any signs that he could be dangerous? Would he harm Melly? Would he harm us or someone else, too? Why had he murdered Tony? What do we do now? Nope. My parents would *never* have slipped a note inside my pillow.

Hannah probably would have told me about her suspicions, too. I could certainly count out *Gus* leaving that note attached to my pillowcase. That narrowed down the possibilities nicely. It had to be either Aunt Melly, Cyril, or Roscoe.

Aunt Melly concerned me. I wasn't sure whether she would be relieved to be rid of Gus or would try to protect him. She had clearly been upset when he mentioned selling her home, but later on when they danced at dinner, it looked as though all had been forgiven.

Relationships were a peculiar thing. There was always the desire to think *he couldn't have done that*. But doubt had a way of wiggling itself into our brains. There was no telling how a person might react. Would Aunt Melly defend her new husband, determined to believe that he must be the good and wonderful man she had married? Would she turn him in, horrified and disgusted to know he could do anything so heinous? Or would she do the passive-aggressive thing and surreptitiously slide a clue into my pillowcase where it would be found and hope that I would take appropriate measures?

I collected my clothes, a white skort and navy-blue top adorned with almost inconspicuous tiny white stars, then quietly showered and dressed. I took Daisy out for an early-morning walk. The summer air felt fresh and cool. That wouldn't last long. So far, the streets were quiet because of the July Fourth holiday. A few bakeries and cafés had opened for business. When I saw cute doughnuts decorated with holiday colors and themes, I almost felt guilty for not making some myself. I bought a couple of boxes of them for my company.

On our way home, I made a point of visiting the alley behind Dollie's house again. I wasn't the only one. Several joggers had slowed to a walk and looked around. There really wasn't much to see. Dollie's red gate appeared to be in perfect condition. The paint wasn't scratched, and I didn't see any smears of blood.

Back at home, Mochie wound around my ankles in the kitchen. I picked him up. "I'm glad you don't keep escaping the house like Georgy. But as one of the permanent residents, I'll feed you breakfast first." He purred his appreciation.

I spooned his favorite turkey mousse cat food into his bowl, and he nestled down to eat.

After feeding Daisy, I made coffee and set out mugs for coffee and tea for early risers. I pulled out a large round red-and-white platter and placed the doughnuts on it with the cheerful red, white, and blue napkins next to it. Anyone who was up early could have a little pre-breakfast doughnut nibble.

I got to work on potato salad and pasta salad for dinner later in the day. Before long, I had a pot of potatoes, a pot of pasta, and a pot of eggs cooking. Meanwhile, I chopped and minced the various things that would go into the dishes. Crunchy celery, savory onions and garlic, sweet and sour pickles.

I was so busy that I didn't notice Cyril standing in the doorway. "Good morning," he said softly.

I squealed. "I'm sorry. I was concentrating and didn't see you there. Come help yourself to some coffee. Did you sleep okay?"

"Mostly. Tony's death weighed heavily on my mind. He was such a nice fellow. So patient and he had a wonderful sense of humor."

"I think we all felt that way. I desperately want to think he died from some natural cause, but I certainly didn't notice anything about him that would have made me think he was ill. Did you?"

"Not really," he said with a hint of hesitation.

"Sort of?"

"Well, I think we can admit that he might not have been in the best physical health, but these things vary so much. I suppose they will do an autopsy."

I nodded as I poured water out of the rotini pasta. "It's a requirement when someone dies who isn't under a doctor's care for a terminal illness."

"I wonder how we could find out what killed him."

"I imagine that Humphrey or Wolf will tell me." I poured olive oil over the pasta and tossed it.

"Tony was in my age group. It can happen to any of us. It's unsettling to imagine that we could simply drop dead. Makes a person think about all the things he hasn't done. All the plans, the places he hasn't seen, the relationships that he wished he had pursued, the things he wishes he had done differently. That'll keep a person up all night for sure."

He'd said one thing that caught my attention. I stopped chopping. "Relationships he wished he had pursued?"

His back to me, Cyril poured coffee into a mug. "I was one of those people who focused on work. My adult life has always revolved around my work and the university. That was my life. I was dedicated to it, and I won't say that it wasn't rewarding. Married friends had to be at their children's activities, but I was married to my job. Now I've reached an age where I wish I had that special someone to share life with. It makes me feel as though life has passed me by, but there's nothing I can do about it. I can't stop time. I should have followed my heart when I was young, but I was completely focused on my career. I admit I enjoyed it very much but now I wish I had found the time, made the time, for someone else." He laughed bitterly. "Remember that song?" He sang on key in a lovely voice, "'I lost my true lover, by courtin' too slow.' I believe that song could have been written for me."

"You were in love with someone?"

He nodded. "But enough about me. Don't let that happen to you. I was surprised to see Humphrey last night. I recognized him by his hair. You don't see such incredibly light hair too often. I only knew him as a child. As I recall, he was quite shy." Cyril bit into a doughnut.

Mom must have heard the tail end of our conversation. She joined us and poured a mug of coffee for herself. "Good morning! I've heard that Humphrey's mother is particularly fond of you, Cyril."

Cyril coughed. "That's a nice way of putting it."

"Oh?" asked Mom.

"Stalker would be more appropriate."

I stopped what I was doing. "She follows you around?"

"And how! I caught her going through my mail one day. She took it out of my mailbox and was flipping through it!"

Mom chuckled. "Single men our age are at a premium in Berrysville."

"That's no reason to hound me. I have made it abundantly clear that I am not interested in her. One doesn't want to be unkind to a lady, but her behavior is outrageous. And she's a bit, umm, pompous for my taste. Humphrey turned out quite well, but I'm sure it was in spite of his mother, not because of her."

Mom sat down at the table and eyed the doughnuts. "I noticed you dancing with Wanda last night."

He chuckled. "I also danced with you. Let's not jump to any conclusions."

His cheeks blazed. I did like a good love story. For a minute there, I thought he might have had a thing for Wanda, but now I had to wonder if he had been in love with my mom!

At that point, Aunt Melly and Dad joined us and the conversation turned back to Tony's death.

I finished the salads, covered them with wrap, and began to scramble eggs and make sheet pan pancakes for breakfast. Mom and Aunt Melly pitched in, which made it all the easier.

In no time, each of us carried something outside to the porch and we sat down to eat. Only Gus, Roscoe, Stan, and Hannah were missing. Clearly the late sleepers in the group. Or maybe the ones who stayed out the latest.

The air had warmed considerably but was still comfortable. We had no activities scheduled until the backyard barbecue with friends and the fireworks afterward.

Old Town had strict rules against fireworks. But who needed them when there would be fantastic professional fireworks to watch? Bernie had made arrangements with a friend whose building offered a perfect view of the Washington, DC fireworks from the rooftop.

I had prepared pies, cake, and snacks in advance and looked forward to homemade strawberry ice cream later in the day.

Hannah finally made an appearance on the porch wearing a jean skirt and one of my white shirts with the cuffs rolled back. She had bothered to curl her hair in loose beach waves and wore a bold gold necklace that I was certain was faux, and dangling red earrings in the shapes of clovers. Several bracelets jangled on her tanned arm. She had taken care with her makeup, too. What was going on?

I thought I might have my answer when Roscoe ambled in a few minutes later in shorts and a T-shirt advertising his craft beer.

Stan showed up again, acted as if he was part of our group, and helped himself to breakfast. "How was the fancy party last night?"

We'd felt guilty for not taking him with us, but we hadn't known he was coming with Gus until it was far too late to bring along another guest.

"It was delightful," said Mom. "I'm sorry you couldn't join us. Even the food was similar to what people may have eaten in the 1820s. Though I suspect the chef had to take a lot of liberties."

Aunt Melly glared up at the window of the bedroom where she and Gus were staying. Probably irate that he was the last to appear.

I doubted that it mattered to anyone else.

I watched for interaction or fond glances between Hannah and Roscoe but didn't notice anything other than an exchange about the doughnuts. It was always a little awkward to reveal a new relationship but there was no reason for them to pretend. Each was single and, as far as I knew, not involved with anyone else.

Gus finally made an appearance. If he had gotten any sleep at all, he certainly didn't look like it. Maybe Tony's death had hit him hard as it had Cyril. That could account for Gus's puffy eyes. He ambled toward us barefoot, wearing jeans and an unbuttoned shirt of tropical palms which revealed a hairy chest. "Mornin'."

"Well, don't you look nice and cool," said Mom.

I thought Aunt Melly might just melt from embarrassment. She got up on the pretense of fixing him a plate of food, but everyone heard her hiss, "For heaven's sake, button your shirt!"

Fortunately for her, we all turned our attention to Wolf as he strode across the lawn. "I hope I'm not interrupting your breakfast."

From the cheerful greeting the others gave him, I knew they didn't realize that his presence meant bad news. For starters, it was a holiday, and most people don't work on a holiday unless there's big trouble. Although Mom immediately offered him breakfast, and he gratefully accepted a plate full of food, I knew without him saying so that Tony had been murdered.

The conversation was light and focused on where one could see the fireworks best from Old Town. We invited him to join us for our backyard barbecue dinner, which I knew he would never do because he wouldn't leave his wife alone on a holiday unless it was an emergency and it would be awkward to bring her with him. I waited, my heart pounding, for the bad news I knew was coming.

"That was delicious. I don't know who prepared it, but I suspect Sophie had a hand in it. Thank you."

He seemed so congenial. Unless you were a murder suspect, he actually was a pretty friendly guy. If I hadn't known him as well as I did, I would have smiled at him like my mother was.

"Is this a good time to ask you a few questions about Tony?" Wolf didn't wait for an answer. "All of you spent time with him in the last couple of days before his death. Did he say anything about his plans?"

"He was excited about the Fourth of July," said Aunt Melly sweetly. "He was very interested in the Declaration of Independence. Did you know that they didn't all sign it at once? It had to travel around for all those signatures!

Wolf smiled at her. "Would you happen to have one in your attic somewhere?"

Aunt Melly smiled. "Don't I wish! The last one sold for nearly four million dollars!"

"Imagine making two hundred copies without a modern copy machine!" said Cyril.

Wolf moved on. "Did he mention what he would be doing today or yesterday?"

"He spoke a good deal with Gus, Cyril, and Roscoe, didn't he?" said Mom.

Wolf watched them all with a pleasant expression. "Did he seem worried? Out of sorts at all?"

"He was most gracious!" Aunt Melly exclaimed. "If he had any concerns about anything, you sure wouldn't have known it. And he was very funny, too. Always interjecting humorous tales."

"Was he taking calls from anyone?" asked Wolf.

My guests exchanged looks.

I answered for them. "He was very professional. I think he may have had his phone turned off. I never saw him otherwise engaged. He took us through museums as if he had worked in each one and knew the details about various paintings and artifacts."

"Definitely," said Dad. "So many interesting facts. I had no idea that nearly half of the signers of the Declaration of Independence were in their twenties and thirties. I guess the pictures of paintings I usually see of men in white wigs made me think they were all old at the time."

"Are any of you collectors of historic memorabilia?" asked Wolf. "The antique fair in town has some incredible things."

Aunt Melly said, "That's right up Gus's alley. We should

poke around a bit. Maybe you can find something that's worth more than they think, Gus."

"I used to be in the pawnshop business, so Melly thinks I'm an expert on everything."

Wolf must have been frustrated but as was his way, he didn't show it. "A man like Tony must have had big plans for the Fourth. Was he going to speak somewhere? Be in the parade?"

I felt a little bit sorry for Wolf. I had asked those sorts of questions many times about murder victims. It wasn't easy to delve into other people's lives. Some people blathered about everything while others, like Tony, kept their private business to themselves. "I'm afraid the topic of interest those two days was history," I said. "Not Tony's personal life."

Cyril, who hadn't spoken much after Wolf arrived, said in a quiet voice, "I gather these questions mean Tony did not die of natural causes?"

Chapter 10

Dear Sophie,
My husband says I get too worked up over having guests for dinner. I just want everything to be perfect, but I find it difficult to pull off meals when people are milling around and trying to chat with me. Help?

Stressed Hostess in Vienna, Virginia

Dear Stressed Hostess,
Do as much as you can in advance. That includes simple things like setting the table, getting out serving dishes and utensils. You could even do a dry run of that in advance, so you'll know what you're missing. Make a list of all the dishes you are serving so you won't get sidetracked and leave something forgotten in the fridge or on the stove. Do not drink any alcohol until everyone is seated and served. Then you can relax and enjoy your guests.

Sophie

Silence fell over us. All eyes were on Wolf when he said, "I'm afraid not."

Cyril paled. "What was the cause of death?"

"I'm not at liberty to say just yet." Wolf scooted his chair back. "Thank you for breakfast. It was delicious. Probably the best meal I'll have today." He looked at me as he rose to his feet. "Please do me a favor and let me know if any of you remember something useful. It might seem unimportant, but sometimes those little things lead us in the right direction."

"Of course," I said. "Although I have to tell you, I was with them and Tony didn't talk about himself much."

"And yet you knew where he lived."

I could feel the blush of embarrassment rising in my face. "Good point. His family must be devastated." I hustled around the table to walk out with him and tell him about the note on my pillow as well as Gus's presence at Dollie's house the previous morning, when his phone buzzed.

"Fleishman," he barked into it. "On my way." He tucked his phone into a pocket and smiled at me. "At least you're not involved this time. Have a great Fourth of July."

I hoped he was right and that Gus had nothing to do with Tony's death. "We're having a big barbecue around dinnertime. If you're in the neighborhood, I hope you'll stop by. And Wolf . . ."

A ruckus broke out behind me at the table. I turned to see what was going on.

Gus was standing and appeared to be arguing with Aunt Melly. Mom and Dad looked upset.

I turned back to Wolf, but he had taken off.

I rushed to the table, certain that I did not want to know what Gus and Aunt Melly were arguing about.

"Melly, we have to go. That's all there is to it. Sorry to cut your vacation short, Stan." Gus rubbed his unshaven face vigorously.

"But it's the Fourth of July! That's why we came," Mom protested. "Melly, honey, do *you* want to leave?"

Aunt Melly appeared conflicted. I hoped she wouldn't cry. I didn't know if I could bear that. She raised both of her hands shoulder height, her fingers curled into fists. "But I'm enjoying myself, Gus. I never get to see Sophie. Besides, we planned to stay a few more days. Why would we leave now?"

Gus chewed the side of his lower lip.

I tried hard to analyze the look on his face. Was he afraid? How stupid of me. Of course! He probably hadn't expected the detective in charge of the case to show up and have breakfast with us. The killer would be flipping out. No wonder he wanted to leave. The author of that note had been right!

I tried to appear calm, even if I wasn't, and poured myself another mug of tea. "It would be a shame if you missed tonight's fireworks. I thought you wanted to see the parade in Washington at noon." Now I was sorry I hadn't run after Wolf to tell him about the note on my pillowcase. No matter. I would call him in a few minutes and let him know. Right now, I needed to stop them from taking off. Or would it be safer for the rest of us if I encouraged them, in an unobvious way, of course, to depart? But that would leave Aunt Melly all alone with a killer. Definitely not!

Everyone watched Gus.

Tension cramping his voice, he said, "I would like to speak with you privately, Melly."

Aunt Melly shook her head. "It's not necessary. We're not going anywhere. This is my family, Gus. This is where I want to be. Now get yourself another one of those cute doughnuts. They're so yummy! That will help you relax. Honestly, I don't know what has come over you."

Gus closed his eyes and hissed, "Please. You don't understand." He reached out and gripped her hand.

Aunt Melly shrugged and rose from her seat. "I do not appreciate the scene you're making." But she went along with him toward the house.

"Well! What do you suppose got into him?" Mom asked.

It dawned on me that it might be better not to tell anyone else what I knew. They wouldn't act normal around Gus. And worse, one of them might tell him.

Mom patted the chair next to her. "Honey, don't you think we should bake a cake or make a casserole for Tony's family?"

It did seem like the right thing to do. And we definitely needed to do it before they found out that my guest had murdered him.

"I'm not much of a cook, so if you don't mind, I thought I'd pay a visit to a college friend who lives in town. Thanks for breakfast, Sophie." Roscoe rose and walked across the lawn with his phone up to his ear.

Hannah's phone jangled. She glanced at it and grinned. "Hiiiii." She drew the word out. It was sultry, almost seductive. She left the table.

Mom gazed from Roscoe to Hannah and back at Roscoe. "I don't think that was a coincidence. Is it possible that Roscoe and Hannah have, what do they call it these days?"

"Hooked up," offered Stan.

"I hope so. They would make a nice couple." Cyril smiled.

If that was the case, I was happy for both of them, but I needed to sneak off and make my own call to Wolf. Right after I eavesdropped on Gus. I excused myself and hurried to the kitchen entrance. I closed the door behind me quietly and listened.

Aunt Melly didn't bother to whisper. "That doesn't make any sense. I just don't understand why you want to leave. What is the problem, Gus?"

Were they in the sunroom? I crept closer.

"I will be the killer's next victim."

"What?!" Melly shrieked loud enough to be heard next door.

"Shh. It's true. Remember when we saw the gemstones at the Smithsonian? Tony told me that a ruby had disappeared and he was on the track of it. His killer thinks *I* know where it is."

"What ruby? No one said anything about a missing ruby. I would have heard about it on the news."

"That's just it. They keep it very quiet and put a substitute in the showcase so people won't realize that it's missing. The thief will probably have it cut into smaller stones to sell so it can't be tracked anymore."

"Oh, Gus. Then it would make more sense to have it all over the news so that jewelers would return it instead of cutting it up."

"Melly, you're so naïve. He's not going to hand it over to an honest jeweler. Tony was hot on the trail and shared his information with me. The killer knows that and will murder me next. Don't you see? *We* have to get out of here to save our lives. You're in danger, too. He had no qualms about murdering Tony. And I'm next on the list."

I didn't hear anything for a minute and started to think they might be hugging or something.

"Why would Tony tell you anything about the ruby? Wouldn't he want it all for himself?"

"I guess he trusted me, Melly. Unlike you, apparently. I

expected my wife to have faith in me. Tony and I bonded over our mutual interest in history and historic artifacts."

"In that case, we should get that nice Wolf back over here and you can tell him what Tony said to you. That way, there's no reason to kill you because the police will already know about it. They will find the ruby and you will be a hero."

"Or the cops will blame me for Tony's death and put me away in the clink for the rest of my life!"

Silence followed. I began to worry that Mom or Dad would amble in and I wouldn't hear any more of the discussion between Aunt Melly and Gus.

"Not if you give them the information about the ruby."

"Are you kidding? They'll think I murdered Tony so I could get the ruby for myself!"

"I see. That *is* a problem. But I don't understand how running away would help. They would certainly find you at home. You're safer here surrounded by so many people."

"But that's exactly why we need to leave right away. I don't know who killed Tony. I don't know who I can trust."

"Well, *I* know who you can trust and who would protect us, and that's my brother and his lovely family. We're staying put and that's that. Now get upstairs to shower and shave. Honestly, you look a mess."

I heard a door snap closed ever so softly.

I hurried toward the sound and was just in time to see Stan returning to the table. I followed him, taking care to close the door silently behind me. Stan had arrived with Melly and Gus so I supposed he had a good reason for eavesdropping on them. If they were leaving, it meant he would be, too. And yet, even though I had eavesdropped, I felt a tiny frisson of suspicion about him doing the same.

Mom, Dad, Aunt Melly, and I cleared the table and brought the dirty dishes into the kitchen.

"I'll be right back to clean up," I promised before I flew downstairs to the basement to make my call.

But Wolf wasn't answering. I heaved a great sigh and mentally kicked myself for not telling him earlier. I was trying again when Mom came down the stairs.

She shot me a funny look. "Hard to get a minute of privacy with so many of us around." She dumped a load of laundry on the folding table and sorted it. "I hope you don't mind if I wash a few things."

"Not at all."

"I was thinking we might make a flag cake for Tony's family but realized that would be way too festive. What a shame that he died just before the day that he loved to celebrate. It will ruin the Fourth of July for his family forever. Like the families of people who die over the Christmas holidays." She held up a red sweater. "Did you wash this?"

"I haven't washed any clothes since you arrived. Is there a problem?" I glared at my phone because Wolf wasn't retuning my call yet. I backed away from Mom and texted him.

Call me ASAP. I have info.

"No. No problem."

"Need any help?" I asked.

"No, honey. I've been washing clothes for a few decades now."

I grinned and returned to the kitchen.

I hated to compromise on a cake for Tony's family, but I had a lot to prepare for our dinner tonight. I took the easiest road and one that made sense in terms of serving people who dropped by their house, a chocolate sheet cake.

The great thing about sheet cakes is that they are almost dump cakes. I placed butter and sugar in my stand mixer and let it do the hard work of creaming them together. Meanwhile, I preheated the oven and loaded the dishwasher with the breakfast dishes. All the while, I kept looking out the window for Wolf. When the dishwasher was running, I added the cocoa, flour, milk, vanilla, and other ingredients to the mixer while it ran, let it mix just enough and poured it into a disposable pan that Tony's family wouldn't have to return, and slid it into the oven. I set the timer so I wouldn't overlook it if I got distracted, which was very likely what with Tony's murder and Gus's desire for a fast getaway on my mind. I wondered if he would leave Aunt Melly and simply drive away in the middle of the night in her car.

Her car. Her house. I hated to be miserly, but it did seem like he had gotten the better part of the financial bargain in their marriage. But maybe his company and love made up for it to Aunt Melly. If his presence offered her security and happiness, maybe that was a fair trade.

Roscoe had left to see his friend and Hannah had taken off around the same time. I doubted they would be back for lunch. Just as I pulled the sheet cake out of the oven, I spied Gus through the bay window. He walked away, looking around nervously. For Stan, perhaps? I was relieved that he hadn't taken Aunt Melly's car.

Still, I didn't know what to do about Gus. I couldn't lock him up in my house. And maybe he hadn't killed Tony. There was that possibility. After all, I had seen him early in the morning and Tony's body didn't show up in the alley until evening. As far as I knew, Gus had been eating and dancing with Aunt Melly and the rest of us last night.

I was a bit skeptical about his ruby story, though. I'd heard that sometimes the police withheld information so they could follow clues without alerting the people involved in the crime. That made perfect sense to me. But Gus wanted to go home. Would someone who murdered a rival give up on his quest to find the priceless ruby that easily? And why would he go home? After my house, that was the next place the killer would look for him.

I peered out the window again. Gus had vanished. But interestingly, Stan walked by in the same direction.

The timer went off. I removed the cake from the oven and placed it on a rack to cool. I grabbed a note pad and wrote on it, *Back soon, Sophie*.

I didn't see Daisy. She was probably with Dad. Besides, it was getting too hot for her. I tucked my phone in a pocket and ran out to the street where I caught a glimpse of Gus ambling along with Stan trying to catch up to him.

Gus glanced from side to side as if he was afraid someone might notice him.

I should have a reason ready in case he saw me. I could say I needed butter for the frosting. As far as I knew, he hadn't looked in the fridge. Or chocolate! That was better. He was unlikely to go through my kitchen cabinets to see if I had chocolate on hand.

I walked on the shady side of the street, hoping I appeared like I was heading somewhere in case Gus or Stan looked back. So far, Gus gazed from side to side but didn't seem worried about anyone following behind him.

He dodged into a store. Stan jogged to catch up and entered the same store. I stood near a tree and waited for them to come out. I checked my watch. It was reasonable for Gus to shop around. I couldn't be impatient.

"Who are you spying on?"

I let out a shrill squeak. But I knew that deep voice.

I turned to Wolf. "Gus. How come you didn't get back to me?"

"I've been a little busy."

I told him about seeing Gus leave Dottie's backyard.

Wolf's eyebrows rose. "Come on, Sophie. I'm sorry for your aunt, but the last time I checked, having an affair wasn't a crime."

"But that was the morning when Dollie thought she saw a dead man in her house."

"The operative words in that sentence are 'when Dollie *thought she saw*.' She calls in false alarms all the time. So why are you following Gus now? This isn't the way to Dollie's house."

At that moment, Gus emerged wearing huge sunglasses with black lenses. Stan wore a similar pair.

I felt like a fool. "Okay, so there's nothing sinister about sunglasses. Especially not in the summer sunshine. However, someone wrote a note that said *Gus murdered Tony* and left it in my pillowcase."

Wolf kept pace with me. "Why would anyone put a note like that in your pillowcase?"

"Because they didn't have the guts to tell me in person?"

"Sounds a little fishy to me. Maybe someone is jealous of him or doesn't like him and wants to get rid of him. Your father perhaps?"

"No." Maybe he *didn't* like Gus. Would Dad do something underhanded like that? "No. Not a chance."

Gus walked along with Stan, still checking the people to the sides of them. I followed with Wolf by my side. And then they popped into a hat store.

"See? Did you notice how Gus keeps looking from side to side like he's worried someone might recognize him? And he told Aunt Melly a story about a missing ruby at the Smithsonian. Do you know anything about that?"

"No. But it's not in my jurisdiction." Wolf checked his

watch. "Look, Sophie, if you see Gus murder someone, then give me a call. Okay?" Wolf turned the corner and disappeared from my line of sight.

Again, it didn't take Gus long. He and Stan hit the sidewalk. But now Gus wore a large brim sunhat. The kind with a longer brim in the back to keep the sun off his neck.

Seriously? More sun cover? It would soon be too late to attend the parade if that was what he had in mind.

And then they crossed the street. For one long breathless moment, I feared that Gus had spotted me.

Chapter 11

Dear Sophie,
My mother gave me a sundial that she says is an antique. It sure looks it. There's greenish-blue grunge on it. Mom says it's bronze and not to scrub it off! Is that how it's supposed to look?
Antiques Neophyte in Old Antioch, Tennessee

Dear Antiques Neophyte,
The greenish color is a patina that develops over time, similar to copper when exposed to the elements. It's a protective layer that shields the bronze. It can be cleaned off, but most people appreciate the beauty of aged items with a greenish-blue patina.
Sophie

When Gus and Stan entered a barbershop, I sighed with relief. Aunt Melly had said Gus *looked a mess.* He wasn't doing anything suspicious at all unless he thought the sunglasses and hat would disguise him.

I figured the barber would take a while. But just to be sure they hadn't spotted me and were trying to put me off their scent, I hung around for a few minutes, in case they popped right back out.

They didn't.

I walked home, thinking I should have worn sunglasses and a big hat in the strong sunshine when I ran into Dad and Cyril exploring Old Town.

"I can see why you love living here," Cyril said. "No wonder Gus would like to move. The old buildings are charming. It's wonderful that they put regulations in place so it wouldn't be a hodgepodge of architecture."

"Is there anything we can do for you?" asked Dad. "Something we can pick up for tonight's dinner?"

"I think we're set, but thanks for asking. You might run into Gus and Stan. Gus is wearing a huge sun hat and black glasses."

"Incognito?" asked Dad, exchanging a look with Cyril. "Do you know what he had to say to Melly in private?"

I weighed whether I should tell them. I looked into Cyril's clear blue eyes. How much did I really know about him? "I think he's scared because Tony was murdered."

"Well, that's certainly understandable. All of us are horrified and very sad. Tony was such a great guy. I can't imagine why anyone would have harmed him," said Dad.

"Maybe we should walk Sophie home," suggested Cyril.

"Nonsense! I'm fine. I think we might order pizza for lunch. Anything special that you'd like?"

"Your mom knows what to order for me," said Dad.

"Anything I don't like, I'll just take off my slice. Paul, we should stop somewhere and buy something for dessert."

I waved at them and headed home to find Mom and Aunt Melly had already made a frosting for the cake. It looked luscious. They were scraping the bowl with spatulas and licking them clean. Mom held out a fresh spatula to me. "Melly makes the best chocolate frosting! Is this for Tony's family or for us?"

Melly had brightened up and seemed much happier than she'd been in the morning.

I licked my spatula. "Mmm. This *is* good! It's for Tony's family. I thought we'd go over there after lunch. Do you want to come along?"

"I think someone should. Not all of us, that might be too much. But Hannah and Roscoe probably won't be back by then anyway."

"I told Dad and Cyril that we would order pizza for lunch."

"Thank goodness. I looked at your list. There's not all that much to do for the barbecue. Between the three of us it shouldn't take long at all."

While Aunt Melly and Mom discussed what kind of pizzas to order, I stewed over Wolf's reaction to my information. It wasn't earthshaking, but someone had accused Gus of murder. I was a little put out by the way he had brushed off Gus's presence at Dollie's house that morning, too. Maybe he knew something that I didn't.

"Aunt Melly, how well do you know Stan?" I asked.

"Hardly at all unless you count the drive up here. He seems nice enough."

"You didn't think it was odd that Gus brought him along?"

"Did he do something offensive, Sophie?"

"No. Not at all. I'm just wondering about him."

Mom frowned at me. "Does this have something to do with Tony's murder?"

"I don't know. He sort of runs around on his own. How long has Gus known him?"

Aunt Melly shrugged. "I never asked. I will say this though. Stan seems a little more polished than Gus. You know what I mean?"

"I know exactly what you're talking about," Mom agreed. "He's very polite. Always thanking us for meals—"

"And the tours."

Mom nodded. "His mama raised him right."

The front door opened, and Aunt Melly called out, "We're in the kitchen."

Dad responded, "Look who we found."

When Dad, Cyril, Stan, and Gus walked in, no one uttered a word. Gus removed his hat and bowed to the ladies. He'd had his hair cut, almost like Cyril's. It even had the gentle wave at the top where it parted on the left side.

"Excuse me," said Aunt Melly, "did any of you see my husband while you were out?"

"It's quite a transformation. You look dashing." Mom glanced at Melly.

At that moment, the pizzas arrived. I hustled to the door to collect them and tip the driver. When I walked into the kitchen, everyone was talking about Gus's haircut. I had to admit that the new style was much more becoming.

Because of the heat, we passed on eating outside and instead, we gathered around the banquette in my kitchen. While we ate, we admired Gus's giant new sunglasses and the hat that almost hid his face from view.

While they discussed the benefits of the big brim, I couldn't help thinking that it would make a clever disguise. Until someone caught on anyway. Once they knew about that hat, he would stand out in a crowd.

I bit into a deliciously savory slice of salami on my pizza and noted that Aunt Melly's initial joy had dimmed and she now looked concerned. She played along, forcing a smile and a chuckle as appropriate, but she wasn't fooling anyone who knew her well.

After lunch, we changed into appropriate attire for a condolence visit.

Mom and I were in my walk-in closet looking for something navy or black for her to wear when Aunt Melly dashed inside.

"Can you believe it? After the fuss Gus pitched this morning, he left a box of beautiful Belgian chocolates on the bed for me."

"Aw, Melly. Maybe we're not giving him enough credit," said Mom. "Paul would never have thought of a sweet gesture like that."

"My dear departed husband wouldn't have, either. The only time he ever bought me chocolates was on Valentine's Day, which was very sweet, but this means more, you know. It was so unexpected."

Both of them borrowed dark clothes from me, but the men were stuck with the khakis and navy blazers that they had packed. Mom assured them no one would expect visitors to come prepared for something like this.

We drove over in two cars and parked along the street. Tony's home stood out thanks to the soft blue exterior and the people coming and going. From the sidewalk, we could see guests milling about inside. I reached for the door knocker and paused. Aside from being surprisingly large, the ram's head with distinctive horns that curled backward had a greenish patina and looked like an expensive antique.

"Maybe you should knock," said Dad. "I'd hate to damage that thing. Bronze, you guess?"

Copper exposed to the elements developed a green patina, and bronze did as well. I heeded Dad's advice and knocked on the door lest I damage a pricy door knocker.

A gentleman whom I didn't know opened it immediately. "Cake or casserole?" he asked.

"Cake," said Mom. "Is that some kind of password to get in?"

Fortunately, the man chuckled. He motioned us inside

with his hand and closed the door. "The dining room is to your left." He ambled off, leaving us in the small foyer.

I carried the cake into the dining room and unwrapped it. Borrowing a knife and cake server that sat on the table, I cut a square piece and placed it on a plate for someone to help himself.

"Do you know what his wife looks like?" whispered Mom.

"Not a clue."

"She must be a country girl."

I nodded. I had expected the current trend of modern décor with a lot of white and clean lines or mid-century modern, but this house screamed country living from the horseshoe mounted over the doorway to the kitchen and the blue-and-white gingham chairs around the dining table. I moseyed into the sunflower-yellow kitchen with a plate rack over the sink and a rod along the ceiling that held an interesting collection of baskets.

"Sophie!"

I turned to find Liam Flynn. An event planner like me, Liam was technically one of my competitors. He air-kissed me on both sides.

"Darling, you must have used Tony for private tours, too. Such a shame. I don't know what I'll do without him. Do you have any idea what happened?"

I wished I didn't have ideas about what might have happened or, even worse, who might have killed him. I shook my head to avoid lying. "He was the best tour guide in town. No one told stories the way he did."

"Don't I know it. He brought the past to life. Have you been in the living room yet? There's an incredible collection of stoneware crocks. We're talking verrrry pricey. Tony had a good eye for antiques. He was always chasing down rumors about valuables. I remember him telling me that he was on the trail of a Fabergé egg. I've been keeping an eye open for one around here but haven't seen any yet. Guess that lead didn't pan out for him. I'm gonna miss that guy."

He excused himself when someone called his name. I made my way into the living room where my parents were engaged with a woman wearing a plain long-sleeved black dress that tied on one side. Other than a pair of pearl earrings, an engagement ring with a bright solitaire set in rose gold, and a matching rose gold wedding band that featured sparkling diamonds, she didn't wear any adornment.

"This is our daughter Sophie," said Mom.

I held out my hand and she shook it. "Sophie? Sophie Winston?"

"Yes. Tony was a wonderful man. I will miss him very much."

"Thank you. He always spoke highly of you." She pointed to her engagement ring. "I think I have you to thank for this. I lost my engagement ring and was distraught! You can imagine that it's not easy to match a rose gold wedding band. But my Tony found one. He had just been paid for a big corporate job that he did for you when he found this one in an antique store. He brought it home and surprised me with it."

We admired her ring.

"I don't know what I'll do without Tony," I said. "His knowledge of history was truly amazing."

"Could I speak with you privately?" she asked.

"Certainly." I followed her outside into her backyard. Mom and Dad followed along.

The grass needed mowing. Yellow squash and zucchini were already crowding a raised garden bed.

"I've been trying to understand exactly what happened," she said. "Tony came home for a dinner break after he left you. Then he was off again in the bus. What time did he bring you home?"

Mom, Dad, and I exchanged worried glances.

"He dropped us off at my house around four in the afternoon. We didn't see him again that day."

She twisted her rings. "He never came back to pick you up?"

"No. He wasn't scheduled to do that. He was finished with our tours when he left at four."

She held trembling fingers over her mouth. "He didn't take you out again? But they didn't find him until the following night. Where was he all that time?"

Mom wrapped an arm around her. "I'm so sorry. He wasn't with us. Did he often stay out all night?"

"Once in a while. Usually when he went on a business trip."

What kind of business trip did a Washington DC tour guide go on? "Business trip?"

"Yes. But he always let me know. I'm sure he said he was going back to pick you up. People love to see the city at night with all the lights on."

"So you expected him home that evening," said Dad.

"Yes, of course." Her eyes widened as she gazed at us with fear. "What did you do to him?"

"Nothing!" Mom protested. "We never saw him again after he dropped us off in the afternoon."

Tony's wife backed away from us, holding her palms toward us as though she didn't want us to chase her. She turned and flew into the house. I was pretty sure I heard a clank that meant she locked the door.

"I think we'd better get out of here," I muttered. "This way." I headed to the gate in the back of the small yard and the three of us hurried through it. I paused and took care to latch it behind us. "That was weird."

"She thinks we killed her husband!" Mom sounded surprised. "Poor woman. Losing a spouse must be so difficult."

"Poor woman?" Dad spouted. "She thinks we're murderers!"

"Dad, calm down. We have loads of witnesses who were with us all evening."

"It's a good thing we went out for Chinese food that night. I'm sure they would remember us at the restaurant," said Dad.

We walked around the block to my car.

"How are we going to spring Cyril, Melly, Gus, and Stan from that house?" asked Mom.

"You text Melly, and Dad, you text Cyril. Tell them we're waiting for them at the cars."

"I feel just terrible for Tony's wife," Mom muttered as she texted. "He lied to her! Do you think he was having an affair and the husband came home and caught them in flagrante?"

I fervently wished that was what had happened.

Aunt Melly, Stan, and Gus emerged from the house. Cyril was right behind them.

As I watched them walk toward us, I wondered if the person who left the note about Gus was wrong. Had I murdered someone, I definitely would not have had the guts to pay a condolence visit to his wife. I would be keeping a very low profile. Hiding out. Leaving town. Wearing big hats and sunglasses . . .

Chapter 12

Dear Natasha,
We're throwing a lovely barbecue for thirty guests in our newly redone backyard. As the chief dishwasher in our household, I say paper plates are the only way to go. My wife is horrified by that idea but says she'll go along with paper plates if you think they're okay. C'mon, Natasha, this is outdoor eating!

Barbecue-Loving Dad in Beantown, Maryland

Dear Barbecue-Loving Dad,
I bring fine china plates and crystal stemware to outdoor picnics. Need I say more?

Natasha

Even though I had invited everyone on our block of the street as well as friends, not too much remained to be done for the barbecue that evening. Almost everyone had offered to bring side dishes or desserts. I cringed when Natasha insisted on bringing baked beans. While I loved baked beans, her food had a tendency to be spicy hot. I had often wished I could put up warning signs. Maybe I could if we labeled all the dishes so hers wouldn't be the only one.

Everyone except Mom, Aunt Melly, and me had left to wander around the antique fair being held in the center of town. Neither Roscoe nor Hannah had come home yet. That suited us just fine. I was grateful to Mom and Aunt Melly for their help,

I was decorating our flag cake with blueberries and strawberries when a commotion broke out in my backyard. Daisy, who wasn't much of a watchdog, barked furiously. Mom rushed into the kitchen and howled something incoherent at me.

I heard voices and screaming in the backyard. Mochie, who had been sleeping in the bay window, flew past me seeking safety. I rushed outdoors.

Two gentlemen appeared to have been unloading an ice sculpture when it slipped and fell. The yelling came from the men and Natasha. What was she doing here?

"Hi!" I waved at them. "What's going on?"

All three of them spoke at once.

"Stop!" I shouted. Pointing to a very handsome man with dark hair who wore a T-shirt that showed off a tight body and muscular arms, I said, "You first."

He shot me a crooked smile. "Hiya. I'm Frankie."

"What, you gonna flirt with her?" his companion asked.

"I could. Ya see, this crazy woman"—he gestured toward Natasha with both hands—"ordered an ice sculpture of the Statue of Liberty. We told her it was gonna be too hot outdoors, but she said she'd pay us double. So I said bring on the money, honey. It's your problem if it melts before your barbecue starts. Just like I predicted, when we delivered her, the lady started to melt." He pointed at the sculpture. "Her. Not the crazy dame. Then she starts yelling at us because she's melting. What did she think was gonna happen?"

I looked to the other guy. "Yeah. Pretty much what he said."

"Natasha?" I asked.

"I ordered her holding an eagle, not a torch."

An odd thing to do. But at that point, it was getting difficult to say exactly what she was holding other than an icy blob that was rapidly changing shape and looked more like an ice cream cone as it dripped on the grass.

Natasha pointed at what was left of the ice cream cone. "That clearly was not an eagle."

"Yeah? Prove it."

Natasha looked to me for help.

I shrugged. "I didn't see it when they first brought it in."

"Okay then. Hand over what you owe us. We did our part." Frankie crossed his arms over his chest and stood with his legs apart as if he didn't plan to leave without his money.

His retort didn't respond to her complaint, but at that moment, I really didn't care. "Natasha, pay them. Gentlemen"—I used the word rather broadly—"please remove this lovely sculpture from my yard."

"You don' wan' it?" asked Frankie.

"I'm sure it was beautiful on the way here. But right now it's making puddles where I'm expecting guests in a few hours. Please take it away?"

"Anything for you." Frankie winked at me.

The two of them rolled it out of the yard. I could only hope the dry soil would suck up the water before guests came.

"Write them a check," said Natasha.

"I didn't order it."

"It's for your party."

I had no intention of arguing with her about this. I tried not to grin as an idea popped into my head. "Fine. I'll call Wanda and ask her to pay them."

"We're not ten years old, Sophie."

"Natasha, I don't care how you handle this as long as it's not in my yard." I could imagine how big a puddle it would have left. As soon as they had it out on the sidewalk, I returned to the house where Mom had finished the flag cake decoration and popped it in the fridge.

"What was that about?"

I told her what had happened.

"Why is Natasha still yelling?" she asked.

Daisy walked out into the blazing sun with Mom and me. From the sidewalk in front of my house we could see Natasha running in high heels and shouting something as the men dumped the now totally unrecognizable sculpture on the tiny lawn in front of her house.

We went inside, and I checked my to-do list. All the side dishes were ready and waiting. Desserts and the traditional carved watermelon basket of fruit had been prepared. Multiple pitchers of lemonade and iced tea were lined up in the fridge.

"Flowers, tablecloths, and candles," I read aloud to Mom and Aunt Melly.

While we set the tables, Bernie and Mars showed up to start the barbecue. The pork butts needed to cook low and slow, which would take a while. We still had plenty of time. Nina came over, too, with Muppet.

I set out casual blue-and-white-checked tablecloths with alternating blue and white stars in the fabric. Nina pitched in and whispered, "What's the scoop on the guy who was killed?"

Mars and I pulled the long tablecloths straight on one side while Nina and Bernie handled them on the other end. Mom and Aunt Melly followed behind us with red lanterns, fitted with battery-operated candles, and short vases filled with blue and white hydrangeas from my yard, and red gerbera daisies I had planted for this occasion.

I asked Mars, Bernie, and Nina to help me with two taller arrangements that needed to be set up on the buffet table on the porch. Safely out of earshot, I told Mars and Bernie that Nina and I had caught Gus leaving the back gate of Dollie's house the morning of the day Tony was found dead. "And now someone staying at my house put a note in my pillowcase that said, 'Gus murdered Tony.'"

"Do you think that's true?" asked Bernie.

"I don't know. I overheard him telling Aunt Melly that he wants to go home because he will be the next victim. Something about a missing ruby?"

Bernie shook his head. "The antique fair has people imagining all kinds of weird things. Stories about hidden treasures in Old Town are rampant but I haven't heard anything about a ruby."

"That's silly," Nina said. "But kind of fun, I guess. I'd love to find some old treasure in my house."

"They say the average backyard in Old Town contains thousands of artifacts." Bernie turned around a tall vase of blue hydrangeas, and gladiolas in red and white, all from my yard. "But there's a catch. They have to be turned in because they're of historic significance."

"Bummer," Nina joked.

Mars laughed at her. "Most of them are little shards of pottery. I think the bigger danger is that people will throw them out."

"I have enough dishes that I don't use, thank you. I certainly don't need any shards," Nina laughed.

Bernie gave me a solemn look. "Did this Gus fellow get into an argument with Tony? What motive would he have to kill him?"

"None that I know of. But someone staying in my house must have reason to think that."

"Maybe Aunt Melly wrote the note?" asked Nina.

"Would you keep sleeping with your husband if you thought he had murdered someone?" I asked.

Nina appeared aghast at the thought. "No! No way. But then he might catch on. I'd have to pick a fight to justify sleeping on the sofa. That could be dangerous, too. But if he murdered someone, arguing about anything with him could be deadly."

"That's what I think. I don't know if I would get a second of sleep. I'd be petrified that he might turn on me! She hasn't been happy with him, but she doesn't seem panicked like I would be if I thought my husband had murdered someone."

I held the door open while Bernie and Mars carried the flowers out to the buffet table. They set them down and headed for the grills to check on them. Nina went home to collect the drinks she had prepared, and I set out glasses, napkins, the blue and white Johnson Brothers Historic America plates I had been collecting, and flatware. Dad and Cyril had set up an extra table with glasses, lemonade, iced tea, wines, and beer. I had found a cute red trash bin and carried it out into the yard near a game table I had covered with a disposable cloth for used plates and glasses.

Guests began to arrive around six o'clock. In spite of the heat, it was a jolly crowd. They downed Nina's cherry-red lemonade, and blue curaçao drinks, and snacked on chips, dips, and assorted cheeses, crackers, and fruit from the charcuterie boards Mom, Aunt Melly, Nina, and I had assembled.

Hannah finally rolled in. Mom, Aunt Melly, and I noticed that Roscoe came back about five minutes later. We honestly did not know why they were keeping their relationship secret.

Natasha arrived with a gelatin mold of barbecued beans. A shimmering, jiggling, brown mess of beans reminiscent of the gelatin molds from the 1950s.

"So you mixed beans with barbecue sauce and gelatin?" asked Nina, who was clearly fascinated.

"I sparked it up with hot sauce, cilantro, and chopped habanero peppers. You'll love it!" Natasha glided over to chat with Dollie.

I didn't think I had time to mark it as a spicy dish but I flashed Mars a smile when he slid it toward the back of the various safer offerings like an interesting salad of corn and cabbage, cole slaw, broccoli slaw, black bean salad, hush puppies, and Wanda's cornbread.

When guests began to help themselves and Natasha was busy flirting with Julian, my opinionated next-door neighbor, Francie, tasted a tiny bit of Natasha's gelatin concoction.

"What was this supposed to be?" she asked in a loud voice. "It looks like a giant po—"

"Francie!" I said as loud as I could to cover up her next word without making a scene. "I'm so glad you could come."

It was too late. Several guests gathered in front of it, all remarking on its unique appearance.

Mars rushed over from the grill and whispered to me, "When I say *now*, flick all but a couple of bites into this bag." He handed me a plastic grocery store bag. "Now!"

He blocked me from view as I hastily scraped almost all of the gelatin into the bag, leaving remnants so the dish would look as if it was popular, and set the platter back in place.

"Aww," said Mars to the next person in line. "Will you look at that. Natasha's dishes always go first."

I tied a knot in the bag and hurried it into my kitchen trash.

When I returned to the lawn, Wanda walked by me. "Good move," she said with a smile. She paused. "Where's Wong?"

"She claimed she had to work, but I think she felt she shouldn't mingle with us until Tony's death is resolved."

When we sat down to eat, I noticed that Hannah sat between Roscoe and Humphrey. I was glad that Humphrey no longer followed me around. He seemed to have matured somewhat over the last few years. I appreciated that.

Stan mingled with everyone but never seemed to be far from Gus. If I were a stranger and only knew one person well at a party, I might stick close to that person, too. I wondered where Stan was staying.

Natasha approached me and I braced myself. Would she be upset about the ice sculpture or her beans?

"Sophie, Sophie, Sophie. You of all people should know better."

I waited for the bomb.

"Using paper napkins is simply tacky. What *were* you thinking?"

I was delighted that I'd chosen to use paper napkins. The table was a mess! But cleanup for dessert took no time at all. "I was thinking they are beautiful and I wouldn't have to wash and iron one hundred barbecue-stained napkins. Are you ready for dessert?"

"They all look so ordinary. I should have brought a dessert. Did you see that my beans were the first dish to go?"

"I heard people talking about your beans. Surely you can find a dessert that you like. Lemon meringue pie, blueberry pie, cherry pie, chocolate cakes, brownies, chocolate chip cookies, and the flag cake. People brought all their summer favorites."

By a quarter of nine, the flames had been extinguished, and the grills were cooling. We all headed to watch the national fireworks from the top of a building owned by a friend of Bernie's. The fireworks were accompanied by the music of John Philip Sousa played by the National Symphony Orchestra, which was live on the west grounds of the US Capitol and broadcast on TV and radio stations. Speakers all around us carried the music so well that it felt as if the band was only feet away.

When the fireworks and music ended, Cyril surprised us with a moving solo of “The Star-Spangled Banner.” He looked a little bashful when we all applauded and cheered but I gave him a lot of credit because it’s not an easy song to sing well.

“I hope that wasn’t too forward of me,” Cyril said shyly.

“It was beautiful! I never knew you could sing like that.”

“The occasion doesn’t rise very often, but I was so overcome by the significance of our wonderful nation. My favorite phrase in the Declaration of Independence is ‘the pursuit of happiness.’ Because that’s what it’s really all about, isn’t it?” He wrapped an arm around my shoulders and gently squeezed as we left.

Afterward, most of the guests went home, except for my houseguests and Stan. We sat outside in the dark, nibbling on leftovers and desserts. One by one, they straggled off to bed. I checked the doors to be sure they were locked, wrapped up the leftovers and found places for them in the fridge, and finally turned in after the very long day.

Chapter 13

Dear Sophie,
Hubby invited a bunch of friends to a Fourth of July barbecue at our house. I would love to indulge in special table settings, but we're on a tight budget. How can I make the table look festive without spending a lot of money?
Blue Hostess in Grill, Pennsylvania

Dear Blue Hostess,
Use what you have and add just a few inexpensive touches. A white tablecloth will work great. You probably have one already as well as clear glasses. Buy bright red napkins. Paper is fine—this is a barbecue! Angle them on your plates. Check your local dollar store for blue glass vases. (Hint: arrangements from florists often come in useful colors. Keep the vases!) Fill them with red and white flowers. Elegant, easy, and it won't break the bank.
Sophie

Daisy pawed at me.

"Mmph. Daisy, go to sleep."

Now half-awake, I heard the creaky stairs.

Daisy nudged me with her nose. I rolled over and covered my head with my pillow. Daisy persisted and managed to get her cold nose underneath the pillow so she could touch my cheek. I pushed myself into a seated position. "Okay, okay. I give up." I threw on a bathrobe, noting that Hannah had not come up to bed, and walked down the stairs as quietly as possible. No one was in the kitchen. So much for midnight snacking.

The door to the den was closed, so I presumed that Roscoe and possibly Hannah were asleep in there. But I found Aunt Melly wrapped up in a blanket in the sunroom, lit only by the light of the moon visible through the glass ceiling.

I turned on the tiny twinkling lights overhead that looked as if they were little stars against the night sky. I sat down in the chair next to her. "Are you all right?"

"Oh, honey, I feel like such a fool. You know what's worse than a fool? An *old* fool!"

"My Aunt Melly has never been foolish."

"She has now!"

My mother appeared in the doorway. "Oh, Melly! I'll go make some chamomile tea. Or would you prefer something stronger?"

"Chamomile would be nice. Thank you, Inga."

I joined Mom and found leftover pies, which I had carefully stashed away. One of the many things Aunt Melly and I had in common was a sweet tooth. I carried the tray of tea into the sunroom and Mom followed behind me with the pies.

I settled in next to Aunt Melly.

"What's troubling you, Melly?" Mom cut slices of lemon meringue pie, cherry pie, and chocolate cream pie.

Aunt Melly helped herself to chocolate cream pie. "I have made such a mess of things. You know, I felt like an eighteen-year-old girl again in Las Vegas. Not a care in the world. I don't think I stopped smiling or laughing the whole time."

"Did you drink a lot?" asked Mom.

"Not all the time, but more than normal I suppose. It was all giddy fun. And now, my whole life has crashed. I feel like Natasha's gelatinous beans looked."

"I'm so sorry, Melly," I said. "I didn't know. I thought you were having a good time with Gus."

"More like Gus has been having a good time with my money. I am too old to be so stupid. I had a good husband. A really wonderful husband, and somehow I suppose I thought marriage to Gus would be the same. I thought I was marrying someone kind and thoughtful. Gentle and caring. Someone who would look out for me, for us!"

So this was about money, not about murder. Maybe she hadn't written that note. "You looked so happy dancing with him. Did something happen?" I asked.

"He started up that business about selling my house and moving into an apartment again." Aunt Melly scowled.

"Melly, a lot of people our age do that," said Mom. "There's even a name for it. They call it downsizing. We don't need so much room anymore. And heaven knows we're better off without stairs!"

Melly's lips drew tight. "There was something about the way he was talking that got to me. So while everyone was out this afternoon and you and Sophie were busy, I snuck into Sophie's office and borrowed her computer." Aunt Melly looked over at me. "I hope that was all right. The passcode was right there."

I smiled at her. "Of course! Hannah has been using it, too."

"I checked my credit card account. I thought Gus paid

for our trip to Vegas. At least he made it sound that way. 'Nothing's too good for you, Melly. I'll pay the tab, Melly. Dinner's on me, Melly.' But every last penny was charged to my account. Everything! I'm not poor, but I don't have money to throw away like that. I remember asking him how we got such a glamorous suite. I've never stayed in a suite before. You should have seen it. There was a bar and the biggest bathtub I have ever seen! He told me it was on the hotel because he was a high roller. Baloney! It was on me. I would have been perfectly content with a regular room. I didn't need a suite like a rock star gets. It's a good thing we weren't there longer. It cost a small fortune."

Mom cocked her head. "Oh, Melly. How could you not know he was using your card?"

"I've been thinking about that. He took care of everything. I thought he was being very generous. Chivalrous, you know? When I saw the charges on my credit card statement, I thought that he must have practiced my signature, but then I realized that most of the time these days, you don't sign anything. You just tap the card. Even if he had to sign something, no one would have looked at it."

In the dim light, Mom's eyes met mine.

"Do you have enough money to pay the bill?" asked Mom.

"Yes, it will poke quite a hole in my savings, though. I can't afford to live that way every month or every year for that matter." Aunt Melly held up a wallet. "After he fell asleep, I swiped his wallet. You know what I found? *My* credit card and *my* debit card." She unfolded a little slip of paper. "And this contains all of my bank accounts and the corresponding numbers and passwords. He must have found the little book where I write them down." She pulled out a wad of cash. "He took this out of my bank account. The man must think I'm made of money!"

"Melly!" Mom tsked. "To be honest, I never pegged him

for a gold digger, either. A little rough around the edges but as long as you were happy, that was enough for us."

"What are you going to do?" I asked.

"Well, I shut down the credit and debit cards and ordered new ones. So he can't use those anymore. I'm hiding this cash to tide me over until we get home. I don't suppose we can throw him out of your house, can we?"

All eyes were on me. "Actually, I think we probably could ask him to leave. I'm only guessing but if he took money or used your credit card without your permission before you were married, that was probably a crime. I don't know about while you were married, but if you like I can set you up with one of my lawyer friends to find out what you can do."

Melly heaved a deep sigh and ate another forkful of creamy pie.

It seemed like a good time to broach the subject of Gus, the possible murderer or unfaithful husband. "When I was out walking the other morning, I saw Gus sneaking out of Dollie Peabody's backyard."

"What? Where was I?" asked Aunt Melly.

"In bed, I presume."

"That can't have been. I would have known if he got up and left. Are you certain it was Gus?"

I nodded. "I'm afraid so. Nina was with me. She can confirm it."

"We've been married for less than a month and he's having an affair with another woman? That woman who showed up here when we were eating breakfast? The one who came to the barbecue with that young man?"

"That's the one."

"That rat!" Mom exclaimed. "What a low-down, filthy, stinking rat! Oh Melly, who is this man? Who did you marry?"

In the dim lights of the sunroom, I couldn't see the color of Aunt Melly's complexion well, but there was no doubt that her lower lip trembled. "Do you think he isn't who he says he is? Did you Google him?" I asked.

"Of course not! Who does something like that?"

I refrained from saying what I was thinking—*any sensible person.*

"Really, Sophie!" said Mom. "Your generation is so untrusting."

"Yeah, to avoid situations like this!" I rose and went to my office. Minutes later, I joined them again. "There are plenty of Guses and Eberles but I don't see a Gus Eberle."

Aunt Melly gasped. "He's using a fake name?"

The room wasn't dim enough for me to miss the annoyed look Mom shot me. "Now, Sophie. I know you think everything is on the computer, but Gus is Melly's and my age. We didn't use computers much. He probably didn't list his pawnshop. Or it might have had a different name, like Ye Olde Pawn Shop or something."

A hopeful note in her voice, Aunt Melly added, "That's right! I'm probably not on the Internet, either."

"Exactly," said Mom. "I don't do Facebook or anything like that."

"I signed up for it, but I'm never on it," said Aunt Melly.

I tried not to groan. "Did you write an obituary when your husband died?"

"Don't be silly. Of course I did."

"Then your name is on the Internet."

"Nonsense. I didn't put it there."

"The newspaper would have." How could Melly and Mom order things on the Internet but not realize that they were on it, too?

Aunt Melly wiped tears from her face. "What does all this mean? He's someone else? Who hides their name or real identity?"

Mom bit her top lip. I guessed she was thinking the same thing I was. A con man or a criminal would do that.

Aunt Melly wrenched her fancy rings off her finger. "Times like this, I wish I were a witch or at least someone who knows how to place a curse on a man."

In spite of the seriousness of the situation, Mom and I giggled.

"But Melly, we do know someone who thinks she can do that," said Mom. "Wanda Smith!"

Melly laughed so loud that she clapped a hand over her mouth to cover up the sound. "If ever a man deserved a curse, it's Gus." When we stopped laughing, she asked, "Do you think Gus knew Dollie before he came here?"

"I don't know. They certainly don't act as though they knew each other." I leaned toward her. "Aunt Melly, did you leave a note in my bedroom for me?"

"A note?"

I nodded.

"No, honey, I didn't. But what a sweet thought. I should do that when I'm a houseguest!"

I whispered, "The note said that Gus murdered Tony."

The two of them stared at me.

"That can't be," said Melly. "I've been with him all the time."

I didn't point out to her that he managed to go over to Dollie's house without her knowledge.

"Do you think that's true?" asked Mom.

"Inga! Of course not. He may be a thief and a liar but . . ." Aunt Melly's voice faded.

I assumed the ridiculousness of her defense was setting in.

"What are you going to do?" asked Mom.

"Wolf sort of blew it off. I don't know why, but he seemed disinterested."

"That's right. He didn't come to the barbecue tonight, did he?"

"I didn't expect him to come. He's a decent husband and he wouldn't have abandoned his wife on a holiday, even if he had time off."

"He could have brought her with him," said Aunt Melly.

"It might be awkward for her. I get that." I shrugged.

"Romance is supposed to be lovely and exciting," said Mom. "How do you two manage to get yourselves into such messes? I think we should get to bed. I'm exhausted." Mom gathered the dirty dishes. "Honey, would you mind if we left these in the sink until morning?"

Mom must have been worn out if she was willing to do that! "Sure. It's okay with me. They won't go anywhere."

I watched Aunt Melly take the first few steps up the stairs slowly. Now that she knew he might be a murderer or a philanderer, and certainly a con man, she probably dreaded crawling back into bed with him. I knew I would. "Aunt Melly, why don't you sleep in my bed tonight? I'll take the blow-up mattress. Hannah won't be back for hours."

Mom whipped around. "Hannah isn't home yet?"

Oops. Shouldn't have let that slip. "She'll be back soon, Mom."

"I have to have a talk with that child."

"She's not a child. It's okay. She'll be back."

"Well, now I'm not going to be able to sleep at all!"

I didn't think that was true. If I had to wait up for Hannah, I would drift off for sure. Mom probably would, too.

I offered to change the sheets on my bed for Aunt Melly but she just laughed. "Do you remember how many times we slept in the same bed when you were little? You used to smack me in the face while you were sleeping! I think I can manage sheets that you've slept on."

The two of them walked up the stairs but I heard the kitchen door open.

Daisy ran toward it. I figured it was Hannah, and I'd better tell her about the new sleeping arrangement.

But it was Roscoe. I needn't have worried about him overhearing us in the sunroom.

He bent over to pat Daisy.

"Hi," I said from the kitchen doorway.

Roscoe gasped and jerked up straight.

"I didn't know you were out. Where's Hannah?"

"She's not here?"

"No."

"I'm sure she'll be back soon." He turned toward the den.

"Did you two have a fight?"

"Fight? Uh, no."

"Then where is she?"

"Probably out at a bar or something. Night!" He disappeared in a rush.

I ran upstairs to retrieve my phone and text her.

Where are you?

I'll be home soon. Go to bed.

Are you all right? Did you have a fight with Roscoe?

I'm fine. No fights with Roscoe or anyone else.

That was weird. At least she was okay. There wasn't anything I could do but go to bed. I knew I would be awakened by Hannah when she came in, but I was too tired to worry about that. I crawled into her bed, which wasn't as uncomfortable as I had feared. Daisy and Mochie snuggled up with me and I dropped off to sleep.

* * *

I overslept. It was past nine when I jerked awake. Daisy and Mochie were gone. I stretched and looked at my bed. Hannah slept in it, emitting little snores. I scrambled to my feet, showered and dressed in a light sheath as fast as I could, and ran downstairs. Everyone except Roscoe and Hannah was up and eating breakfast outside. The temperature was refreshingly crisp and the scent of bacon hung in the air.

"Good morning!"

They all responded and continued with their breakfasts.

I poured myself a mug of hot tea and added milk before settling in a chair next to Dad and stealing a slice of bacon off his plate.

"Hey! Get your own bacon," he said with a grin.

"I'm sorry that I overslept."

"You needed your sleep," said Mom. "Can you believe that your dad and Cyril cooked breakfast on the grill? Bacon, and eggs sunny-side up!"

"You're kidding."

"She's not! The next time the electricity goes out in Berrysville, I know where to go for meals," Aunt Melly teased. "And they're pretty good cooks at that!"

Cyril blushed. "It was the least we could do. You ladies have been doing all the cooking."

I grabbed a plate and headed toward the grill to get my own breakfast. It turned out that Dad and Cyril were pretty good cooks. I wasn't halfway through eating, when Daisy loped toward the side of the house and returned with Wolf. They were followed by two uniformed police officers.

While his face showed little emotion, Wolf seemed oddly formal. "Good morning."

"Won't you have some breakfast? We have plenty." I smiled at him.

"Not today, thank you."

"Do you have news about Tony's murder?" Mom asked eagerly.

"Yes. I do. I'm very sorry to do this, but I'm afraid I have to ask Paul to come down to the station with me."

Chapter 14

Dear Natasha,
I met a guy who I thought was "the one." He started staying overnight with me, but a proposal was not forthcoming. I'm paying for all the groceries but he's the one eating them. He even moved his pet snake in. I'm done with both of them. How do I get rid of them?

Ready to Exterminate in Snake Creek,
South Dakota

Dear Ready to Exterminate,
Sounds like two snakes have moved in. Change the lock on the door. You can buy one and install it yourself. Leave the snake in its cage in a safe place outside the door. When the other snake knocks, do not answer. Without food, a bed, running water, or electricity, they will soon look for another person to wrap around.

Natasha

"Dad?" Of all the things in the world that Wolf could have said, I never expected that. "What for?"

"I'm very sorry." Wolf swallowed hard. "Please don't make this more difficult than it already is."

"Make what difficult?" asked Mom. "I don't understand. What's happening?"

"They're arresting Dad." I could hardly breathe.

Aunt Melly screamed, "Nooooooo!"

"Melly, hush. Nonsense. Whatever for?" Mom picked up her coffee mug with hands trembling so hard she had to hold it with both.

"Paul, would you come with us, please?" Wolf sounded almost friendly until he said, "Now."

I grabbed Dad's arm. "Don't answer any questions or say anything."

"Honey, I haven't done anything wrong. If I can help the police, then I'm glad to do it."

"You don't understand. They think *you* murdered Tony. Do. Not. Say. A. Word. Do you understand me? Anything you say, no matter how innocent, can be twisted and used against you. Not a word! I'll get a lawyer to you as soon as I possibly can."

Dad kissed my forehead. "Don't worry about me, sweetheart. I have a completely clear conscience."

Mom leaped to her feet and faced Wolf. "This must be the doing of Tony's wife! She thinks we killed her husband because Tony told her that he was coming over here. But he never did. That was a total lie. We all have ironclad alibis. We went out to dinner. There are tons of witnesses who know we were there. They saw Paul. Should I call the restaurant?"

Gus remained in his seat. His head bent, he stared down at his plate as if he didn't want to be noticed.

Cyril stood. "I'll come with you, Paul." He looked to Wolf. "May I ride with Paul?"

Wolf raised his chin ever so slightly. "I'm afraid not. But I'll give you a lift."

"Wolf," I said, "I know you're going to read him his rights. Don't ask him anything until his lawyer is present."

"And who will that be?"

"Whoever I can get on a Sunday morning. Dad is officially exercising his right to remain silent." I had a strong feeling that didn't make any difference at all. Dad had to tell them that himself. Or just not say anything. I couldn't imagine Dad keeping quiet. He would probably chat with the police officers in a friendly way, meaning to be helpful.

Wolf beckoned to Dad.

Oh no! Dad actually smiled at him! Cyril joined them and the three of them walked out to the street, followed by the police officers.

"I should go with him, too." Mom burst past me and ran to join them.

I picked up my phone and called Alex German's office. A recording informed me that he was on vacation. Swell. We didn't have time to wait. I pressed Ronin Walker's office number. Thankfully, it rolled over to his cell phone. He was available and promised to meet Dad at the police station. With any luck, and Dad's super clean record, Mom could post bail and have him out of there in time for a late dinner.

Aunt Melly began to cry.

Stan Cox rounded the corner. "What's going on?"

Gus quickly filled him in. Then he turned his attention to Aunt Melly. "I told you we should have left yesterday." He spoke far too harshly. "But noooo. You wouldn't believe me. Pack your bags. We're going home in half an hour."

Stan appeared to be uncomfortable. He wolfed down bacon and eggs.

Aunt Melly dabbed at her tears with a napkin. "How dare you, Gus? It's my wonderful brother who is in trouble, not you. I know about you. I know what you did!

Everything you do is for *you*. It's all about Gus, all the time." She wrenched her engagement ring and wedding band off her finger and flung them onto his plate. "I want an annulment. And I can get one, too. I read about the law in Las Vegas. I don't know how often you have done this to women, but you picked the wrong one this time. How stupid do you think I am? Already having an affair! Shame on you! You're a fraud who married me for my money. And the silly thing about it all is that I don't even have much money! You want to go home? *I* have a home and you're not getting that or going there. I want my money back. Every last cent of it and you will leave this house immediately."

Aunt Melly lifted her chin and stalked into the house.

Gus picked her rings out of the food on his plate and slid them into his pocket. He ate the last piece of his bacon. "Thank you for your hospitality."

We heard the creak of an upstairs window opening.

Daisy ran to my side. A good thing as it turned out.

As if it came from the heavens, a suitcase slid off the walkway roof and landed on the grass in my yard. It bounced once and split open, spilling clothes.

"Whoa!" Stan gawked at his friend.

Gus's eyes met mine. "I guess I won't have to go back into the house. Except for the car keys. Maybe you could bring them out to me?"

"I believe you arrived in Aunt Melly's car."

"Aha. Yes, I suppose we did." He collected the items that lay on the lawn, latched the suitcase which looked far worse for the fall it had taken, and walked around the corner of the house, followed by Stan.

And suddenly, I was alone. "I did not see that coming," I said aloud. She talked about throwing him out, but I never imagined she would do it.

Aunt Melly yelled from the window, "Is he gone?"

"I think so." I walked inside to make sure they had left. With Mochie and Daisy by my side, I watched from the bay window.

Gus paused when he reached the street. He appeared to consider something, turned right, and strode in the direction of Natasha's house.

Stan watched him, evidently wondering what he should do.

I wondered if Gus was headed to Dollie's place. I supposed it wasn't really any of my business, unless the author of the note in my pillow had been correct and Gus had murdered Tony.

I was on the verge of checking on Aunt Melly when Roscoe and Hannah appeared in the foyer.

"What was that noise?" they both asked.

Aunt Melly ran down the stairs. "That, ladies and gentleman, was the sound of a con man being dumped."

The four of us returned outside. I wanted to rush to the police station, but I knew there wasn't a thing I could do there. And I desperately needed a very strong mug of tea to think straight.

Aunt Melly asked if there was any more bacon because Gus had stolen all of hers. Roscoe and Hannah took over the grill and delivered more eggs and bacon to the table.

"Where is everyone?" Hannah passed me the salt.

Aunt Melly explained what had happened to Dad.

Hannah let out a little scream and turned to me. "And you didn't tell me?"

Roscoe stopped eating.

"I'm waiting for a call from Ronin. He'll be able to tell us what's going on."

"Why are we here? We should go to the police station!" Holding a piece of crisp bacon, Hannah shoved her chair away from the table.

"Mom and Cyril are there. There's nothing you can do right now. It's wait there or wait here."

"We should all go, if only to show our support." Hannah gulped her eggs and grabbed a muffin. "I'll get dressed. It'll only take a few minutes."

Roscoe ate slowly. "I'll stay behind. Make sure the grill is out and keep an eye on things. Right, Daisy?"

She wagged her tail when he offered her a bite of bacon.

"Thank you, Roscoe." Aunt Melly took a deep breath. "Be sure Gus doesn't return. Don't let him in the house, even if he claims he forgot something. The man's a thief"—she lowered her voice—"and a murderer! There's no telling what he'll do."

Aha. Aunt Melly was not good at keeping things secret. "We don't know that yet for sure," I clarified, "but it's a possibility."

Roscoe nodded somberly. "A murderer. You're better off without him, Melly. To think he has been in the house with us this whole time! I thought there was something creepy about him."

Hannah quietly finished her breakfast and excused herself.

The rest of us put on a very bad show of remaining calm. Aunt Melly and I carried the dishes into the kitchen. I was cleaning up when Aunt Melly returned to the kitchen.

"Have you seen Hannah?" she asked.

"No. Did you check my bedroom?"

"I did. I even went up to the third-floor bedroom. She's not there."

The two of us looked in the backyard but there was no sign of her.

"Do you suppose she went ahead to the police station?" asked Aunt Melly.

"It's possible, but why wouldn't she wait for us, or at least tell us she was going?"

When we returned to the kitchen, Hannah was seated at the banquette. "There you are. Ready to go?"

Aunt Melly and I exchanged a look.

"Where have you been?" demanded Aunt Melly.

"I just stepped outside for a few minutes."

I loved my sister but this new habit of sidestepping information about where she was going, and with whom, was beginning to be tiresome.

"Hannah, this isn't like you," said Aunt Melly. "What's with all the secrets?"

"Aww, Aunt Melly, you're sweet to worry about me. Let's go already."

Ten minutes later, I opened the front door to leave with Aunt Melly and Hannah. A police car and an evidence van pulled up in front of my house. That could only mean one thing. Goose bumps prickled on my arms.

An officer handed me a warrant to search my house. I knew Ronin was with Dad, but I phoned him anyway and left a message to let him know about the search warrant.

Hannah grabbed hold of Mochie, and at my bidding, Roscoe put Daisy's harness on her and held on to her leash.

Many years before, a killer had entered my house while I was in the bathtub. I didn't think anything would ever feel as violating. But I had been so wrong. People whom I didn't know, dressed in white Tyvek coveralls, ran through my house all but ransacking it. Closets were opened. Drawers were searched. Even my kitchen cabinets were inspected. I supposed people hid things in their freezers, but the fridge?

I didn't understand what they were looking for. What could they want? Had the killer stolen something from Tony? A watch? A wallet?

As I observed them collect all of my kitchen knives, I knew Tony must have been stabbed. "When will you return those? I have guests. How am I going to make meals without knives?"

A Tyvek-clad person shrugged and muttered, "Sorry."

Aunt Melly followed me around holding Mochie in her arms. He didn't mew. Even Mochie felt the tension.

"Where's Hannah?" I asked.

Aunt Melly shrugged. "She handed me Mochie. He's such a good boy. He isn't even wriggling to get away."

Eventually, a couple of white-clad people appeared in the foyer with bulging evidence bags that appeared to hold clothes, including some of mine! Did they think Dad wore my clothes to sneak around and kill Tony? What in the blazes was going on?

As soon as they departed, I locked the door behind them and leaned against it.

I punched Wolf's number into my phone with no small amount of anger. When he answered, I hissed, "I think I have the right to know what is happening."

He answered in an irritatingly calm voice. "Your father's DNA was found on Tony."

Chapter 15

Dear Sophie,
I love open airy spaces, but hubby prefers dark colors. Believe it or not, this has turned into a huge fight. I don't know if I can live in rooms with dark drenched colors. How do we resolve this?
No Dark Caves for Me in Weyers Cave, Virginia

Dear No Dark Caves for Me,
There are a few possibilities. A sole wall in a bold drenched color is very much in vogue right now. The rest of the room should be a light beige or white, which would appeal to you. Or you could put in chair rails. Above the chair rail and on the ceiling, paint your light airy color. But use a comforting bold color below the chair rail. Cozy underneath but airy on top!
Sophie

I reeled from that one bit of information. DNA? There had to be a mistake.

I flinched when my phone rang. Finally, Ronin was calling back.

"I hope things are going better for Dad than for me," I said.

"Want the good news first or the bad news?"

Good grief. How could it get any worse? "Bad news. Let's get it over with."

"They found some fibers on Tony. Specifically on his clothing. DNA testing showed that they were from your dad."

"Stop right there. How can they possibly know it's Dad's DNA?"

"Looks like his sister, Melinda, submitted her DNA to one of those genealogy sites. But they knew the person they were searching for was male, so it was an easy jump to your dad, who just happened to be here in Old Town at the time of the murder. They've asked him for a DNA sample to make sure there's a match."

Fibers with Dad's DNA were damning. But they had to be completely innocent. No, they *were* completely innocent. I babbled an explanation. "We spent two days on his bus. I'm sure all of us left some DNA behind. Some of our DNA could have made it onto Tony's clothes when he cleaned the bus or maybe they hugged or brushed by each other at some point."

"We will definitely be arguing that. There are many means of transmission, so that's a possibility. On the bright side, your mother is paying the bail bondsman right now, so hopefully, they'll be home in a couple of hours."

I relayed the good news to Hannah, who had returned, Roscoe, and Aunt Melly. But I left out the part about Aunt Melly's DNA submission to a genealogy group having led the police to Dad. That information would come out soon enough. She had enough troubles with Gus and her distress about Dad's arrest. She didn't need to feel like it was her fault.

Each of us coped in our own way. Roscoe scrubbed the

grill. Hannah, Aunt Melly, and I roamed the house cleaning up the mess left by the police and making beds. I was collecting towels to wash when I began to laugh.

Hannah shot me a dirty look. "There is nothing funny about this."

"No? Apparently, the Bauers and Roscoe clean when they're feeling stressed."

It broke the tension a little bit.

Hannah giggled, which appalled Aunt Melly and Roscoe as they returned to the kitchen. Hannah explained and then said, "Okay super snoop. You've solved a lot of murders. This may be the most important one of your life. How do we figure out who really killed Tony?"

She was right. I made fresh coffee and tea, and set out cubed watermelon squares with toothpicks for spearing them, bright blueberries and raspberries, rich purple grapes, and leftover pie sections on the kitchen table, along with plates and napkins.

"We just ate breakfast," said Hannah.

"You can't think through a murder without food."

Daisy wagged her tail, and I thought Mom and Dad might have returned, but it was Nina, Mars, and Bernie who showed up unexpectedly at my kitchen door.

Nina opened the door and Muppet ran inside. "Is this a bad time?"

"Mars edged past her and embraced me. "We heard. I'm so sorry. But anyone who knows your dad knows it can't be true."

"Wow, this place is worse than Berrysville," Hannah groused. "At home it would have taken at least until lunchtime for that news to get around."

"I heard everything at The Laughing Hound." Bernie rubbed my back. "No worries. We'll figure it out."

Nina blushed. "I confess that I heard through the gossip grapevine."

Mars forced a sad smile. "I learned about it from these two."

"You've timed it perfectly. Coffee or tea?" I asked.

Minutes later we all settled around the banquette in the kitchen. Out of habit, I handed Mars a pad of paper and a pen. I knew he would ask for them.

I took a seat, hoping it would calm me to think things through. My heart felt like it was beating out of control. "Basics first. We need to know when Tony died. That would be in the autopsy report."

"Good point," said Bernie. "If we can establish where Paul was at that time, complete with witnesses, then your dad will be in the clear. I bet Humphrey can get that."

"I can ask him," Hannah offered.

"Ask him *how* Tony died, too," I said. "I saw blood on his clothes around the level of his abdomen."

Hannah nodded.

Mars made notes and asked Bernie, "What's the scuttlebutt on Tony's killer at the restaurant?"

"I haven't heard anything particularly helpful. An unnamed possible mistress, of course. Dollie Peabody's name has been mentioned. But that's because of where the body was found. It didn't go unnoticed that the house on the other side of the alley belongs to Elwin Martel. One fellow said Tony owed him money for a painting he commissioned. I'm not saying Elwin killed Tony because of that but it made me wonder if Tony was experiencing financial issues. Someone might have gotten rough with him over an unpaid debt."

"But does the location of the body really mean anything?" asked Nina. "Someone could have murdered Tony in another county and dumped him in that location."

I nodded. "Good point. That would explain why there wasn't any blood in the alley."

Hannah huffed. "I thought you guys were good at this. So far all you have is a bunch of nothing."

"Call Humphrey. Or would you rather I did that?" I picked up my phone.

"No, no. I've got it." Hannah took her phone and left the kitchen.

"I think a visit to Elwin would be in order." I bit into a grape.

Bernie nodded. "I'll go with you. I know him. Not very well, but enough to be a familiar face. He's a regular at The Laughing Hound's bar. Scotch on the rocks."

Daisy leaped to her feet and whined.

The kitchen door opened. Mom, Dad, and Cyril walked in. Dad immediately became the center of attention. Happily, Dad looked none the worse for his terrible experience, but I had never seen my mother look so haggard. We all moved to the living room to comfortably accommodate everyone.

After Dad told us the basics of what happened—the fingerprinting, being questioned but not answering anything because I told him not to, I asked, "What questions did they focus on?"

"Well, not many. They weren't happy that I wasn't being more helpful. Let's see, when was the last time I saw Tony alive? They asked that a lot. And they sort of reworded it, as if they thought that would make a difference. I found that intriguing. Why would they care about that so much? It made me wonder what Tony was up to. Do you suppose someone saw him come here while we were at dinner? It's curious."

"What else?"

"Why was it that Sophie and I were present shortly after the body was reported? They asked me where I was that day. All day! What time I got up. What did I do? Who did

I talk to? But they gave up fairly early on and just let me sit there to stew. To be honest, I think they were perturbed that I wasn't shaken. As I told you when I left, I have a completely clear conscience. I could have answered their questions, but you said not to."

"Why you?" asked Aunt Melly. "That's what I don't understand."

Dad's eyes met mine. Ronin had probably told him how the police identified his DNA. "Because, somehow, my DNA got on Tony's clothes."

"Red fibers they said." Mom sat with her hands in her lap, looking hopeless. "I know I'm too rattled to think straight, but I can't even remember anything your father packed that's red."

But I could. Dad had worn a red cotton sweater when we left on our tours in the chill of the early morning. The last time I saw it was when I tried to call Wolf from my basement. I excused myself. As soon as I hit the foyer where they couldn't see me, I ran through the kitchen and down the stairs to the basement. Daisy galloped after me as if we were on an adventure. But the sweater wasn't there. Mom probably washed it and took it back up to their bedroom when it was dry. Either way, it had probably been collected pursuant to the search warrant.

I trudged up the stairs and returned to the living room.

"They asked us not to leave town." Mom looked exhausted. "I'm so sorry, Sophie. I don't know how long we'll have to stay."

"Stop that. I wish it were under better circumstances, but I'm happy to have you here."

"Where's Gus?" she asked.

"I kicked him out for good." Aunt Melly forced a smile.

"You did?" Mom asked. "Really?"

"You would have been so proud of her," said Roscoe.

"Melly dumped his suitcase out of the window. Scared the rest of us half to death when it landed on the roof of the walkway and flew to the ground!"

Mom finally smiled. "I'm sorry I missed that!"

Hannah returned to the living room, her face flushed. "Got it! Humphrey says the body was in early PMI, which means"—she looked at a paper that she held—"postmortem interval and he was still in rigor mortis, which means it was probably less than twenty-four hours after death, but definitely longer than six to eight hours after death. Most likely more than twelve hours after death based on"—she paused and pronounced it carefully—"li-vor mortis. He also said that Tony's size and age can make those numbers vary a little bit."

She smiled and plunked down on the sofa next to Dad. She slid her hand into his.

"Thank you, Hannah. Did Humphrey say the cause of death?" he asked.

She looked at the paper where she had made notes. "Yes. Manner of death is homicide. They think he was stabbed by a knife, probably serrated."

"Eww." Nina wrinkled her nose. "That means a pretty deep cut that hit a bone or something."

"How in the world would you know that?" asked Mom.

"I'm married to a pathologist who testifies about this stuff. He talks about it at home endlessly. There are all kinds of theories. You'd think it would be very straightforward. Some of it is, I suppose, but there are always new studies and developments. I only listen half the time. But I do know about this. A serrated edge isn't smooth, it's like a bread knife with curves in the blade. If it only hits organs, sometimes they can't tell if it was serrated, but when it hits a bone, it usually leaves a mark that is different from a straight knife. He likes to tell me that every time he slices bread."

"I'm quite impressed, Nina." Bernie gave her a thumbs-up.

"I knew there had to be bleeding," I said. "I'm trying to work backward. It sounds like they don't know exactly when he died. We returned from the party around eleven-ish. Right? So that would be the twenty-four-hour mark. He would have died between then and eleven o'clock the night before. But given what Humphrey told you, he had probably been dead for more than twelve hours, so he must have been killed sometime between eleven the night before and noon-ish the day he was found."

"That's a pretty big window. I wonder where he was in between," said Dad.

"That's why they kept asking you when you last saw him. They don't have a handle on when he died or where he was before he lay in the alley," said Mars.

"If he was alive at eleven p.m., why didn't he go home to his wife?" asked Mom. She waved her forefinger. "He was up to no good or he would have gone home."

"You are my alibi, Inga. Half that time I was asleep in the same bed as you," said Dad.

Aunt Melly scowled. "I was certain that I would wake if Gus left our bed, but Sophie saw him at that Dollie woman's house early in the morning. I never knew he was gone!"

"Then Gus likely murdered Tony," said Bernie. "He was there at the right time."

"It was the morning of the day his body appeared. Nina was with me. I didn't notice any blood on Gus, did you, Nina?"

"It's not as though he turned around in a circle so we could examine his clothes, but I didn't see anything that caught my attention. I agree that it sounds like blood would have been on the killer's clothes."

"Could Tony have been the dead man Dollie claimed to have seen in her house?" asked Mars.

"That would make sense, but Gus was leaving when we saw him," Nina clarified. "And he wasn't dragging a dead Tony behind him."

"Or carrying a knife," I added.

"And Dollie said she didn't know Tony when she saw his corpse in the alley," Dad pointed out.

Mom's lips tightened. "I'm sorry but I have to say this. I don't like to speak ill about people though I probably do it more than I ought to, but here's the thing. There's something weird going on with that Dollie. She claims she sees a dead man in her house, then less than twenty-four hours later Tony is lying in the alley behind her house—dead? There has to be a connection. That woman is involved."

She had a point. There was one other thing that bothered me. "Where is the knife?"

When no one said anything, I added, "I'm going to have to buy new knives this afternoon. I'm afraid the police raided the house while you were gone. They took all of them, even the butter knives! Dad, you'd better check your clothes. I have a bad feeling they took everything. Actually, all of you should check to see if anything is missing."

"My clothes?" Dad shook his head. "I'm so sorry, everyone. I thought this would be a wonderful little trip. I never dreamed anything like this could happen."

"Dad, it's not your fault. We know you did not murder Tony. There's no doubt in my mind about that. So where do we go from here? Bernie and I will pay Elwin a visit, maybe he noticed something. While we're gone, Mom and Dad, see if you can write up a precise schedule of Dad's whereabouts and who was with him for the twenty-four hours preceding the discovery of Tony's body in the alley."

"I can help with that," offered Cyril.

"Neither Hannah nor I have met Tony's family and we're not regulars here," said Roscoe. "Maybe we can ask around about a mistress? It would seem conversational, not as if we're investigators."

"Great idea, Roscoe. We can hit some bars and find people who knew him. I'm in," said Hannah.

"Sorry but I'm out for the next few hours." Nina stood up. "My husband is leaving for a trial that begins tomorrow in Taos. But I'll join you for dinner to catch up with any developments, if that's okay."

"It's better than okay. We have tons of leftovers. Bring your own knife. We reconvene around six?" I asked.

We split up to go our separate ways.

I sprinted upstairs to run a brush through my hair. From my bedroom windows, I saw Cyril walking toward the river like someone who had somewhere to go. Maybe he just needed fresh air after being in the police department for hours.

Fifteen minutes later, Bernie and I strode up to Elwin's house. Three stories tall, it was brick, painted beige. The front door bore a shiny forest-green color, but the narrow shutters were navy. We had discussed whether we should call ahead, but feared he might come up with an excuse not to see us.

The door knocker looked to be an antique style, but unlike Tony's, it wasn't old. An oval handle featured a quirky face, reminiscent of an old elf with large ears and a beard.

When Elwin opened the door, I was surprised by his resemblance to the door knocker. His beard was shorter and quite neat, but his face was weathered. He had a bulbous nose and generous lips.

"Bernie!" he exclaimed.

"Hello, Elwin. Have you met my friend Sophie Winston?"

"Ahh, the sleuth! I have not previously had the pleasure, but I have heard many tales about you. You are far more attractive than I imagined. Somehow, I had a notion that you wore a Sherlock Holmes–style hat and carried a magnifying glass at all times," he laughed.

I could feel my face flushing. I shook his hand. "It's a pleasure to meet you."

"Come in, come in. Could I offer you a scotch?"

He showed us into a room with a white marble fireplace. White walls helped it feel airy but a rich green wainscoting around the entire room gave it a comfortable, cozy feeling. Books packed the shelves. An oriental carpet in greens and blues with a touch of burgundy nearly covered the entire hardwood floor.

Bernie declined his offer of a drink. I did, too.

"I expect you've come about the grisly death in the alley behind my house?" asked Elwin.

"I'm afraid so," I said. "Did you see or hear anything unusual that night or during the day before the body was discovered?"

"Not really. As you can see, this room, as well as my home office, face the street, not the alley. My kitchen and bedroom windows look out that way. But I can't see the alley from the kitchen because of my wooden privacy fence. So I would have had to be upstairs to see anything at all. I'm sure you have noticed that it has been warm, to say the least. I keep the windows closed and the air-conditioning on. It cuts down on outdoor distractions as well, like noisy trucks or children screaming as they play."

"By any chance, did you notice a man in the early morning? Sort of a hefty guy?"

A smile crept over his face. "The one you were spying on?"

Chapter 16

Dear Natasha,
Our kitchen window overlooks the neighbor's house. My wife spends a lot of time in the kitchen for legitimate reasons, but I think she spies on him. Noticing that he has a new outdoor table is one thing, but she's obsessed. She knows when he's out and when he comes home! How do I stop this highly inappropriate behavior?
Concerned Husband in Good Neighbor, Texas

Dear Concerned Husband,
For starters, you could install curtains. Or you could plant a large bushy pine tree between your homes to block the view. Are you certain there isn't more to their relationship?
Natasha

Well, well. Elwin saw a good bit more than he was letting on. "Yes, that one. Did you see him arrive at Dottie's house?"

"I did not. She has a number of gentleman callers. I'm

not sufficiently interested to keep up with her carryings-on, of course."

Did I detect a bitterness in his tone? Jealousy, perhaps?

"Gentlemen callers? Really?" asked Bernie in his delicious accent.

"Oh my, yes. Especially the fellow next door. Justin? Judd?"

"Julian?" I suggested.

"He helps her quite a bit. Takes her trash out to the alley. Borrows her Mazda convertible, for what reasons I'm not certain, perhaps to fill it up with gas. It's sort of an aubergine shade that one wouldn't think would appeal to him. Besides, one would imagine he could use his mother's vehicle for most errands. He mows that tiny bit of grass she has back there, as well. Waters her plants when it's dry. The sort of helpful things a manservant might do. I don't know quite how far their relationship extends but it's a curious one. She has children, so I can't imagine he expects to inherit anything from her, but you never know."

"Would you mind showing us the window from which you see all this?" I asked, smiling sweetly.

"Yes, I suppose that would be reasonable. The police weren't as thorough. This way."

Bernie and I followed him upstairs and into his bedroom. Heavy ornate furniture crowded the room. The walls had been painted a dark, rich teal which was interrupted by heavy burgundy curtains. Blackout drapes, I suspected. I noted binoculars on a nightstand and sidestepped a telescope to peer out one of the windows. Didn't see anything, my Aunt Fanny! He was up high enough to see inside Dollie's backyard. Her garage opened to the street but was closed at the moment. I was slightly aghast about the telescope. He could see straight into Dollie's house with that thing. Fortunately, her bedroom was on the other side of the house.

"So you think there's something going on between Julian and Dollie?" Bernie asked.

"It's not as preposterous as one might think. Especially not if he expects something out of the arrangement."

"You mean money," I said.

"I don't think he's doing it for her cat."

"Does she let the cat out in the backyard?" I asked.

"No. I see it out there sometimes, but I don't think it's intentional. She's a bit older than I, so she may be getting forgetful."

"What is it that you do?" I asked, still observing Dollie's house. I felt a bit of a voyeur because I could see her in the kitchen putting something in the fridge.

"Me? I'm retired now, but I restored paintings for the government. These days, I restore them for private citizens."

I whirled around. "That must be very fulfilling."

"I suppose so. I'm often asked why I don't paint original paintings. Perhaps I still will. But private restoration brings in some nice money and that is also rewarding."

"Pardon me for being impertinent, but have you dated Dollie?" I asked.

His face grew taut. "Inquiring into a person's private affairs is a bit rude, but yes, we were once close. I know what you're thinking. It's hard to imagine flashy Dollie with her fine clothes and huge jewelry having anything to do with a fellow like me. But it happened, nonetheless. She's entertaining, and quite interesting."

"Did you paint the portrait of her that hangs over the fireplace in her living room?"

"No. I wish I had. She was quite beautiful."

Whoa! He was in love with her. I wondered if she knew that he spied on her. I picked up the binoculars and as I suspected, he could see everything she was doing in her kitchen very clearly. I moved my view slightly to where the dead man had allegedly lain. He would have seen it for sure.

Goose bumps prickled on my arms. Could Elwin have killed the man? I was glad Bernie was with me. I didn't have to watch my back out of fear Elwin might stab me from behind. Nevertheless, I set the binoculars down and turned to face him.

"Did you know Tony Fontana?"

"Not well. We shared an interest in antiquities so our paths crossed occasionally."

"In what way?" asked Bernie.

"We were members of some of the same online groups. People who collect antiquities. It's quite a popular pastime. It's truly amazing to hold something in your hand that is hundreds of years old. It's a remarkable feeling to have that connection to something someone held and used two hundred years ago. I think that's why we like these old houses so much. They represent another era with all their odd nooks and crannies. When I sit by the fire reading on a cold winter night, I feel like I'm part of something special. I'm certainly grateful for electricity, but I feel a special kinship to those who sat there before me."

"Sorry to bring up old wounds," said Bernie, "but I'm wondering if you can give us some insight to Dollie. You must have split up for a reason?"

"I suppose we didn't have much in common. She used to accuse me of living in the past while she lived in the present. Always going out to fancy events dressed in glamorous gowns. That's Dollie. I don't have much interest in every charity someone can think up. She loves that stuff."

"You must be quite an early riser to have spotted me spying on Gus," I observed.

"The penalty of drinking too much the night before. Nature calls. I saw you from the bathroom. But your friend went on his way and so did you. I went back to bed."

"Thank you for your time. If you think of anything that might be helpful in the matter of Tony's death, I hope you'll let us know."

"Of course."

We followed him downstairs to the front door. I handed him a card with my number on it. "In case you remember something."

He nodded and closed the door behind us.

Neither Bernie nor I said a word until we were well out of hearing range.

Bernie broke the silence first. "Odd fellow, what?"

"I'll say."

Bernie headed for his restaurant, and I went home to another calamity.

My parents, Cyril, and Roscoe sat around my kitchen table. They clammed up when I walked into the house.

"What's going on?"

"Uh, I don't mean to add stress here." Roscoe cleared his throat. "We were planning to drive back to Berrysville today. I rode up here with your parents, so now I don't have a ride home."

"Perhaps I could drive you home in their car and then drive back here," Cyril offered. "Assuming you don't mind me borrowing your car? Maybe I can find a short-term rental where I can stay while this is cleared up?"

"Don't be silly, Cyril. You're more than welcome to stay here." As houseguests went, he was pleasant to have around.

The knocker on my front door sounded. I opened it to find a police officer. He handed me a document. "Sorry, ma'am." He walked back to the street. I glanced at the paper in my hand. The police were impounding my parents' car!

A tow truck rattled on the street as it backed up toward

the car. Two men jumped out and hooked it up. The police officer observed.

Behind me, Dad said, "Just when I thought it couldn't get any worse."

The two of us watched until Mom and Dad's white Lincoln sedan vanished from sight.

We returned to the kitchen.

"They took the car," said Dad.

"The police?" asked Cyril.

"I'm afraid so." I leaned against the kitchen counter and smacked my forehead with my palm. "I should have expected that. They're checking for evidence of Tony in your car."

"He was never in our car," Mom protested. "He always brought his bus."

"When he was dead, Mom. Remember how there wasn't any blood in the alley? They think someone killed Tony, then transported him there. It's hard to lug a dead body around. So they're checking cars for evidence of Tony's presence."

"Oh, thank goodness." Mom relaxed a little. "We're in the clear on that then. Will they drop the case against your dad?"

"I doubt it. They still have the DNA."

Dad embraced me. "Don't look so gloomy, Sophie. It's just a matter of time before they find the real killer."

I didn't want to shock everyone with the truth. If they had Tony's DNA on Dad's clothing, they weren't looking for another killer. They were building their theory of what happened, and in that scenario, Dad was the bad guy.

Chapter 17

Dear Sophie,
I love browsing through antiques stores. I've heard stories about people who bought an item for next to nothing and found out that it was worth thousands! But there's always so much stuff that I'm afraid I'll walk right by the bargain of the century. How can I tell what's worth a lot of money?
Clueless About Antiques in Table Grove, California

Dear Clueless About Antiques,
Educate yourself in one or two areas that you like. For example, period furniture, paintings, jewelry, dolls, vintage toys, or pottery. You'll be better equipped to identify what you see and know a fair price for it.
Sophie

Mom pressed her fingers against her temples. "When will this nightmare end?"

Aunt Melly jumped to her feet and with forced cheerfulness said, "It's the last day of the antiques fair. They always have great prices on the final day so they'll have less stuff to pack up. Let's go!"

If there was one thing my mother loved, it was shopping. For practically anything. "Great idea," she uttered sarcastically. "I can buy something to remind me of this terrible time when my husband was accused of murder and could be going to prison."

Cyril placed his hand over Mom's. "I think it's a good idea. Come on, we'll get some air and stretch our legs and browse. Maybe you'll see some clothes for Paul."

Reluctantly, she agreed, and we all trooped down to the fair. We stopped at a store where Dad shopped for clothing necessities. I took that opportunity to dash across the street to buy steak knives and a few kitchen knives because I had a feeling my knives were going to be in police custody for a very long time. Afterward, we strolled along the tents and gazed at jewelry, pottery, art, and assorted old items that we couldn't figure out. I was admiring a painting of peonies when Cyril called to Dad.

The two of them examined a map in a locked shadow box display case. The proprietor eyed them with great interest. I walked closer to see what the fuss was about.

"This is John White's map of Virginia. A truly remarkable piece dating 1585."

It barely looked like Virginia as we know it today.

"It is the first known use of the word *Chesapeake*," continued the salesman. "As you can see, it is adorned by the Royal Arms of England. A must for any serious collector of maps."

It was old, for sure. Possibly brittle.

"This should be in a museum, not a private collection," said Dad.

"How much is it?" asked Cyril.

"Fourteen thousand dollars."

My breath caught in my throat.

Dad took it much better. "We'll take two of them."

For one moment, the salesman appeared to take him seriously. He sighed. "You won't soon find anything like it. This map was discovered right here in Old Town. It's a miracle that it survived in this condition."

"I'll say." Cyril smiled wistfully. "I feel honored to have seen it but I'm afraid it's a bit pricey for me. I hope the person who buys it will take good care of it."

I saw Dollie out of the corner of my eye.

She must have spotted me at the same time because she rushed over. "My psychic says your father didn't murder Tony."

Her psychic? That was interesting. I took a deep breath to give me a moment of time to think of a kind response that wouldn't sound snotty. "That's great. But we already know Dad didn't murder anyone."

"Oh, then who did?"

I was sorely tempted to suggest she ask her psychic. "We would love to know that."

Dollie pointed toward a gilded clock on display. A cherub was checking the time and touched the clock portion. "Oh my word! We had a clock like that when I was growing up. Two hundred fifty dollars! Who would ever have thought that. I bet my mom donated it to some charity."

Aunt Melly studied the woman Gus had visited while Melly slept. Her eyes narrowed and her jaw twitched. "What does your psychic say about carrying on with other women's husbands?"

Dollie didn't appear at all taken aback by the question, which was clearly directed at her. "You should ask her! She's right over there."

I wasn't a psychic, but I could see what was coming.

"I've always wanted to have a reading. Can you set one up?" asked Aunt Melly.

"Of course! Come with me."

"Inga, Inga. Don't you want to come?" Aunt Melly prompted.

Mom paused briefly. "Yes, I'd like to know who murdered Tony."

Why did I think it would be a good idea to come here? I thought it would be innocent. Something to distract us all from Dad's terrible situation. I followed them over to a tent where a slender, stylish woman with jet-black hair pulled back in an elegant bun smiled at us.

"Oh, my dear Dollie. You have brought your friends to me. Who is first?"

Other than the many bracelets she wore on both wrists, she looked fairly average. If I had met her in the grocery store, I wouldn't have thought she was a psychic. No interesting headgear, dramatic makeup, or flowing robes.

"Come, come. Please have a seat."

Mom plunked herself into a chair across a table from the psychic. A banner behind the psychic read:

MISS LI
THE PSYCHIC WHO KNOWS ALL

She lowered her head and turned her eyes up at me. Raising her eyebrows, she said, "Aah! You have big problems in your love life." She frowned and squinted at me. "And murder. You must be very careful."

Okay, enough already. She was putting on an act. I exhaled a deep breath and drew back. I might as well let Mom and Aunt Melly have their fun.

Miss Li took Mom's hands into hers. "I feel great sadness in you. You are worried about your family. But you have a trustworthy husband to help you through difficult times. He is in grave danger though."

"What kind of danger?"

"I see him wearing red. He is in a very small space with people yelling at him. They want to keep him there. He will be very unhappy. I see that your son has brought you great joy. But you worry about your daughters who are not married. One of them has finally found the right man. But the other one"—she peeked at me—"is troublesome and cannot find a man who accepts her shortcomings. But do not despair for although she is bossy, nosy, and should not eat so many doughnuts, she means well."

Aunt Melly burst out laughing.

Miss Li pointed at her. "You now. Sit here."

Mom stopped her. "No. I want to know who murdered Tony."

Miss Li reached for Aunt Melly's hands. "You have many problems with money and a family member. I see police in your life. You have issues to overcome and must be careful that you are not arrested."

Aunt Melly interrupted her. "Arrested? Me? Oh no! But I haven't done anything! What I want to know is will I ever find a good man again?"

Miss Li smiled at her. "You already have. He loves you very dearly. You are lucky because you are deeply loved. And now you. The bossy daughter."

"No, thanks. You've already said that I mean well. Thank you for that."

"You must be very careful. I see you in grave danger also. People do not like when you peer into their lives."

"Uh-huh. Mom, pay the lady and let's go. I'd like to buy that painting I saw."

"Wait!" cried Mom. "Who murdered Tony?"

Miss Li closed her eyes and leaned her head back. Suddenly she snapped her head forward, her eyes wide with fear. "I am through. I must go."

"What did you see?" Mom demanded.

Miss Li shook her head but accepted her payment. She

looked up at me with a cruel gaze. "You are surrounded by liars and thieves. Do not trust anyone. Even those you love. You know too much and one wishes you dead."

Hah! I didn't know enough or Dad wouldn't be a suspect anymore. I backed away from her and ushered Mom and Aunt Melly toward a tent selling antique quilts.

Across the street, a storefront that had recently been empty bore the name AMERICANA BY NATASHA.

Mom saw it at the same time. "Do you think that's *our* Natasha?"

We entered the huge store. A portion of it was devoted to 1800s gowns and menswear. Not antiques, though. They were new and lovely with staggering price tags. One section featured patriotic T-shirts, another was decorated for the holidays with Christmas trees that showed off blown glass ornaments in the shapes of the Capitol building, the Washington Monument, and other DC buildings and monuments. Similar items were featured on nearby displays as paperweights and decorative bric-a-brac.

Two bored salesladies wearing 1800s gowns informed us that the owner of the shop wasn't in.

Our little foray wasn't a total loss. Dad picked up some clothes. I came home with a wonderful old painting of peonies and new kitchen knives. Mom found a piece of pottery that she loved. Aunt Melly bought an amethyst ring from 1920 and a few small gifts from Natasha's store for her neighbors and friends back home.

She dashed upstairs to stash them away and returned to the kitchen holding a red rose. "Gus was here. Look what he left on my bed! Maybe I shouldn't have thrown him out. Was I too quick to judge?"

"Melly, how can you even think that?" asked Dad. "A man who takes your money is no good."

"But he loves me. Deeply!"

"Melly!" He sounded exasperated. "Do you really think lying to you, stealing from you, and cheating on you are what a good man does when he loves you?"

"No." Aunt Melly pouted. "But he left me a red rose! Maybe it's my destiny to change him. Maybe if I love him enough, he won't be that way."

Everyone in my kitchen groaned. While Gus hadn't been a terrible person to have around, I didn't miss him, but mostly I didn't want him taking advantage of Aunt Melly. "Frankly, I'm a lot more concerned that Gus was able to get into the house while we were gone."

"We must have forgotten to lock one of the doors. Maybe the one to the sunroom?" Dad's eyes met mine. "We'll be more careful."

Roscoe brought up the subject of going back to Berrysville again. Cyril agreed to drive Roscoe home in the morning in my car, so that was settled, and Roscoe could get back to his brewery. I wondered how Hannah felt about that.

I was making a huge salad for dinner when I heard a funny noise. A thunk upstairs, as if someone was moving furniture. And then another thunk. Gus! He must have come back and sneaked into the house.

I took one of my new kitchen knives and walked up the stairs slowly, trying to determine where the sound came from. I peeked in Aunt Melly's room. Everything was in order. My room looked fine. That meant it had to come from the guest room where my parents were staying.

I crept up to the door and flung it open.

Cyril turned and smiled at me. "Sophie! Sorry about the noise. Your dad asked me to help him move the desk. Apparently, they stumble into it at night."

I wasn't buying that. Where was Dad? And why wouldn't he have asked me to help him move the desk?

Cyril held something in his hand.

"Oh. What's that you have there?"

"My phone. If I don't take it everywhere with me, I can never find where I left it."

What was he doing in their room? Searching for something? Or worse! Planting something incriminating?

"You look worried, Sophie. And downright dangerous the way you're holding that knife! Can I give you a hand with dinner?"

"Um, okay." But I made sure he walked down the stairs in front of me, just in case he was planning to push me.

I went back to making the huge salad. We also indulged in a final night of ribs and leftovers from the barbecue and hit the sack early, even Hannah!

I was in bed, wondering what Cyril had done in Mom and Dad's room, when Hannah slid between the covers of the blow-up bed.

"Are you upset that Roscoe will be leaving tomorrow?" I asked.

"Not particularly. I'm more concerned about Dad. I need to get back to work, too. But, luckily, I can work from my laptop. It doesn't matter where I am. I hope I won't be in your way. You probably have a lot of work piling up, too."

"I'm okay. Feel free to work in my office so you won't be interrupted constantly."

"Sophie?"

"Hmm?"

"I'm scared for Dad. This isn't something that will just blow over. How do you get around DNA on something? I thought that it was sort of conclusive. They've solved murders forty years later based on DNA!"

"I know. There has to be a way to explain the presence of Dad's DNA on Tony. For starters, the mere presence doesn't mean Dad killed him. I probably have Mom's DNA on me. She's still alive. And I know one thing for certain. Dad did not murder Tony." But I was beginning to wonder about Cyril.

Daylight was just beginning to peek over the horizon when we woke to a rumbling noise on the street. Simultaneously, someone rapped the knocker on the front door. In the silent house, it seemed to echo in all the corners.

I threw on a light robe and scrambled downstairs to the foyer. Daisy beat me there.

Dad was right behind me. "See who it is first."

Some habits die hard. He couldn't help it. I was still his little girl. I looked out the peephole. My heart sank. Now what? I opened the door to a uniformed police officer. He handed me another paper exactly like the one from the day before except this one had *my* name on it.

"Sorry to disturb you so early, ma'am. I'm under orders to take your vehicle in. Is it in the garage?"

"What? Why? I haven't done anything."

"Yes, ma'am. I'm just following orders."

After all I had been through with Wolf, I now truly despised him. A fury rose in me that made me want to scream at the poor young officer in front of me. What would happen if I slammed the door in his face? It was awfully tempting.

Dad placed his hand on my shoulder. "I'm sorry, Sophie. I don't understand all this. Open the garage door for him."

He was right, of course. For just a moment I wished I was the kind of person who could punch that kid in the nose. But that wasn't me and I knew it. Besides being quite inept at punching, I would end up in jail, making things even worse. As if they weren't bad enough now.

Wolf would certainly hear from me, though. I couldn't believe he was doing this to me.

I grabbed a key to the garage and led the way through the living room outside onto the porch and over to the garage door. To my surprise, the garage door wasn't locked. I must have forgotten to lock it what with life in chaos over the last few days. I opened the door.

But the garage was empty.

Chapter 18

Dear Sophie,
My best friend moved in with me when she broke up with her boyfriend. I don't mind having her around but when I come home from work, exhausted, I find the table set for dinner! The last thing I want to do is cook. If it were just me, I would make a sandwich. But now I feel obligated to cook. How do I handle this without hurting her feelings?

Too Tired to Cook in Ham Lakes, Florida

Dear Too Tired to Cook,
You need to sit down with your friend and determine whether she is a guest or a roommate. Determining that will allow you to better define responsibilities and expectations for both of you. And it might be a good way to broach the subject of just how long she will be staying with you.

Sophie

"Ma'am, where is your vehicle?" asked the young police officer.

That was a very good question. "I have no idea."

He took a deep breath. "Did you hide your car?"

I glared at him.

"Sometimes people do that to conceal evidence."

My tone terse, I said, "I had no reason to hide my car because I didn't think anyone was coming to take it. As odd as that might seem to you, it never occurred to me that you would appear here to demand my vehicle!"

"Ma'am, there's no reason to get testy with me."

"Hey!" Dad glared at him. "We have every right to be annoyed. We haven't done anything wrong. My daughter isn't even a suspect. Now do your job and report this car stolen."

I had never heard Dad so angry. He took the sheet of paperwork that I held and thrust it at the police officer.

"There is no point in being upset with me," said the officer.

"That's where you're wrong. We have every right to be angry with you and the entire police force. Now, if you don't mind, and it's all right with the police, we're going to have breakfast." Dad stood his ground.

"I'll find my way out."

"You will not!"

Dad was beginning to scare me.

"Show him the door, Sophie."

No one uttered a word until the police officer had left, and the front door was closed behind him.

Dad grumbled, "I'm not giving them a chance to plant something in your home. I don't know what's going on here, but I've had about enough of this nonsense."

I thought about how many times people had asked me to help them when someone was murdered. Then they showed up twenty-four hours later frustrated that no progress had been made. Being unjustly accused of murder or losing someone dear to murder was unbelievably stressful. I turned to Dad and hugged him. We stood in the foyer that way for a few minutes.

Mom, Cyril, and Aunt Melly joined in our big hug.

Hannah ambled toward us barefooted. "Uh, what's going on?"

We finally let go and began to chuckle.

I hustled into the kitchen and put on coffee. Mom heated water for tea. Mochie mewed for his breakfast, and through the bay window, I could see Nina running across the street in a silk bathrobe and fuzzy slippers. Muppet scampered toward my house a few feet ahead of her.

Hannah opened the kitchen door for them. Daisy trotted out to play with Muppet, and I fed Mochie kitty salmon.

Everyone talked at once until Nina had been filled in. I wished I had leftover doughnuts. They would be stale by now, but I wanted one just to spite that awful psychic, Miss Li. Instead, I settled for fruit salad, blueberry pancakes, and bacon out on the porch. I gazed around at my guests as I ate. Everyone was on edge. The level of tension was palpable.

"What do you think happened to your car?" Nina asked, looking directly at me.

"I wish I knew. I haven't driven it recently because I've been busy with company." I looked around the table at my family and friends.

But her question prompted me to think about it. I excused myself and dashed into the house. The easiest way to steal it would have been to take my car fob. I located the purse I had carried to the antiques fair and pawed in it for my keys. I let out a breath of relief when I found them, but that was immediately replaced with horror. Most of my house keys were there, but the car fob and one key were gone. During the barbecue, loads of people had access to my house. They went in and out and any one of them could have easily found my car fob and keys and taken them.

I returned to the porch. "Maybe we can hire someone to drive Roscoe home. An Uber or something. I'll make some calls." But not until I called Wolf and gave him a piece of my mind!

Hannah poked a square of watermelon with her fork. "Could Cyril take Aunt Melly's car? We wouldn't have a vehicle available to us unless we borrow Mars's car but we could probably manage."

"Mars's car?" While it was a possibility, I didn't want to impose on him.

She shrugged. "You know he or Bernie would help us out. Or Humphrey."

Dad smiled at me. "It's good to have friends who can help you in a pinch."

"Hannah, how did it go when you and Roscoe chatted up bartenders about Tony? Did you learn anything?"

Hannah scowled. "It was kind of fun but not at all helpful. Apparently, Tony gabbed a lot about historic stuff. Remember how he went on and on about the copies of the Declaration of Independence? What were they called?"

"The Dunlap Broadside," said Cyril.

"Yeah. Apparently, someone found one in a box in the basement of a bookstore somewhere up north and got millions for it. I swear Tony and all the local bartenders dream of finding a copy. So there was a lot of discussion about stuff people had found when they were renovating houses in Old Town. Dolls and old newspapers and magazines that are now valuable. Apparently, even buttons and toys can fetch a lot of money."

"Nothing about Dollie?" I asked.

"Not that any of them knew about. Tony didn't come in with his wife, either. No women at all."

"Well, that was a waste of time! Sorry, Hannah." Nina excused herself and went home to get dressed.

While Mom and Aunt Melly cleaned up breakfast, I dashed upstairs to change into a coral sleeveless dress. I pulled my hair up in anticipation of the hot weather. Everyone was having another cuppa when I returned to the kitchen. I poured myself a very strong mug of tea, disappeared into my office, and closed the doors.

Something was missing. A shudder ran through me. On my desk, a tiny bit of dust surrounded the area where my computer had been. The cops! They took my computer! New rage welled up in me. I had to remember not to shout because it would only make things worse. Holding my breath, I opened the drawer where I kept my laptop. It was gone.

I pulled out my phone and punched in Wolf's number.

"Hello, Sophie," Wolf said softly.

He had to know what was coming. "How dare you? Taking Dad's car? You know he didn't murder Tony! I can't believe you're allowing this to happen. You know us! I'm furious. I understand that some things have to be cleared, but this is outrageous. And then sending someone for my car, too? How did you think we would get around? I wouldn't even be able to make it to my events for the rest of the summer. Not to mention my computers. My father doesn't use those. How am I supposed to work? And now my car has been stolen!"

"Stolen? When did that happen?"

"I don't know. I opened the garage for that policeman this morning and my car wasn't there!" I paused. "How could you not know about that? You sent him. Didn't he report back to you?"

"I've been removed from the case."

"Removed?"

"They think I'm too close to you and your dad. Look, I can't imagine your dad murdering anyone, either. But I've been wrong about people before. They can fool you by putting on an act. I always have to consider that there's a lot I don't know about a situation. Not everything in life is as it seems. I admit that I was hesitant about bringing your parents' car in. But if there is no sign of Tony or a murder in that car or yours, then the case will have to take a new turn. And that could be to your benefit."

"You mean because he wasn't killed in the alley?"

"I did not say that." He paused briefly. "How did you know?"

"There would have been blood in the alley."

Silence. I could picture him smiling. "I can't interfere. They're not going to tell me anything. I wish I could help you, but I can't. I shouldn't even be talking to you."

So much for ranting and raving. "Thanks for taking my call."

"Sophie?"

"Yes?"

"Your dad is a decent guy. Good luck." The line went dead.

At least I knew he wasn't ghosting me. But there was no doubt that unraveling this mess would be more difficult without Wolf's help.

I wanted to check my work calendar but it was in my missing computers. I would have to take some time each day to keep up. First, I would have to buy a new computer!

Mental images of my reliable car upside down in a creek with shattered windows haunted me. It might not even be in Old Town anymore.

Trying to calm down, I called my insurance company and was glad to learn that they would cover car rental starting in forty-eight hours. It wasn't great, but it was something. Then I arranged for a rental car and added Cyril's name so he could drive Roscoe home. How did everything get so complicated?

Having done all that, I returned to the kitchen. Mom, Dad, and Cyril sat at the banquette.

"I have a little good news."

"Did they find the killer?" Mom asked.

"Not that good. I rented a car. It will be delivered this afternoon. Cyril can drive Roscoe home."

"One problem solved," said Dad.

"Where is Roscoe?" I asked.

"I haven't seen him this morning." Mom frowned at me. "Take a peek at him. He's probably just exhausted."

"No point in disturbing him. We can wait for the car to be delivered," said Cyril. "And we can always go tomorrow if that's okay with everyone."

Dressed to the nines with full makeup on, Aunt Melly entered the kitchen.

"Melly, you look lovely. Are you going somewhere?" asked Mom.

"Yes. To find Gus. He has to be around. He didn't have enough money to leave town."

"Melly, you ended it." Dad spoke to her firmly. "Now leave him alone. Or do you want him to take everything you have?"

Melly sucked in her lower lip. "You don't think he loved me?"

"Not one single bit," said Dad.

"Especially not deeply!" added Mom.

Dad sighed. "You're smarter than this, Melly. You were his target. I don't understand why you can't see that."

Cyril rose to his feet. "You look so lovely that you really should go somewhere. How about having lunch with me?"

"Oh, Cyril. That's so kind." Melly blushed. "But it's not necessary to distract me. I understand what everyone is saying. I guess all those nice things Gus did for me like the wrist corsage, and the chocolates, and the rose were so thoughtful and romantic. Maybe I've just watched too many romance movies. Life isn't like that. Wouldn't it be nice if it were?"

"What a pity," said Cyril. "I had my eye on a nice place down by the river, near the Torpedo Factory. I was eager to look around there a bit."

"Go ahead, Melly." Mom took a deep breath. "Paul and I think it's wiser for him to stay put for a few days. But be back by three. I invited Natasha and Wanda over for afternoon tea."

I opened the front door for Melly and Cyril. "Have fun!"

But then, like a dark cloud ascending, Dollie walked up to my house. Trails from tears cut through her thick foundation.

"Sophie!" She held out her arms for a hug.

I obliged her reluctantly.

"Darling, I need you again."

Chapter 19

Dear Natasha,
My husband inherited the family home where he and his siblings grew up. His parents never moved out so everything they owned is there. His siblings drop by constantly asking for their dad's chain saw or their mom's punch bowl. I understand sentimentality but I can't live like this. How do I get rid of their stuff short of divorce?
Cluttered to Death in Old Dime Box, Texas

Dear Cluttered to Death,
It all belongs to you and your husband now. Hold a big garage sale and throw out anything that doesn't sell.
Natasha

"Please don't tell me there's a dead man on your floor."

Dollie looked like she might cry. "All right. But there is! There's a dead man, but he doesn't look like the other dead man I saw."

I didn't know what to think and could only hope that

there would be no dead man this time, either. I poked my head into the kitchen. "Dollie has a problem. I'll be back soon, I hope."

When we passed Nina's house, she came running out to us. "What's happening?"

I shot her an unhappy look.

"You're kidding me. Another dead man at Dollie's? I should come along. You might need me. As a witness if nothing else."

When we reached Dollie's house, the first thing I noticed was that she hadn't locked the front door. "Dollie, maybe you should be more careful about keeping your doors locked."

She flicked her hand. "He's already dead. He's not going anywhere."

She opened the front door and as I stepped inside, I realized that something wasn't right. The elegant demilune table was gone. The mirror still hung in place, but the table had been moved somewhere else.

Nina and I followed her through the house to the kitchen. Once again, there was no sign of anyone, dead or alive. "Dollie, where was he this time?"

She sniffled. "Oh, we're not there yet." Dollie rounded a corner and opened a door. She went first, stepping carefully down twisting narrow stairs in her spiky heels.

While the main floor was elegant and spotless, the basement hadn't been renovated. Pipes and beams ran across the ceiling. Large antique trunks were stacked against the walls two and three thick. It was a claustrophobia-inducing space if ever there was one. Daylight leached around the edges of tiny ceiling height windows that were mostly blocked by boxes that lined high shelves. Light bulbs flickered as if we were in a horror movie. I had never seen anything quite like it but soon realized that this was the result of multiple generations of one family living in the same house for decades. This was their storage area and no one had cleaned it up. I had to suspect that ancient treasures and historic documents must be hiding in some of the boxes and trunks.

"Wow," Nina uttered. "Do you know what's inside all these trunks?"

"Not all of them. When I was a little girl and when my kids were young, it used to be an adventure to come down here and open a trunk to explore. It was rainy-day fun to dress up in old clothes and hats. They wore a lot of hats. But there are also tons of papers. The deed to the house is probably in one of them. We never have found it."

She flicked on another light and it illuminated a man on the floor.

My breath caught in my throat. "Roscoe!"

He lay on his back. I scrambled to kneel beside him, but it was hard to wedge close to him with trunks on both sides. I was pretty sure he was dead. "Roscoe!" I patted his cheeks to see if I could revive him. "Roscoe!"

He wore a black T-shirt with a small insignia below the left shoulder. Two arrows were crossed with the heads pointing up. Two words printed in arcs, one above the arrows and one below read *Fratres Perpetua*. Beneath the insignia, a spot grew in size and blood trickled to the floor. Not unlike Tony's wound. I felt his neck for a pulse. It was cool to the touch. Abnormally cool. He had no pulse at all. Not on his neck and not on his wrist. I felt sick. How could this have happened?

"Nina! Call nine-one-one."

She pulled out her phone, put it on speaker, and pressed the numbers.

I looked over at Dollie. "You know we have to call the police."

"Okay. But you do the talking. What's he doing here?" She began to cry.

Nina gave the dispatcher the address. We all heard when she asked, "Is this at Dollie Peabody's house?"

"Yes, ma'am," Nina had to confirm.

"You say there's a body?"

"Yes, ma'am. It's Roscoe . . . Sophie, what's his last name?"

"O'Brien."

"I'll send someone right over."

"Did you let him in your house?" Nina asked Dollie.

"Of course not. I don't even know him. He does look sort of familiar, though."

"That's because he attended Natasha's party and Sophie's barbecue."

"That explains it. I didn't remember him. He's a friend of yours, Sophie?"

"Yes. How did he get into your house?"

"I can't imagine!"

"Nina, take Dollie upstairs. Then let the police and emergency guys in and show them how to get down here."

Minutes later, I heard footsteps on the stairs and Wong asking, "Sophie? Are you down there? Is there really a dead guy this time?"

Her shoes clunked on the stairs.

"Unfortunately, yes. Sadly, it's one of my houseguests. He was planning to leave to go home. We don't know what he's doing here."

Wong kept her cool when she saw him. I left his side so she could reach him. "No pulse. He must have been here for a few hours already. I'm sorry about your friend but I can't believe that after all those false calls from Dollie that there's actually a body."

Emergency responders clattered their way down the stairs. I gladly retreated to make room for them.

"I need to speak with Dollie." Wong followed me up the stairs.

We found Dollie at the kitchen table with Nina.

Wong didn't bother to take a seat. "What is the victim's full name?"

"Roscoe O'Brien," I said.

"Address."

"I don't know. He lives in Berrysville."

Dollie sniffled and dabbed under her eyes with a tissue.

"Dollie, how do you know this man?"

"Nina tells me I may have seen him at Natasha's party or Sophie's barbecue. But I don't remember him. I thought he looked a little bit familiar. I guess that would be the reason."

"When did he come to your house?"

"I don't know. I didn't let him in."

Wong scowled at her. "Now, Dollie, there's a dead man in your basement. How did he get into the house?"

"How would I know?"

"Is there another entrance to the basement? From the outside, maybe?"

"Not that I know about. I don't think so. It's mostly underground."

"So there could be one."

"I don't think so, but these old houses, you never know what you might find."

"How long have you lived here?"

"Most of my life."

"And you don't know if there's a door to the basement?"

"I don't recall seeing one. And I never used one."

"Is there a broken window?"

"I don't think so."

"What did you do yesterday evening?"

"I went out to The Laughing Hound for dinner with my next-door neighbor Julian Kowalski."

"And then?"

"And then I came home and got ready for bed. Oh! And I watched a movie that was very funny. It had Tommy Lee Jones in it. He really needs to use sunscreen. He's all wrinkled."

Wong shot me an annoyed glance.

"Did you lock your doors?"

"I always do."

I doubted that.

"Did you hear anything unusual?"

"No." Dollie spun a ring with a large vivid purple-blue stone around her finger.

"Did you hear anyone else in your house last night?"

"No."

"Then how did you come to find him?"

"The basement door wasn't completely closed. Georgy was pawing at it and ran downstairs. I went after her."

Dollie's door knocker banged. I hurried to the front door.

A large bald man in plainclothes flashed a police badge at me. "Detective Morales of the Alexandria Police. Are you Dollie Peabody?"

"No. Follow me, please." I closed the door behind him and walked toward the kitchen.

"Are you a relative?"

"No. I'm a friend."

"Name?"

"Sophie Winston."

He stopped in his tracks. I turned around.

His eyes narrowed and a sly grin crossed his lips. "So, you're Wolf's girlfriend. The one whose father is a murderer. They warned me about you. I guess it should not come as a surprise that you are now involved in another murder."

I'm short but I drew myself up as far as I could and met his deep brown eyes without wavering. "I haven't been

Wolf's girlfriend in years. He has a wife. And my father is not a murderer. He is currently a suspect but that will be cleared up very soon."

I turned and marched into the kitchen. "Dollie, this is Detective Morales. He would like to speak with you."

Dollie seized my arm. "Sophie! You're a lawyer. Don't leave me alone!"

"Dollie, I'm not a lawyer! Should I call one for you?"

"No. I want you to stay with me. Of course you're a lawyer, you've solved a bunch of murders."

Dollie was confused and scared. I wrapped an arm around her shoulders. "We'll get you a lawyer. You'll be okay." Unless you stabbed Roscoe—but I stopped myself from pointing that out.

Dollie gripped my arm with the force of a bald eagle. "What do you want?" she said to Morales. "She's with me." Dollie pulled me close. "You do the talking." She pressed her thumb to her forefinger and pulled them across her mouth as if she were zipping it shut.

"It's okay, Dollie. Just tell him what you told Wong and me. What did you do last night?"

"I went to dinner!" That brought on a new flood of tears.

Nina patted her hand.

"She had dinner at The Laughing Hound with Julian Kowalski. Maybe you'd like to see the body while she collects herself?" I showed Morales to the stairs.

As he disappeared, Nina asked, "What's his deal?"

Wong whispered, "He's trying to make a name for himself. Word is that he's delighted to have this case. He's after you, Sophie."

"Why? Why me?"

"You heard what he said to you—Wolf's girlfriend. You would be a prize perpetrator and that would also nail Wolf."

"The other cops don't like Wolf?"

"Most of us do. But the jealous ones wouldn't mind if he got into trouble. You know how it is. In any group when one of them gets to the top, gets recognition, and is the big dog, others want to take him down."

It was a rat race. Someone was always trying to get ahead.

At that moment, Georgy had had enough. She wailed in a high pitch and shot toward the stairs. Dollie screamed.

I tore away from her, leaped forward, and barely caught Georgy before she could disappear into the basement.

Heavy shoes clunked up the stairs in a rush and Morales's head appeared. "What's going on?"

"The cat got loose," I said in as calm a voice as I could. "Dollie, do you have a carrier for Georgy?" I asked.

"Of course."

"Maybe it would be a good idea to put her in it right now so she won't escape again."

She acted as if I had made the most brilliant suggestion in the world. "You're so right. This way."

Morales said, "Hey! You can't wander off. Stay right there."

"We're just going to secure the cat," I said.

"Lock it in a closet."

Dollie drew a sharp breath. "You beast!"

We waited until Morales vanished from sight down the stairs. "Take off your shoes," I whispered to Dollie.

Chapter 20

Dear Sophie,
In our household, we wear indoor slippers or go barefooted. We ask our guests to do the same and even have slippers ready for them. A couple we like refuse to remove their street shoes. I think that's silly. My husband says we shouldn't invite them to our home anymore. But I hate to do that! We all agreed to abide by what you have to say on this subject.
Shoes or No Shoes? in Wooden Shoe Village, Michigan

Dear Shoes or No Shoes,
Your house—your rules. In your home, you get to decide how you prefer to live. If they are insistent, then they lose out. Enjoy their company outside of your home.
Sophie

"We don't want them hearing our footsteps downstairs." All we needed was Morales thinking we were leaving the premises. He would slap handcuffs on both of us!

She slipped them off her feet and led the way to a tidy laundry room. The cat carrier was neatly stashed on a low shelf.

I took it out for her and unzipped it. Georgy didn't fuss when I placed her inside. I wondered if Georgy was glad to be in a familiar, secure place and a quiet room.

"There you go, sweetie," cooed Dollie. "I'll close the door and you can take a nice nap. Those dreadful people will be gone soon."

I closed the door to the laundry room so it would be quiet for Georgy.

"Thank you, darlin'," Dollie said. "This is why I need you."

We returned to the kitchen, where Dollie donned her shoes and Nina whispered, "You've got to get Georgy out of here. And unless you have recently gone to law school and passed the bar, we don't belong here, either."

Dollie flashed pleading eyes at me. "Don't leave me!"

"I'm not going anywhere until I have Dollie set up with Alex." I searched my phone for Alex's contact number. Hopefully, he had come back from his vacation. I clicked on his name and the phone began to ring on the other end. Alex's assistant picked it up. I explained what was happening and asked if Alex was available.

Morales reappeared and addressed Dollie. "Ma'am, I'm going to have to ask you to come down to the station so you can tell us exactly what happened."

"But I don't know anything," Dollie protested. "He was lying there just like that when I found him."

"Yes, ma'am. We still have to take you down to the station."

"Am I under arrest?" Dollie shrank from him.

"Not at this time."

Alex took my call. "Sophie! I hear you have a problem?"

I explained briefly what was happening.

"Sure. I can meet her at the station."

"Dollie, I'm on the phone with a lawyer who will meet you there. In the meantime, don't say anything to anyone."

"Oh, tosh! Everyone is making such a fuss about this. I don't even know that man!"

I walked out of the kitchen so Morales wouldn't overhear me. Alex was a highly respected criminal attorney and from the sound of it, Dollie was going to need someone smart to get her out of this mess, although I really couldn't imagine that she killed Roscoe. Even if she had thought he was an intruder and managed to clock him with a frying pan, he would surely have been able to overpower a frail older woman.

Nina and I watched her walk to the police car. She stood on the sidewalk with her hands on her décolleté, waiting for a cop to open the door as if she were getting into a limousine. When it drove away, she waved at her neighbors like she was the Queen of Alexandria.

"I'm going to get the cat," I said to Nina.

She nodded. "Probably a good idea. Is Dollie having mental issues?"

"Not that I've heard. We can ask around. You mean because she seems so confused?"

"She's kind of, I don't know—imperial?"

"That's how she is."

"Maybe she murdered her husbands!"

"I don't think so. I'm told that, sadly, the first one died in the Vietnam War. Number two was zapped by touching a live electric line that was knocked down in a storm, and the third one liked to fly his own plane and crashed in the ocean just off Myrtle Beach."

"Given that kind of bad luck, I'm surprised the third and fourth husbands took a chance marrying her."

We retrieved Georgy and started to walk home.

"Nina, yesterday evening, I was in the kitchen and

heard some loud noises. I went upstairs to check them out and found Cyril in Mom and Dad's room. He made up a bogus story about Dad asking him to move the desk."

"Cyril? Oh no. I like him! Even my husband enjoyed meeting him. How do you know his story was bogus?"

"I don't think the desk had been moved even half an inch. Why wouldn't Dad do it himself or ask me for help? I don't know what he was doing there."

"Do you think he was planting something to make your dad look guilty?"

"I don't want to think that. But why make up a story?"

"We haven't considered Cyril being involved at all. Maybe we should!"

As we walked, Nina rambled on about Dollie and her house.

But I was wondering how to break the news about Roscoe. Hannah was bound to take it hard. And I wondered where to put Georgy. I didn't know how Mochie would respond to another adult cat, and I most certainly didn't want Georgy escaping under my care.

We reached Nina's place. "Keep me posted, okay?" She placed her hand on my arm gently. "I'm sorry about Roscoe. We're going to figure this out."

I forced a smile and walked on, my thoughts returning to Roscoe again. Why had he been at Dollie's house? It seemed unlikely that he would be in her basement at all. I didn't know what to think. Had he broken into her house? Crept in through an open window? If Dollie was lying and had invited Roscoe to her home, though that seemed unlikely to me, why would he be in the basement? Unless she had asked him to help her with something there. Whatever happened, Dollie was definitely involved now.

A shiny Toyota was parked on the street in front of my house.

Mom opened the kitchen door for me. "Good news! The rental car is here. Maybe you can pick up some groceries for us." She took a step back and peered into the carrier. "You got another cat?"

"She belongs to Dollie." I let Mochie sniff Georgy's carrier so he would know who was behind closed doors. I took her into my small home office and closed the doors to the living room and sunroom before letting Georgy out. She carefully placed one paw on the floor and then another, gazed around, and leaped onto a chair, probably fearful that I would shut her in the carrier again.

I left the room to retrieve water and food for her. On my return, I wrote two signs for each door—DO NOT LET THE CAT OUT!—and taped one to each side of the office doors. I took comfort that even if she escaped my office, she would still be inside my house.

It was the best I could do with so many people visiting. Besides, I thought it likely that the police would send Dollie home. I didn't understand what had happened, but I wondered if a woman her age had the strength to murder someone with a knife. She was very thin but maybe she was more powerful than she appeared? Some thin people were wiry and strong. But Roscoe had youth going for him. Had she somehow managed to surprise him when he was creeping through her house in the dark of night dressed all in black? Did his dark clothing indicate malicious intent? Was there another good reason to dress in all black and sneak out at night?

I meant to tell Mom, Dad, and Hannah about Roscoe's death. But then it dawned on me that the police would descend on my house for Roscoe's belongings very, very soon. Possibly in minutes. Part of me knew I shouldn't touch anything of Roscoe's but the other part of me worried that his death might have some connection to Tony's and the more I knew, the more I could help Dad. I hurried to the kitchen, slipped non-latex gloves over my hands, and headed for the little den where Roscoe had been staying.

The bed had been made. Either Mom or Aunt Melly made it after I left, or else he hadn't slept in it at all before going over to Dollie's house. The good thing about Roscoe's messiness was that I didn't have to be precise about placing things back where they should have been. I picked up the clothes he had tossed over chairs. I found gum, forty cents, AirPods, and a slip of paper in his pockets. I unfolded the paper. It was a receipt for a beer, a hamburger, and fries from Roscoe's brewery. On the back, someone had written *cream colored, red door, gray roof and shutters*. I peered at it for a long moment before I realized that it described Dollie's house. I took a quick picture of it before returning it to his pocket.

The date on the receipt was from May. Why would he have written a description of Dollie's house on the back of a receipt before he came to Old Town? I had to assume that he might have had the receipt in his pocket and wrote on the back of it more recently because it happened to be handy. I jammed everything back into his pockets for the police to see.

I couldn't locate his phone. Pity. It must be loaded with interesting information. There were books and pamphlets on the chair. I hadn't gotten to his bags yet when I heard the murmur of voices in the kitchen and slid off the gloves. No time for more snooping now. I had to tell them before the police arrived.

"Mom? Dad? Where's Hannah?"

"Upstairs, I think," said Mom. "Is something wrong?"

I nodded and fetched Hannah.

"I saw the cat in your office. I adore that cat! What's her name?"

"Georgy."

"She's so sweet! Are you going to adopt her?"

"I hope that won't be necessary."

When the three of them were seated, I said, "Unfortunately, there really was a dead person in Dollie's house this morning. Someone we all know and are very fond of. I'm so sorry to have to tell you that Roscoe has passed away."

The three of them all murmured his name. "Roscoe?"

"I can't believe it! What happened? He's far too young to die." Mom was tearing up.

"What was he doing at Dollie's house?" Dad looked at me with disbelief.

"I have no idea. Dollie didn't recall having met him. She *says* she didn't open the door to him. He appears to have been murdered in a similar manner as Tony."

"Murdered?" Mom croaked. "They'll blame it on your father again!"

"That's a possibility," I acknowledged. "Maybe if we can prove he was here, they'll have to pursue other avenues."

I glanced at my sister. "How are you doing, Hannah?"

"I'm in shock. Who would want to kill Roscoe? He's such a nice guy. He took me to one of the local breweries. They gave us a tour and everything. It was so much fun!" She sniffled and dabbed at her eyes with a tissue. "But then Tony was really nice, too."

All things considered, Hannah was taking the news better than I expected. No one had said it, but we all seemed to be thinking there was an attack on "nice guys."

"I don't understand," said Dad. "It makes no sense for Roscoe to be over at Dollie's house. What interest would he have in her? She's my age and I don't find her particularly interesting or attractive. What would a man his age want with her? Unless he intended to burglarize her house? I shudder to imagine that."

"I don't know. He had a description of her home scribbled on the back of a receipt from his brewery in his pocket. But I do know that the police will be here, probably soon, to look through the house again. Especially Roscoe's belongings."

"His poor, poor mother." Tears ran down Mom's face. "Should I call her or wait until the police break the news to his family? What is one supposed to do in a case like this?"

Hannah groaned. "I'm sure there is no Southern Guide to Etiquette that covers *this*."

Mom winced. "Oh, Hannah, this isn't the time to be sassy. His parents will never forgive us. We were supposed to take care of him. Show him a good time."

"It's not our fault, Inga," Dad pointed out.

"Of course not. And I'm certain that will be a huge comfort to his parents." Mom's tone oozed with sarcasm.

"Shouldn't we get in there and rifle through his belongings before they do?" asked Hannah.

I plunked the box of non-latex gloves on the table.

Mom gasped. "We're not really going to do that, are we?" But then she looked over at Dad. "Hand me two gloves. Paul, you stay here and let us know if anyone comes to the door."

"Now wait a minute—" said Dad.

"Hush. We're doing this for you. Who do you think their first suspect will be?" Mom pulled on the gloves. "I'll give you one hint. It won't be Dollie."

The three of us left Dad sitting in the kitchen with Daisy while we marched into the den to search. I lifted up the pullout part of the bed while they scanned the hardwood floor and throw rug underneath.

"All clear." Mom moved on to shake his clothes and examine the contents of the pockets like I had.

Hannah picked up a booklet called *Little-Known Facts About the Declaration of Independence* and a book titled

Valuable Antiques & Collectibles and How to Recognize Them. She rifled through the pages. "Nothing here."

And then I recalled the note in the pillow. "Check the pillowcases."

Mom made a face at me. "He wasn't four years old."

Hannah picked one up and I yanked the pillow out of another one.

"Nothing here," Hannah said.

"Nor in mine, either." I peered in the wastepaper basket. It was empty, except for one slip of paper. I pulled it out. It was about the size and shape of the note I found in my pillowcase. I switched on a small lamp and held it up to the light. It was the same kind of paper the note in my pillowcase had been written on. That was meaningless, of course, because printer paper was available everywhere. But Roscoe had used that slip of paper as a blotter. I felt certain that if I held it against the message to me, the little ink blots would be a perfect match to *Gus murdered Tony*.

Chapter 21

Dear Sophie,
I adore tea parties! But I don't have the time to bake and cook everything I would like to serve. Especially those adorable French macarons. Is it considered in poor taste to order the goodies from a baker?

In Love with Macarons in Paris, Illinois

Dear In Love with Macarons,
Of course not. It's perfectly acceptable to have all sorts of functions catered.

Sophie

"Inga! Girls! The police are here." Dad stood in the doorway frantically gesturing to us.

"Hand me your gloves." I returned the piece of paper to the trash and reached out for the gloves. I added mine, ran into the kitchen, and mashed them back into the box they came in. At least they wouldn't be obvious there.

Someone pounded on my door with a fist. "Alexandria Police! Open up!"

Very nice. Was this how they were conducting themselves?

I opened the door to find Morales standing on my doorstep. "I *have* a door knocker."

He walked past me and glanced in the kitchen. "Are you Paul Bauer?"

"I am." Dad got to his feet and held out his hand for Morales to shake.

Morales scowled at him and ignored his hand. "Where were you last night?"

"Right here. We were all pretty tired."

"How convenient."

"I presume you want proof that I didn't leave the premises?"

The muscles in Morales's cheeks twitched. "I don't know what's going on here, but I assure you that I will find out."

Dad smiled at him. "Won't you have a seat? I believe I can clear this up."

"I'll stand." He said it gruffly and reminded me of a grouchy ogre who found fault with everything.

"Very well. Cyril?"

I turned to find Cyril had been standing in the doorway to the kitchen, listening in. He wordlessly handed a rectangular object to Dad, who placed it on the table and pushed a button. We all clustered around to see what it was.

An image appeared in black-and-white. I recognized my guest room. Two people were getting into bed.

"Paul!" screeched my mother. "Is that us? What were you thinking? Does my hair always look that bad when I'm sleeping?"

"What is this?" growled Morales.

"It's a nine-hour video of my lovely wife and me sleeping

last night. Feel free to fast-forward. I believe you'll find proof that I was here, in bed, asleep."

"Good try. This could be manipulated."

"If I were savvy enough to know how to do that, I suppose it could be. But it records to a cloud, and I'm told the videos are often used for police purposes, so I think you'll find that it's adequate proof of my whereabouts last night." Dad picked it up and touched a few symbols. "What's your email address? I'll send you a copy so you can review it in the comfort of your office."

Morales rattled out his email address.

"And just so everyone is on the same wavelength and it can't be altered by one of the recipients, I just sent copies to my attorney Ronin Walker, Detective Wolf Fleischman, whom I'm sure you know, and my daughter, Hannah who is a computer whiz."

Hannah raised her hand and gave Morales a little wave.

Morales grunted and called in two officers wearing Tyvek outfits. "Where was Roscoe O'Brien sleeping?"

Dad led them to the den. It didn't take long for them to pack up every last one of his belongings in their bags. As they walked through the kitchen with Roscoe's things, Mom said, "Take good care of those. Roscoe's mother will want to have them."

Morales glared at Dad before heading to the front door.

I hurried after him. "You don't have to be so angry with us. We also want to find the killer. Seriously, what would you do if you were wrongly blamed for a murder? Dad did the right thing."

Morales turned and looked me up and down for a long moment. "You cannot overcome DNA." He walked away.

I closed the front door and leaned against it as if that would keep them from rushing back inside. At least Morales hadn't carted Dad down to the police station again. There had to be an explanation for Dad's DNA on Tony.

In the kitchen, Mom flung her arms around Dad. "While I would have appreciated knowing I was on camera, you are the most brilliant man I have ever known. What on earth possessed you to do that?"

"After they questioned me about Tony, and I had no proof other than my lovely wife's potential testimony about where I was, I got to thinking that it could happen again. So I discussed it with Cyril, who is more savvy about these things than I."

Cyril grinned. "It was a piece of cake. When I was out on a walk about town, I stopped in a store and asked if they had a camera that could record for eight to ten hours. Did you know they make them to watch nannies?"

Hannah shook her head. "Pure genius. Maybe we should all get one."

"Please!" I protested. "Heaven forbid that anyone else be murdered or accused of it."

Mom giggled. "I'm just lucky that I was tired and didn't get frisky."

"Ugh. Mom! Please! We do *not* need to hear about that." Hannah shot me a sick glance and stuck out the tip of her tongue.

The subject turned back to poor Roscoe as I fed Daisy and the cats. We finished up bits and bites of leftovers for lunch, leaving the fridge looking hollow. I set out to the grocery store to stock up on food since I still had a houseful of guests.

My mind should have been on the shopping list Mom and I worked out over lunch, but the truth was that I couldn't get over the shock of Roscoe's death. I pushed my cart along, wondering why Roscoe would have been in Dollie's house and even more peculiar, why would he have been in that rather creepy basement?

I paused for a moment in front of the cheese selection. Could Dollie have lured Roscoe and Tony into her house and stabbed them? Was it some kind of retribution against men? The problem with that was I just couldn't imagine she had the strength to overpower them let alone the character to kill. But sometimes people weren't as they seemed.

I selected an assortment of cheeses and moved on to pork loins, hamburger, whole chickens, fruit, and vegetables.

After unloading the groceries in the kitchen, I headed for my bedroom.

Hannah was focused on her phone. "Need something?" she asked without looking up.

I sat down and Mochie jumped up on my lap. Hannah's eyes weren't red. I didn't see wadded up tissues anywhere. She was acting as if nothing had happened. "Are you okay?"

"Sure. Why do you ask?"

"Losing Roscoe must be hard on you."

"Well of course it is. It's just awful. Mom and Dad called Roscoe's parents while you were out. They were on speakerphone. You've never heard so much crying. Our parents feel responsible."

"I can understand that. They brought him up here for a fun Fourth of July and look what happened. He was an adult, not a child, though. And what was he doing at someone else's house anyway? That's what I don't understand. Why was he there? You've been out all hours of the night. Are you sure you weren't with him?"

"Sophie! I cannot believe you even asked me that. Of course I wasn't with him. If I had been, I would probably be dead, too."

"Why on earth would anyone be in the basement of a virtual stranger?"

"Afraid I can't help you there. If you ask me, it's totally bizarre. Personally, I think Dollie is at the root of this."

I focused on Hannah. "Why?"

"For starters, how many people have you known who found a dead body in their house? Not to mention, how many of them came to you *instead* of calling the police? That alone is weird enough for me to think she's involved. Maybe someone else does the murdering. I don't know about that. But she's knee-deep in this."

Hannah had a point. But it wasn't fully fleshed out. "So she's some aging siren with high heels and too much makeup who lures men to her house and has them killed?"

"When you say it that way it sounds stupid, like a really bad movie." Hannah leaned toward me. "You know what I think? Dollie isn't as clueless as she portrays."

Hannah could be right about that. "How were Roscoe's parents?"

"Bereft. He was their golden boy, what with the brewery and everything." She looked sad, but she wasn't crying or even sniffling. She let out a little snort. "What gave you the idea that I was going out with Roscoe?"

"He *was* cute."

"You think I chase after every cute guy? Seriously, Sophie, I don't see you telling anyone about your love life."

"That's because I don't have one."

"You think we don't see how Mars looks at you? And poor Wolf got kicked off Dad's case because of you."

"We're not talking about me. But that was a very good try at changing the subject. Please just tell me that you are not involved in these murders somehow."

"I am not."

"Would you tell me if you were?"

"Probably not."

"That's what I thought. Have you been inside Dollie's house?"

"Nope. Do you really think I was there? That I had something to do with Roscoe's death?"

"No. But you're being so evasive about where you've been at night."

"I've been here. I wake you up nearly every time I come in."

"Then why can't you just tell me where you've been? Or who you've been with?"

"It's not Roscoe, okay?"

Experience told me I had pushed her to the limit. She would only be sassy with me now. "If Roscoe wasn't spending time with you, then who was he with?"

"Good question."

"Coming to tea today?"

"Absolutely! I love teatime. Wanda is such a hoot!"

"If I recall correctly, Natasha thought you were adorable and wanted you as her little sister."

"Well, I *was* adorable."

I rolled my eyes at her and left. I strolled into the den. For heaven's sake! The cops even took the sheets that were on the bed. I folded the bed up so that it was a sofa again.

Someone pounded the door knocker. I stiffened. It seemed as if it was always bad news these days. I hurried out to the kitchen and saw Natasha and Wanda greeting my parents. Aunt Melly ran down the stairs. I took a deep breath to calm my nerves before I joined them.

Cyril hugged Wanda. "The diner hasn't been the same without you."

"Aww, I miss you, too. I have a sweet spot for everyone in Berrysville. But to be honest, I'm making a lot more money here with my store than I did as a waitress. At my age, I never thought I would be able to start something new and be successful. It just goes to show that anything is possible." They walked into the dining room while she told him about her life in Old Town.

Natasha gushed about how pretty Hannah was, which

Hannah sucked up like strawberry lemonade on a hot summer day.

Mom beckoned to me. "Could you bring in the tea?"

I fetched it and poured it into the cups. While I'd been shopping, Mom had set the table with the Lady Carlyle Royal Albert tea set I had collected at yard sales and small antiques shops.

"When did you find time to bake all these goodies?" I whispered to her.

"I ordered them, silly. With all that's been going on there was no time for baking," she whispered. "And even if there had been time, I wouldn't have been able to focus."

I eyed the delicate triangular sandwiches. Egg salad, something with stacked slices of turkey, and another with pimiento cheese peeking between two slices of white bread. French macarons, petit fours, and a variety of square cakes, some chocolate and some with raspberries.

"It's beautiful, Mom."

"After all we've been through, I think we deserve a little treat."

I supposed it wasn't really time to discuss something macabre, but Mom jumped right in with a long recitation of my parents' call to Roscoe's parents. While they talked about Berrysville and gossiped about the residents, I watched Cyril. Ever the gentleman, he ate a dainty sandwich with sliced turkey in it and politely listened to the conversation. I had dismissed him as a possibility, then wondered if he might be involved. But now that he had helped Dad by installing a camera in his room, he had saved Dad from what might have been a revocation of his bail. I was enormously grateful for that! But I also wondered if I had been too hasty to dismiss him as a suspect. No one was perfect, yet Cyril had been helpful and polite, even when things got rough. He was staying here longer, ostensibly to be of assistance to Dad. I had readily accepted that explanation. They were old friends. Wouldn't I do the same for Nina? But now I wondered if I could be overlooking something about this thoughtful and tidy man with a remarkable singing voice.

When I heard the door knocker, I froze. Not the police again! I excused myself and went to answer the door. To my surprise, Alex waited at my doorstep with Dollie. He sported a just-back-from-the-beach glow.

"Hi, darlin'." Dollie kissed my cheek. "I hope it's okay that I came here. I'm so upset about all the things that are going on." She tented her fingers and slid them nervously back and forth. "I couldn't go home without you. I'm afraid of what I'll find."

Alex shot me an apologetic look. "I'm sorry, Sophie. She insisted on coming here."

"That's fine. Come in, both of you. We're just having tea. Please join us."

I led them into the dining room and pulled up two more chairs. "Perfect timing. Some of you know Dollie and Alex."

My parents looked straight at me, and I knew what they were thinking. *Why did Sophie break up with this handsome man? And a lawyer at that!* I had thought there would come a point when my parents would accept my life decisions. Alex wasn't the right man for me. But he was a good lawyer. I forced a happy face.

"It's good to see you again, Alex," declared Mom. "Dollie, I'm so sorry about what happened. Roscoe was a dear friend, and we can't imagine what possessed him to be at your house."

I fetched additional plates and teacups.

"How did it go with the police?" asked Dad. "I found it nerve-racking even though I knew I was innocent."

"I clammed up," Dollie confessed. "They take one look

at me and assume that I'm an old blithering idiot. I really don't know why. And they twist everything I say, so why say anything at all?"

"Maybe they're intimidated by you," said Natasha. "I love your dress!

"This old thing? Aren't you sweet." Dollie sipped her tea. "The police think I imagine things. They asked me if I invited that fellow, Roscoe, to my house." She laughed when she said, "They intimated that I was having a romance with him! At my age with that young man? Honestly, if that was my intention, then why would he be in my basement, which is only storage space?"

"Did they mention how he died?" asked Dad.

"Not to me." Dollie bit into a little pimiento cheese sandwich.

Alex selected an egg salad sandwich. "As far as I can ascertain, they think he was stabbed like Tony was. They collected all the knives from Dollie's kitchen, which is a fairly good indication."

Wanda seemed on the verge of tears. "Roscoe used to come to the diner with his parents every Friday night. He was a darling boy with all those floppy curls. Carried a rock with him everywhere he went. It was nothing but gravel with a streak of white running through it, but it was his treasure! He showed it to me every time they came to the diner. Just adorable. Did you know him, Dollie?" asked Wanda.

"Sophie says I met him but honestly, I don't recall." Dollie cut into a square of chocolate cake with her fork.

"How did he get into your house?" asked Natasha.

"You sound like the police. How should I know?"

"Didn't you hear him walking around?" Wanda asked.

"Sometimes I think I hear voices murmuring, or whispers, or footsteps. But the police and my children think I'm imagining things. They claim I'm not right in my head.

But I know I'm not losing my mind. I *know* it! My psychic, Miss Li, says I'm an empath. I can feel things that others can't. My children think I've gone bananas. Sophie is the only who believes me."

I was glad she took comfort in that, yet I felt guilty that I, too, had my doubts about Dollie's grasp on reality.

"As we get older, we do have to focus more. I have to be careful about locking the doors," said Wanda.

Natasha deftly changed the conversation by announcing, "You must all come to my new Americana store! It's around the corner from Mom's store and it has been a wild success. I'm thinking about starting a chain of them."

"We saw it yesterday," I said. "It's huge!"

"A chain?" asked Dad. "That's very impressive, Natasha. Will the shops be limited to Washington, DC, or will they be all over the country?"

Natasha seemed uncomfortable. "You were there, too? I really can't have accused murderers in the store. Maybe you can visit again when you're out of prison."

I thought my mother might faint dead away, but Wanda beat her to it.

Chapter 22

Dear Sophie,
I was lucky to inherit the family homestead where I grew up with my siblings. My wife says the house is too cluttered and not her style. Of course, it seems like almost everything has a sentimental value for me and my siblings. I don't want to throw it all out, but I need to keep my wife happy, too. Suggestions?

Sentimental in Old Dime Box, Texas

Dear Sentimental,
You can probably let go of many things. There must be a lot of items that your siblings and nieces and nephews would want, so begin with them and give them the things they treasure. Then consider those in need and donate items that you don't use to a local church or charity. That should clear up your home considerably and make your wife very happy.

Sophie

"Mom! Mom!" Natasha rushed to Wanda's side. Wanda lay on the floor, motionless.

I joined her and felt Wanda's wrist. Her eyes were closed but she had a nice strong pulse.

"Natasha, would you get a cold, wet paper towel from the kitchen?" I asked.

I thought Natasha would knock Aunt Melly down the way she flew through the dining room.

Wanda opened her eyes and winked at me. "Is she gone?"

I nodded.

She reached out her hand. "Help me get up, will ya?"

By the time Natasha returned, Wanda was sitting on her chair again. She accepted the paper towel and held it against her forehead. "Don't make such a fuss, Natasha, it's just one of my spells."

"You've been having those spells for years. You're going to see a doctor about them."

"Nonsense. I'm fine now."

"We'd better get going," said Natasha. "Thank you so much for the tea. It was a delight up until you poisoned my mother."

Mom's eyes widened. "I did no such thing!"

I ushered the two of them to the door as fast as I could. Wanda took a minute to hug my mother, and they left.

"I guess you're glad you ordered the food," I whispered.

Mom started to laugh. "I am, indeed. I have to be honest, right now I couldn't focus enough to bake all those goodies. Your father's situation has me completely distracted."

Alex joined Mom and me at the door.

"I'm sorry, Sophie. I owe you an apology," said Mom.

"Oh?" Maybe she had finally realized that I didn't have to be married. Aunt Melly's situation with Gus might have opened her eyes. It was far worse to be wed to the wrong man.

"I don't recall Natasha being so impudent."

I snorted.

Alex laughed aloud.

I hadn't seen that coming. "Oh, Mom. You and Dad never knew her like I did. What did Wanda say to you?"

"She apologized for her daughter and wants to have lunch. Just the two of us and Melly."

Alex shook his head. "Natasha is something else. Promise me that when she needs a lawyer, you'll call Ronin, not me. Okay?"

I walked outside with Alex while Dollie chatted with my mom. "So how was Dollie?"

"Fine. She followed my instructions precisely. You know what she said about the police thinking she's nuts? It's true. That's exactly what they think. They said as much to me. She calls them too often and when they get there, whatever it was is gone, or never happened in the first place. They have lots of theories like squirrels in her attic or loose shutters that bang in the wind."

"Are they going to arrest her for Roscoe's murder?"

"It's hard to tell. I mean, the guy *was* in her house. And no one else was there. I can't imagine a situation where someone else stabbed him to death and left her house without her knowing anything about it. It doesn't look good for her."

"Do you think she did it?"

"I think I'm going to send her to a doctor for a consultation. The thing is that she makes sense to me when she's talking. She's not showing signs of being forgetful or acting inappropriately. Maybe you can get more information out of her. So this guy, Roscoe, was staying with you?"

"Yes. His parents are longtime friends of my parents. I

feel just awful. They came up here for the big Fourth of July celebration and this happened. What I don't understand is why he was at Dollie's house at all. We thought he was here in bed and hadn't gotten up yet."

"Was he a thief?"

"No! He owns a brewery in Berrysville."

Alex rubbed his head. "Something's wrong with the whole picture. Let me know if you come up with any viable theories, okay?"

"Will do."

Alex called to Dollie while I fetched Georgy. The two of them climbed into his car and I placed Georgy's carrier on Dollie's lap. I hoped that if anything else went awry, Dollie would call Alex instead of coming to get me.

"Well! Wasn't that interesting?" said Aunt Melly, watching them drive away. "That Dollie woman insists she didn't have anything to do with Gus. She acted as if she didn't even know who he was!"

"You sound like you don't believe her."

"You betcha I don't. You're the one who saw him there. I have no reason not to believe you. What else would he have been doing?"

What indeed?

That night after dinner, I texted Mars, Bernie, and Nina.

Anyone know the owner of Royal Dog Brewing? I'd like to ask some questions tonight.

Not surprisingly, Bernie knew the owner. But Nina and Mars wanted to come along for the beer. I suited up Daisy and met with Nina and Mars. Bernie arrived before we did and found a table outside where Daisy could sit with us. Lights hung overhead and lively music played in the background, but not so loud that anyone had to shout.

The three of them ordered beer but I was concerned about the goings-on and declined alcohol, opting instead for lemonade. I had to keep my wits about me!

The owner, Karl Hofmeister, spotted Bernie and came out to join us. "Playing hooky from your own restaurant?" he asked Bernie.

"Something like that. Taking a breather." Bernie introduced us. "We have some questions, if you don't mind."

"Sure." He held a paper cup with something in it. "Can your dog have a hamburger?"

Daisy's nose twitched. She focused on the cup in his hand.

"She would love it," I said.

Karl ruffled the fur on Daisy's head and held out the cup to her. She licked it clean.

"What's up?" Karl asked. "Sounds serious."

"I believe Roscoe O'Brien came by to see you the other day," I said.

Karl grew rigid. "Are you a cop?"

"No. Roscoe was staying with me."

"The cops were here about Roscoe?" asked Bernie.

"Not yet. But I remembered him when I heard what happened. It's all anyone can talk about. I don't mean to sound rude, but what's it to you?"

"My father has been blamed for the murder of the first man to be killed, Tony Fontana. But it definitely wasn't my dad who killed him. We're trying to find out what was going on with Roscoe."

"You think there could be a connection?"

I shrugged. "Possibly."

"Okay. Well, he was here with a pretty blonde. Hannah, I think."

"That would be my sister."

"Interesting. Was she dating him?"

Aha! Maybe she *had* been seeing him, despite her denials. "I'm not sure. What did you think?"

"They didn't act like it. But a lot couples who come in are dating or at least getting to know each other. He told me he owns a brewery in some little town. So I gave them a tour of the place. Professional courtesy you might say. He was observant, smart, and seemed to know his stuff. I thought maybe he was trying to impress his girl. He was different when he came back alone."

"He came a second time?" I asked to be clear.

"Oh yeah. Wanted to sell me his brewery. He had a bunch of different scenarios. I could buy it outright. Or we could merge, which involved me putting some serious money into the project. Or I could invest in his brewery and he would provide me with beer."

"What did you say?" asked Mars.

"I wasn't interested because I've got my hands full here but I asked him a few questions. I'm not one to turn down opportunities. The guy was broke. Dead broke. He owed a lot of money to a bank and an investor. I didn't see any way for him to climb out of the hole unless he could get an extension on the payments."

"I guess you didn't plan to go into business with him?"

Karl shook his head. "I wouldn't have touched that brewery. Even if I had been interested, I know better. When someone owes that kind of money, there's stuff that hasn't been updated or repaired. I'm no dolt. And I'm not in the business of absorbing other people's debts. I have enough of my own, thanks. I felt for him. Really, I did. But I don't know anyone who would have anted up the kind of money he needed to stay in business."

"He didn't mention any of this in front of Hannah?" asked Nina.

"Not a word. At least, not while I was around."

A dish crashed to the floor in the kitchen. Karl winced. "If you need anything else, stop by. Okay?"

He rushed to the kitchen.

I eyed the diners. No sign of Hannah. There were loads

of restaurants in Old Town and more in Washington, DC. It was a long shot that she would happen to be there.

My house was quiet when Daisy and I returned. Only Mochie mewed a greeting when I walked in. I heard voices outside and joined them.

The evening air brought welcome relief from the heat. Fireflies gathered above us as my family and friends moved on to dessert and after-dinner drinks. I worried about Dollie alone in her home. It seemed that most of the sounds she heard came at night.

Hannah had gone out for dinner, prompting a good deal of discussion about exactly where she was going and who she was with since we knew it couldn't be Roscoe.

"Now, Inga and Paul," scolded Aunt Melly. "Hannah is an adult."

"Says the woman who married a total stranger," snorted Dad, which wasn't at all like him. The stress of being accused of murder must have been getting to him.

"I made one big mistake in my life and now you're going to remind me of it at every turn?"

Dad patted her hand. "I'm sorry. This situation is getting on my nerves. And I don't see how it will be resolved. The police have clearly made up their minds about me. They're going to run over here believing I committed every crime that takes place in Old Town. I almost wish I was wearing one of those ankle bracelets so they could see that I haven't left Sophie's house."

"Aww, Dad! I haven't given up yet," I assured him. "You shouldn't, either."

When my guests decided to retire, I ran upstairs to put on sneakers, just in case I had to run. I wasn't much of a runner, but if I needed to move fast or sneak up on someone, I'd rather be prepared.

When I left my room, I caught Cyril quietly closing the

door to Aunt Melly's room again. Why was he always nosing around in other rooms? Surely, he wasn't planting nighttime cameras in each of our bedrooms. I smiled at him as if I hadn't seen him exiting her room. "I'm taking Daisy for a stroll now that it's cooler."

"The daytime heat is hard on dogs."

I walked down the stairs, relieved that he followed me instead of snooping in someone else's room. Aunt Melly was in the kitchen with Mom.

I couldn't stay home all the time, but Cyril was making me feel like someone ought to keep an eye on him. When Daisy and I left, we crossed the street and I watched my bedroom windows for any sign of a light being switched on or a flashlight moving about. No one stirred in my room. Maybe he decided against more snooping because I'd caught him leaving Aunt Melly's room.

Daisy ambled along, pausing regularly to sniff scents. We strolled toward Dollie's house. Across the street from her front door, I stood near a tree and observed for a few minutes. It was so quiet that I could hear crickets chirping. The sound and comfortable warmth of the summer night relaxed me. Nothing was happening at Dollie's house as far as I could tell. The lights on the sides of her front door were on. Her bedroom windows were dark, as were the third-floor windows. Dollie was probably still out at dinner.

It would be a perfect time for someone to enter her house. Out of curiosity, I crossed the street and tried the door handle of the front door. It was locked. Daisy and I walked around to the back of the house, where Tony's body had been found. Nothing stirred in the alley. I opened the red gate and walked into Dollie's garden. I didn't see anything of interest. I did note that all the lights were off in the house. I tried the back door. It was locked.

Daisy and I left the backyard and returned to the dark

alley. I heard the crunch of tires as an otherwise soundless electric car turned into the alley. Daisy and I were squarely caught in the headlights.

The car idled and someone stepped out.

"Sophie, darling!"

I recognized Dollie's voice. She crossed in front of the car, carrying a leftover box from a pizza place in town.

"You brought Daisy with you!" She leaned over and kissed Daisy's forehead. "I love dogs. She's too big for me, though. I would need a little-bitty dog. One that could fit into my handbag. Were you looking for me?"

I tried to act casual. "Daisy and I were just out for a walk."

"Well, come on in! I don't get much company except for Julian. I don't know what I would do without that boy. I should call him a man, of course, but he's about the age of my sons and they will always be boys to me."

She opened the gate while Julian's garage door, next to hers, opened and he drove the car inside.

Dollie unlocked her back door and switched on a light in the kitchen. Daisy and I stepped inside. I looked across the alley and up at Elwin's bedroom windows to see if he was watching. It was hard to tell. They were dark. He could easily have closed the drapes and positioned his telescope in between them.

I turned just in time to see Dollie open her refrigerator. It was nearly empty. I didn't want to embarrass her, but I wondered if she ever bought groceries. She said she didn't cook, but she had to eat something. She placed the pizza box inside and closed the refrigerator.

"May I turn off the lights for a moment?"

Dollie gripped the countertop. "Sure. What for?"

I switched them off. "Did you know that Elwin across the alley can see straight into this room?"

She shuffled over next to me and held on to my arm.

"That's disturbing. His house has been there all my life. I hope he's not a voyeur."

"Can you see into his house from your second floor?"

"Let's look!"

She turned on a light so we could see where we were going. But she didn't switch on any upstairs lights. She followed nightlights along the wall, which appeared to be automatic. I followed her into what must have been her sons' room, and we peered out the window.

"The lights are off in his kitchen," she said.

But I was more interested in Elwin's bedroom. It was completely dark, as if he wasn't home. But then a vehicle turned into the alley and for just a second, the car's lights caused a reflection. A very small one, like the lens of a telescope.

Chapter 23

Dear Sophie,
My mother-in-law is always inviting us to do things with her, mostly meals. But we're not interested, don't have the time to sit around and chat, and we have to attend the kids' activities on our days off. How do we get that across to her?
No Time for Grandma in Busy, Kentucky

Dear No Time for Grandma,
Invite her to come with you. Grandma would probably love to attend the kids' games and activities. Include her in your busy days and pizza runs. She might even love driving the kids to their events, thus opening up a little spare time for you.
Sophie

Elwin had to know more than he was saying. His spying habit was certainly distasteful, but he might know something helpful.

"Thanks, Dollie."

"You will be happy to know that I had the locks on the doors changed."

"Good for you! I'm glad to hear that."

Daisy and I took off for home. On the way, I texted Mars, Bernie, and Nina. Even though we'd just been together, we hadn't had a private moment to discuss the situation.

Early breakfast at my place tomorrow? We need to regroup.

They all agreed.

To my surprise, Hannah was home when I returned. She greeted me with "Thank heaven, you're home! Mom has been trying everything to get me to tell her who I'm hanging out with. It's driving me bananas."

"You could just tell her."

"I'm an adult. I don't have to tell her anything."

"Oh, Hannah. You might be an adult, but you're acting a like a teenager. Just tell her already."

"I don't think that's wise."

Oh no. There must be something majorly objectionable about the guy she was seeing.

I was up early in the morning, mostly because I couldn't sleep. All the bits and pieces of what had happened were swirling in my head. I needed to make some connections. At the very least, get Dad off the hook.

Only Daisy and Mochie were awake when I tiptoed down the stairs, put on tea, and let Daisy out. I fed Mochie breakfast, checked the time, let Daisy in, and took a pot of tea and a mug to my office, where I used my phone to do some research on DNA.

There were a few major factors that could play a role in Dad's case. I hoped it would never go to court. I wrote them down so I wouldn't forget when I called Ronin. He probably knew a lot more than I did about DNA, but it was worth pointing out these facts to him anyway.

One: DNA can transfer to you from brushing against someone. So if Dad was wearing his red sweater and Tony backed into him or placed an arm around him, his DNA could have transferred to the sweater.

Two: DNA may wash out eventually, but putting a garment in the wash probably will not wash it out. So Tony could have made contact with Dad days before his death. It did not indicate Dad was present when Tony died.

Three: Someone else's DNA could be on the sweater. If so, whose?

I felt enormously relieved just to know these things. But finding the real killer remained imperative.

Checking the time, I rushed to the kitchen and started a blueberry buckle. When it was in the oven, I turned my attention to breakfast potatoes, cutting them up and tossing them on a tray with rosemary and garlic. I slid that into the oven on a different rack. I carried an April Cornell sky blue and cottage rose tablecloth outside and spread it over the table. The lighter blue accented by pink and red roses was the perfect summer switch from July Fourth colors. Matching napkins, a few fresh roses from my garden in a vase, and square white dishes looked fresh and appealing. Next, I brought out cutlery and mugs, and then finally, the coffee machine and two huge pots of tea, cream, milk, sugar, and lemon slices.

The blueberry buckle was nearly done. I started the baked scrambled eggs. They were in the oven when Nina, Muppet, Mars, and Bernie arrived.

Bernie carried the eggs out to the porch. Nina brought a selection of breakfast rolls and set them on the table. I gave Muppet and Daisy hard biscuits to eat, and we sat down.

Mars pulled out his list and a pen. "Who in the house can hear us from here?"

"The air-conditioning is running, so the windows should be closed." I stepped out to the garden to check. "I think we're safe as long as we don't speak too loud." I poured coffee and tea before sitting down.

"What smells so good?" asked Nina.

"I suspect that's the potatoes."

"Mmm. I think you're right."

"Well," said Mars, "I have Gus at the top of my list. Does anyone even know where he is?"

"According to Aunt Melly, she took his cash when she threw him out, so he should still be around here somewhere."

Bernie nodded. "I saw him yesterday. He ducked around a corner when he spotted me. He's growing a mustache and a beard."

"Was Stan with him?" I asked.

"No. Why do you ask?"

"We've never considered him. At least, I haven't. There was something different about him. He sort of appeared and disappeared with Gus."

"He was surprisingly quiet. Didn't say much." Nina clutched her tea in her hands. "And he didn't seem to know anyone from Berrysville or here in Old Town."

"I'm pretty sure that Roscoe wrote the note that said, 'Gus murdered Tony.' I found a slip of paper in his wastebasket that looks like it touched the ink of his note." I tasted the eggs and wondered why I ever bothered making them on the stovetop.

"I guess there's no point in discussing why Roscoe wouldn't have come right out and accused Gus," Bernie said. "But I do wonder how Roscoe knew that."

"Now I feel guilty for not having accused Gus publicly." I speared a potato. "But when Wolf dismissed what I told him, I thought I must be wrong. Roscoe might be alive today if I had handled that differently."

"So true," said Nina. "*You* would be dead. I wonder if Gus and Tony knew each other before they came to Old Town." Nina waved her fork around. "They could have had a grudge against each other that started way before they ever came here. Maybe Gus posted a negative review about Roscoe's brewery? I'll search the comments and see what I find."

"It makes a lot of sense that Gus killed Tony and then also killed Roscoe because he knew about it," said Mars.

"But why was Roscoe in Dollie's house?" asked Nina. "Why not kill Roscoe here in Sophie's house?"

A deep male voice can from the doorway. "Because Roscoe was looking for something." Cyril walked toward the table. "May I join you? Or is this a private breakfast?"

"Of course you may join us," said Nina, rising to get a plate for him. "Help yourself."

Cyril sat down next to Nina. I tried to calm my nerves with tea. We should have met at a restaurant away from my house. Cyril could very well have killed both Roscoe and Tony. I didn't know of a motive but the way he was sneaking about snooping in the bedrooms disturbed me.

"Why do you say Roscoe was looking for something?" asked Bernie.

Cyril sipped his coffee before responding. In a thoughtful tone, he said, "By all accounts, Roscoe was in the basement. He clearly didn't go there to harm Dollie, or he would have been upstairs looking for her. So, he must have had a reason to be in the basement."

"Roscoe was broke," said Bernie. "He was about to lose his brewery."

"And Gus may have been, too," Nina pointed out.

"But why would they be looking in the basement?" I asked. "Valuables like paintings, jewelry, or cash would be upstairs, not in the basement."

"Maybe not," said Mars, "but I think Cyril makes a good point. Both Roscoe and his killer had some reason to be down there."

"He could have gone there to hide," I suggested. "Maybe he heard the killer enter the house and he stepped into that stairwell. Which reminds me that Elwin spies on Dollie. I was over there last night, and I'm pretty sure I saw a reflection off his telescope."

"Eww." Nina wrinkled her nose. "That's disgusting. Do you think he's some kind of pervert?"

"He wouldn't see much. Her bedroom is on the other side of the house." I looked at Bernie.

He shrugged and said, "Could be that he has an issue of some sort. He's a bit of an odd fellow, I think. Worth keeping in mind."

"Motive?" asked Mars.

"Maybe she spies on him or reported him to the police for some reason, and he resents her?" Nina suggested.

"He said they dated. Maybe something went haywire between them. Put him on the list, Mars. But we only have speculation as to the motive." I cut the blueberry buckle and placed a cake server next to it.

Mars asked, "How about the next-door neighbor, Julian, who does so much for Dollie?" He wrote his name on the list. "This is the most pathetic list of suspects ever. Three people. All men. None have a good motive."

"It's better than what the police have," said Bernie, helping himself to a piece of blueberry buckle. "They only have two suspects, Sophie's dad and Dollie, and neither of them has a motive, either."

"We're overlooking something," I grumbled. "But what?" I tried the blueberry buckle and savored the sweet, delicious fruit. "Maybe we have to go at this from a different angle. We have two victims. Maybe we need to treat them separately."

"Okay," Nina said, nodding. "That makes sense to me. Where was Tony's body between the time he was killed and the time he reappeared? And why did the killer bring him to the alley behind Dollie's house? Why not take him out in the country and dump him somewhere?"

"And the big question," said Bernie. "Why was Roscoe in Dollie's basement?"

"You notice," said Mars, "we haven't mentioned Dollie as a suspect. What if she killed them? I know she's not young or strong, but she probably could have driven a knife into Roscoe if he wasn't paying attention or didn't know she was there."

"Or if she was trying to seduce him," said Bernie.

"Oh, that's awful," Nina complained. "Why must men always jump to those conclusions? For pity's sake, she's the age of your mother, Bernie."

Bernie nodded. "My mom would have no problem stabbing someone if she were attacked."

"That's even worse," said Nina. "Now I hope I never have to meet her."

Mars laughed. "She's quite lovely and very refined. I can assure you that Bernie is exaggerating although it wouldn't surprise me a bit if she were a fencing expert and could hold her own."

Cyril set his mug on the table. "I agree. I don't think you can eliminate Dollie. What if I go over there and chat her up a bit? Maybe Sophie could arrange that. She appears to trust Sophie."

Nina gasped. "Do you think she's using us? Coming to Sophie to clean up her messes? Pretending to be innocent?"

We all looked at Cyril, who simply said, "It's possible."

Mars shook his head. "It's too dangerous for you to go over there by yourself. If Dollie is the murderer, then you could be her next victim."

"You could always spy on us from across the alley," said Cyril.

My parents ambled in with Aunt Melly. We must have looked guilty because everyone stopped talking.

"You're up early," Mom observed.

Mars quickly tucked our pathetic list of suspects into his pocket and offered his seat. "I'm afraid I have to get off to work. Thanks for breakfast, Soph." He kissed me on the cheek.

Mom elbowed Dad. As soon as Mars was out of earshot, Mom said, "You two act like you're still married. It's very sweet."

"Oh, please! He was being polite. I'm sure Bernie will do the same when he leaves."

Bernie laughed. "I will now!"

I sighed, not worried about being kissed by either of them. I was far more concerned that Gus was our only viable suspect but we didn't know where he was or have anything that tied him concretely to the murders.

When Aunt Melly sat down to eat breakfast, I cut myself another piece of the blueberry buckle and had another cup of tea. "Aunt Melly, I want you to think very carefully. Did Gus ever mention Dollie Peabody to you?"

"Nope. Well, not until after we met her. He called her a 'pretentious society lady' and I said I didn't think that was fair because we didn't know her. She might be very nice and he was being a snob. And then Sophie told me about seeing him at her house and I realized that he was trying to keep me from getting friendly with her because they were having an affair."

"What about Roscoe? Did Gus talk about him at all?"

"Not that I can recall. Gus was more interested in history than in people. Wait! He did mention something else about Dollie. Something about her great-great-great-grandfather living here and being a doctor way back then. So it wasn't really about Dollie but the fact that her family has been here so long. I thought he might be envious because his family moved around so much that he doesn't feel a historical connection to a particular place."

I felt frustrated. At ten o'clock I phoned Ronin's office to see if he had a few minutes for me. He agreed to see me, and I rushed over. I perched on the edge of a chair and asked if he could find out if anyone else's DNA showed up on the same garment as Dad's.

"I see what you're getting at. If there is another person's DNA, that would go a long way toward reasonable doubt. Especially since they're relying on DNA in your Dad's case. They don't even have a motive. If we can open the possibilities to one or maybe even two other people, that could change everything."

"I'm beginning to think that the real killer may have worn Dad's sweater and then washed it in the belief that it would remove his DNA. I saw it in my basement, but I know I didn't wash it, and I don't think my mom did, either. It could have had Tony's blood on it."

I walked home trying to figure out why Gus would have murdered Tony. If Roscoe witnessed Gus killing Tony, then Gus had a motive to kill Roscoe. But why murder Tony to begin with? It seemed to me that most of the usual reasons, like a romantic affair between Tony and Aunt Melly or some conflict from their past, just didn't exist.

And there was one other major issue. Where would Gus have hidden Tony's body between the time he was killed and the time his body was discovered in the alley? I smacked my own forehead. Of course! How could I have overlooked such an obvious thing? Aunt Melly's car!

As I walked, I passed an antique store that I knew well. A stunning demilune table with a graceful leaf design in the shop window caught my attention. I backed up and looked at it more carefully. It certainly looked like Dollie's. I entered the store and greeted the saleswoman. Pointing at the demilune, I asked, "Is that Dollie Peabody's table?"

Chapter 24

Dear Natasha,
I love pink. But on your show, you said no one should ever paint a bedroom pink. Why not?
Pinkie in Blue Springs, Missouri

Dear Pinkie,
Unless you are under the age of twelve, you must choose a more mature color for your bedroom. Grays are still popular and olive greens offer a calm atmosphere.
Natasha

The saleswoman hesitated. "I'm not supposed to say. Why do you think the table belonged to Dollie?"

"I saw it in her house."

"It's in such great shape. It's unbelievable that it's from the 1880s. They took great care of it. Interested in buying it?"

I didn't need it, but I looked at the price tag anyway. It was well out of my price range! "Did she mention why she was selling it?"

"Something about redecorating." She cocked her head and smiled. "That's what most people say."

I knew what she meant but wasn't rude enough to say—*she needed the money*. I thanked her and left the store but stopped cold when Gus's friend Stan Cox crossed the street and ambled into an upscale hotel. The kind of boutique hotel that didn't come cheap.

I hurried across the street and followed him inside. Either Stan had money and he was Gus's current target, mooching off him for a pricey room, or something else was going on. Unfortunately, Stan spotted me the second I entered the hotel.

He did a double take and I overheard him say to the desk clerk, "Thanks, Marci." He ambled over to me. "Looking for Gus?"

I wished I'd had something clever prepared. Instead, I blurted, "Is Gus staying here?"

For a long moment, I thought he was holding his breath. "No, he's not. Look, I'm really sorry about the way things turned out. You have a nice family." He winced. "I never expected anything like this to happen. I truly am sorry, especially for your Aunt Melly. She's very sweet. How's she doing?"

"How do you think? She's kicking herself for getting involved with a guy like Gus."

He nodded. "Understandable. And your dad? He's a great guy. I was very sorry that he was accused of murder."

There was something about the way he said it—regret, maybe? "Do you know something about the murder? Did your buddy Gus kill Tony?"

He took a deep breath. "Really? That's what you think? Gus is the murderer?" His forehead wrinkled as if he hadn't considered that possibility and had to think it over.

I tried not to show any emotion. I didn't respond in the hope he would continue to talk.

He ran a hand through his hair. "I don't think Gus would do that. He's an . . . unusual guy. But I never anticipated anything like this. You have to believe me."

I didn't believe him at all. "Are you staying here?"

His eyes widened. "Uh, no. I'm meeting someone."

That was a huge lie! Odds were that he wouldn't know the desk clerk's name if he wasn't staying there. I forced a smile at him. "Take care."

He nodded at me, and I left to find Dollie.

I didn't have to look hard. She was on the front stoop of her house talking with her neighbor Joanna Kowalski. I waved and walked over to them.

"Is there any news on the death of your houseguest?" Joanna fanned herself with her hand.

"I'm afraid not."

"This is all so frightening. I was so thankful when Julian moved in to help me. All that knee surgery really helped. My knees are great now and I don't need him anymore but I'm relieved that he is still living in the house! I feel so much safer having him around. Poor Dollie. You must have been scared to death when you realized that a strange man was in your home! He could have killed you while you were sleeping in your own bed!"

Part of me wanted to defend Roscoe. But he had no good reason for being in Dollie's house. I couldn't even say something about him being a nice guy because nice guys didn't sneak into other people's homes. "Did they ever figure out how he got into your house?"

Dollie shook her head. "The police always put the blame on me. They're saying I must have forgotten to lock the back door. But even if I did forget, that doesn't give anyone license to enter."

"Well, if you ask me," said Joanna, "you had every right to defend yourself and kill that man!"

Ouch! But she had a point. While I doubted that Dollie

had the strength to overcome a man, I knew that a well-timed smack over the head with a heavy vase could knock a person out. Had Dollie murdered Roscoe? One had a right to defend oneself from an intruder. But Cyril's words ran through my head. *Roscoe didn't go there to harm Dollie or he would have been upstairs looking for her.* I couldn't help feeling Roscoe didn't deserve to die. Of course, they didn't know him. And I didn't know him well.

If I encountered an uninvited stranger in my house, I would have done my level best to subdue him. But sneaking into someone's house didn't sound like the Roscoe who had stayed at my home. Now I had to question whether he had been putting on an act for everyone all along.

A Toyota drove up and parked on the street.

"That's Julian." Joanna waved at her son, who came dashing toward us.

"Sophie! I'm glad to see you. I've been meaning to call. Would you have dinner with me tonight?"

Dollie clasped her hands and held them beneath her chin looking very pleased with herself.

"What am I? Chopped liver?" asked his mom.

"Now, Joanna," cautioned Dollie, "don't go interfering with young love!"

"That's very kind of you, Julian, but my parents and houseguests are still here. I don't see them as often as I'd like so maybe I could have a rain check and take you up on that after they leave? But I could sneak out for a drink at The Laughing Hound around five."

He chuckled. "Here we are at our age, still sneaking out." He winked at his mom.

She held up her palms. "Never let it be said that I would stop you from going out. I think it's wonderful."

I cringed a little when he said, "It's a date, then!" While he was friendly and rather nice-looking, I was more interested in hearing what he knew about Dollie.

"How are you coming on the case against your father?" asked Joanna.

I didn't want to say anything discouraging in front of Dollie. She might *see* more dead people in her house. "I'm working on it," I said brightly.

"Good luck, honey. Julian, we have to run," said his mother. "I'm glad that you're okay, Dollie. If you need anything, just give us a call." Joanna motioned to her son and hurried toward the car.

As it left, I noticed a circular emblem on the back in white with two crossed arrows. I couldn't quite make out the words, but I didn't have to. I knew they spelled out *Fratres Perpetua*.

"Let's go in where it's cool. I just stepped outside to water my geraniums and Joanna wanted to know everything about what happened here." Dollie opened the door and the two of us stepped inside the comfortable house.

I looked for Dollie's demilune table. It had been replaced with a narrow black console table with curved legs. It looked lovely. "New table?" I asked.

"Oh, I like to switch things up now and then. So much of my furniture is stuffy. It does me good to have something new."

I took a chance at the truth. "You needed the money to pay Alex's fee?"

Her shoulders sagged. "It breaks my heart to give up any of the treasures my family bought decades, even a century, ago." She dropped wearily into a chair in her living room. "The insurance from my husbands' deaths ran out years ago. Sadly, the wrong ones died. The first three were good men. They would have looked out for me. It would never have come to this."

"The fourth one, the one you divorced. What happened to him?"

"Nothing. He was the one who should have died. He was

a rat fink all along. Never changed a bit. He could sweet-talk anybody into thinking whatever he wanted. I'd never seen anything like it. Do you know I had to fight to keep *my* house? He was a liar and a cheat. Sometimes I think he only married me for the house. He was a rotten person, through and through. That was when I changed my name back to Peabody, my maiden name. I didn't even want to use his name!"

Could he be trying to scare her out of her home? "Where is he now?"

"I have no idea. And I don't care as long as he stays away from here. He was a conniving liar." Her eyes met mine. "Don't look at me like that. I wasn't the only one he fooled. I told him one of these days the devil would catch up to him and he would pay dearly for his lies and swindling."

Dollie gazed up at the painting of her on her wedding day. "I thought life would always be like it was when I was young. I had two brothers, but I was the only girl. My daddy used to tell me that I was a princess. I knew I wasn't. I'm not that naïve, but I thought there was family money. He always said I would never have to worry about money. *That* was wrong! You know, back then a girl had four choices in life. She could marry and be a wife, or she could be a nurse, a teacher, or an assistant but they called them secretaries back then. I wasn't trained to do *anything*. So I kept getting married and for a while, things would be fine, and then I would be a widow again. I always had food and a roof over my head, which is more than some people have, so I don't want you to think I feel sorry for myself. It's just how my life was. Now, all that's left is this house and the things in it. And if I sold the house, I wouldn't have anywhere to live. But many people are far worse off than me. I am grateful for what I have."

I hated to question her spending habits when she was down, but I asked, "What about the designer clothes?"

Dollie snickered. "Good clothes stand the test of time. Everything I wear is old. I haven't bought a new outfit in years. If someone asks me, 'Isn't that Gucci from the eighties?' I say, 'You have a great eye!' It's called vintage, and it's as chic now as it was when it was new. When I look back, I realize how much money I wasted on things that *had* to be expensive. The latest shoes. The newest fashions. None of it matters, although it does make me feel better when I can wear something pretty. You know the dress I wore to Natasha's party? I found it in one of the trunks downstairs. I'm surprised it held up so well. Once I had it dry-cleaned, it was perfect. It even fit me! I think it must have belonged to my great-great-grandmother."

Dollie gazed at me. "I never was one of those women who wears sneakers and blue jeans. I don't think I ever will be. So, when I need money, I find something in the house that I can sell. I thought I was putting on a pretty good front."

"You were. I had no idea until I saw your beautiful demilune table in the window of a store. How can you afford a housekeeper?"

"Oh, that! Sheila and I have been friends for the longest time. She doesn't have a driver's license. So she cleans my house, and I drive her wherever she needs to go, like to the doctor's office or a shopping mall, or to take her chihuahua to the vet." Dollie pressed her hands together. "I am determined not to be a burden on my children. They have their lives and that's how it should be."

"I can understand that."

"I'm too old to go to a job. Ugh. I can't imagine working. I don't have the energy for it."

"Is that why you don't eat breakfast? There's no money for it?"

Dollie nodded. "It's fine. All I need is my coffee. And I'm often invited to special events. All of them include something to eat."

"Maybe you should learn to cook."

"Heaven forbid! I would probably burn the house down."

I hadn't taken that into consideration!

"And now I'm in trouble because of that guy Roscoe dying in my house when I didn't even know him!" Dollie looked me in the eyes. "You don't think I killed him, do you?"

"No, Dollie. I don't think that at all. But you know what that means."

"That you're a good friend to me."

"It means someone else was in your house that night. The person who killed him." If nothing else, maybe she would take more care about locking her doors.

Back at home, I baked a peach crostata, all the while thinking about Gus. Leaving the crostata on the kitchen counter to cool, I dashed up to Aunt Melly's bedroom to search for her car keys. Luckily, she had left them on the desk.

I slid a harness on Daisy and took her outside with me. It was hot, but we weren't going far and I thought she would appreciate getting out a little bit. Aunt Melly must have parked her car somewhere nearby. Her powder-blue Volkswagen convertible was easy to spot. I unlocked the driver's side and checked around for any signs of blood. If Gus murdered Tony and transported his body somewhere in this car, there had to be some blood. I didn't see any. Daisy wanted to jump into the car, which made me realize how difficult it would have been to get a big guy like Tony in the car when he was dead. Unless a person could manage to sit Tony's body upright, which I seriously doubted given rigor mortis, this could not have been the car used for transport. I suspected that the trunk was too small and opened it for a look. I was right. A couple of tennis rackets and a small suitcase would have fit nicely.

So much for that theory.

Daisy and I walked home, glad to be out of the heat. But Daisy didn't head to her water bowl in the kitchen as I had expected. She loped upstairs. I followed her, thinking my parents and Aunt Melly had come home.

Daisy stood outside Aunt Melly's room. I could hear someone moving about inside. The door stood ajar about two inches. I was about to knock and ask Aunt Melly if she needed anything, but out of an abundance of caution, first I cocked my head to see inside.

It was Gus!

Chapter 25

Dear Sophie,
My husband and I bought a small house with a tiny kitchen. We're pinching pennies and planned to paint the cabinets. My husband wants it all white because it's so small. I think that's too plain and would love some color but everything we consider seems overwhelming. What color won't make the kitchen feel even smaller?

Itching to Paint in Paint Town, North Carolina

Dear Itching to Paint,
Your husband is on the right track with white. But you can combine white upper cabinets with pastel or light-colored lower cabinets for a lovely look. Consider very pale blue or green and use the same color for accessories.

Sophie

I grabbed Daisy's collar and tried to coax her toward the stairs. She balked immediately. I gave her the hand signal for come and she reluctantly scrambled down the stairs making the biggest racket I could imagine. I followed on her heels.

Gus appeared at the top of the stairs. "Where is it?"

"Where is what? I don't know what you're talking about."

"Put your phone down."

I laid it on the foyer console but stood next to it so I could grab it immediately if he started down the stairs.

"Look, Sophie, you're a good person. Your whole family is nice and decent, and I really appreciated being treated like a member of the family. I'm not going to hurt you. Okay? Just tell me where it is."

"I truly do not know what you want."

"The necklace. The necklace Melly wore the night we all dressed up."

I was so confused. "You murdered Tony over a necklace? It's not even real."

"That's what you think? I didn't murder Tony. Don't mess with me, Sophie. Remember, I was here when they arrested your dad. Just tell me where the necklace is."

"How would I know? Aunt Melly is furious with you. She might have given it away."

"And whose fault is that? Your father tried to make me look like a fool by leaving gifts on our bed for her. That rose and the corsage and the chocolates."

"Dad did that?" I asked innocently. He was thoughtful but he didn't like Gus. And if he had done something along those lines, he would have given the same things to Mom. And probably to Hannah and me, too.

"Well, it sure wasn't me."

"Maybe he was trying to make you look good. As if you were apologizing for the things you did." That didn't actually make sense to me, either. Dad was glad Aunt Melly had ditched Gus.

"You think?"

For a moment, I thought he might just leave. But then he growled, "The necklace. Where is it?"

"I don't know. She's very upset with you. She might have thrown it out."

"No! She can't have done that. No, no, no! Listen, I don't want to be here any more than you want me here. Just hand over the necklace and I'll get out of town. You'll never see me again. Do you have a vault? A safe? Is it under a picture?" He began to lift pictures and paintings off the wall and fling them crashing to the floor.

I picked up my phone and dialed 911.

"Where is it?" he shouted.

When the dispatcher answered the phone, I rattled off my address. "There's an intruder in my house." I dashed to the kitchen in the hope that Mochie was lounging in his favorite window. Alarmed by the noise of glass breaking upstairs, he was standing in a position that suggested he was going to seek a safe spot to hide. I grabbed him and called Daisy to follow me out the kitchen door.

Mochie was not happy being held outside. He squirmed as if he had eight legs. Poor guy. I tightened my grip and waited for the police.

Two officers arrived in a matter of minutes and drew their weapons as they entered my house. They returned shaking their heads. "There's no one inside. Do you know who it was?"

"Yes. Gus Eberle. He's, uh—" How could I explain this? "He's separated from my aunt. She's getting their marriage annulled."

"Do you have an address for him?"

"Not really. Now that they're separated, I don't think my aunt's home address is where he'll go anymore."

"There's not much we can do. How do you think he got in?"

"I don't know. He could have swiped a key. But I have

family visiting and not everyone has been locking doors. He might have walked right in."

"Call us if he comes back."

Even though they had been through the house, I entered reluctantly. What if they missed a closet or he jumped out a window and was on the roof? Daisy sniffed the floor. She found him last time. Maybe she would do it again.

I shut Mochie in my den and put up a dog gate at the bottom of the stairs so Daisy wouldn't walk on the broken glass that I knew lay on the floor upstairs. Out of an abundance of caution, I located the Taser Mars had given me and tucked it into a pocket. Then I began the tedious job of cleaning up the mess Gus had made.

I was just finishing when I heard Mom's voice downstairs. "I'm up here!" I gathered my equipment, trudged downstairs, and removed the dog gate.

"Did you bake that crostata?" asked Mom.

"I did."

"Perfect! It smells so good. Cyril gave us a ride around Old Town in the rental to see if we could find your car. No luck, I'm afraid. We picked up Chinese takeout for lunch, though. Are you cleaning?"

"I'll tell you over lunch. Aunt Melly, do you still have the necklace that Gus gave you?"

"Yes. I considered throwing it out but it looks so good with my dress."

"Where is it?"

"I hung it on the hanger with the dress so I wouldn't have to search for it if I ever wear the dress again. Maybe for a costume party or something."

"Would you mind bringing it down here?"

"Sure." She shot Mom a bewildered look on the way to the stairs.

As beautiful as the day was, Mom decided it was too

hot to eat lunch outside. She set the kitchen table with a light green tablecloth and blue Famille Rose plates from Williams Sonoma. I added cutlery and chopsticks and fetched a pitcher of iced tea from the refrigerator.

As we sat down to eat, Aunt Melly came running down the stairs and handed me her necklace.

I turned the large blue pendant over. "It's a good thing you kept it. It's marked seven hundred fifty, which means it's eighteen-karat gold."

"No! It's real?" Melly squeezed her eyes shut. "Do you think those are really diamonds around the stone? I thought they were paste."

"Could that be a real sapphire?" asked Mom. "It's awfully large. It must have been very expensive."

"Something else he bought with my money, I'm sure," Melly complained.

"Gus paid us a visit today. He was in Aunt Melly's room when I came home. He wanted the necklace. In fact, he said I would never see him again if I gave it to him."

"He came here?" Melly stared at me, her eyes huge. "I didn't think he would have the nerve to do that."

"Melly, didn't you say you took all the cash out of his wallet when you threw him out?" asked Dad.

She chuckled. "I sure did!"

Dad helped himself to lo mein. "If he has no money tucked away somewhere, he probably can't get out of town. He wouldn't have money for a bus, much less for a flight somewhere."

"I wonder where he's staying," said Cyril. "This isn't the kind of neighborhood where you could hide in an abandoned house and the hotels are pricey. At the least, he would have needed a credit card to check in."

"I took those, too. Because they were mine," Aunt Melly said.

The kitchen door opened abruptly. Natasha stormed in.

"You will not believe what happened to me!" She plunked two laptop computers on the island.

"What are those for?" I fetched another plate and a glass of iced tea and set them in front of her. While I gathered a napkin and cutlery, she downed half the iced tea.

"I was almost arrested for driving a stolen vehicle!"

"Oh, Natasha! That's terrible," my mother said. "How on earth could that happen?"

"I don't understand," said Dad. "Why were you driving a stolen vehicle?"

"Well, that's the odd thing. I wasn't! I was driving my own car when lights started flashing behind me. I saw that it was a patrol car and was certain the flashing lights were meant for someone else. But the officer kept waving at me. I thought I was in the way and the car he was after must have been ahead of me. He even turned on his siren! So I turned at the next corner to get out of his way and he followed me! I'm telling you, everyone was looking at me. Just everyone!"

"And you had no idea what he wanted?" asked Aunt Melly.

"I thought he must want one of my gorgeous dresses for his wife or maybe he wanted me to sign something. You know, a fan of my show. His face was so red I was worried that he might have a medical emergency right then and there. He asked for my driver's license and the papers that I ignore and throw in the glove compartment. When he flipped through them, I could see he was confused. He asked my name and address and then told me to stay in the car. Well, luckily Wong came along and straightened everything out. The car belongs to me, of course, but someone put the license plates of a stolen car on my vehicle!"

"Why would anyone do that?" asked Aunt Melly.

"I haven't the faintest notion. It was lucky that Wong was on duty and knew who I was."

"What was the license plate they put on your car?" asked Dad.

"I don't remember. Maybe SBW?"

Dad's eyes met mine. "I think we know who has your car, Sophie. What do you bet that Gus is living in it?"

"Of course! He had easy access to my keys. He must have returned to the garage and taken my car. That way he didn't need a pricey hotel room. And if someone recognized the make of my car, the plates didn't match."

"Sophie." Aunt Melly placed a hand on her chest and gazed at me apologetically. "I love you to bits. Can you ever forgive me for bringing Gus into your life and home? He has created so much chaos for all of us."

Okay, so it *was* her fault for marrying Gus, but I loved her far too much not to forgive her. I reached for Aunt Melly's hand. "You didn't know. You thought he was a wonderful man."

Clearly eager to change the topic of conversation, Mom asked brightly, "So how is your business going, Natasha?"

It was the wrong thing to ask.

Natasha held the back of her hand against her forehead like a drama queen in an old movie. "Sales of my dresses have plummeted. They're historically correct and so gorgeous but they simply aren't selling. The only things that people buy are the little ornaments and T-shirts."

Mom clucked sympathetically. "Oh my. And such fine fabrics, too! I didn't realize you could sew."

"I'm an excellent seamstress! Mom couldn't afford all the clothes I needed in my pageant days. She can sew anything. She taught me how out of necessity. But I hired professionals to make the 1820s dresses so I would have time for the business end of the store. I thought they did a fine job. Why don't you come by the store? All of you? You can try on some dresses!"

After a painfully awkward silence, Mom finally said,

"Natasha, you're a dear and I wish you all the best in this endeavor, but I have a fancy 1820s-style dress that I wore to your charming party. Honest to goodness, I don't know where I would wear another one."

It became instantly evident that no one had suggested this to Natasha. She seemed surprised by the revelation that my mother had nowhere to wear such a gown.

I was beginning to think that she hadn't considered just who might be the target market for expensive dresses in 1820s style. Hoping to blunt the news that *we* weren't her target market, I said, "Perhaps you can sell them to theater troupes, or reenactors, or living history type places like Williamsburg?"

"Theater troupes?" Natasha said softly as if it was some kind of insult.

No one said a word.

Mom broke the silence. She sounded positively cheery when she said, "You didn't wear one of your historic dresses today, Natasha."

She was right. Good call, Mom! Natasha wore a sleeveless black top with a hemline on a slant and a cream-colored skirt that jutted out at her waist into rounded pleats that would have made me look twice as wide as I was. It screamed designer.

Natasha took a deep breath.

Mom smiled brightly. "It could be worse, Natasha. You could have married a man who stole all your money."

Aunt Melly gasped and glared at Mom.

Cyril groaned. "Melly, I saw a nice jewelry store just off of King Street. How about I take that sapphire necklace down there this afternoon and find out what it's worth?"

"I'll go with you. It would do me good to get out and walk around a bit." She shot a look of daggers at my mother.

"And when we return," said Cyril, "would you mind if I did a little laundry? I wasn't planning to stay this long."

"Of course," I said. "The washer and dryer are in the basement."

"Paul and I are still keeping a low profile," said Mom. "No happy wanderings about town for us. I'd be happy to do your laundry, Cyril. Just bring it down here and I'll take care of it."

"Cyril," Natasha cooed. "Won't you join us for dinner tonight? Mother was so pleased to see you again."

"That's very kind but I would hate to put you out."

"Not at all. It would be our pleasure. You know Mother missed you when she moved up here. I understand you were one of her Wednesday night regulars."

"The diner will never be the same without her."

"Do you think she could get her old job back?" asked Natasha.

"I thought she was enjoying her new business," Mom said, blinking at Natasha.

"The problem is that it just doesn't suit my reputation. I can't have her selling questionable CBD products and medicinal herbs. But she won't listen to me. She would be so much happier back in Berrysville again."

"Really? She seems so content here," Dad pointed out. "From what Sophie tells us, she's now in a financial position where she never has to work again if she doesn't want to. Running that store must be enjoyable for her or she wouldn't do it."

Natasha winced. "I have to be so careful about my reputation but she's oblivious to that and does whatever she wants."

"I'm sure Wanda means well," said Mom. "Cyril, why don't you run upstairs and get that laundry for me?"

"So we'll see you for dinner, Cyril?" asked Natasha.

He looked as if he might choke.

I thought I'd better rescue him. "Pity. Bernie is bringing his famous pulled pork for dinner tonight, just for Cyril.

What if Cyril went over to your house for a cocktail, and then you all came here for dinner?"

"Well, all right. I can bring dessert. You owe me anyway."

"Owe you? For what?" I asked.

"Your laptops, silly."

I rose to take a closer look at the ones she had placed on the island. The top one belonged to Hannah. I recognized the business label she had affixed to it. And when I opened the one on the bottom, I knew it was mine immediately. "What were *you* doing with them?"

"Hannah asked me to keep an eye on them."

"Hannah?"

Natasha nodded, acting as if people made that sort of request of her on a regular basis. "I'll see you around five, Cyril." She waved at him and left.

That was our cue to disperse. I took over cleaning up the kitchen, while Mom waited for Cyril.

He brought her a pile of clothes. "Are you certain you want to do this? I've been doing my own laundry for years. It's not as though I'm a novice."

"Don't be silly. I'd much rather have you find out about that necklace."

I turned to say goodbye, but my breath caught in my throat.

Chapter 26

Dear Sophie,
My husband inherited the family home where he grew up along with all the furnishings and contents. I'll admit that it's a bit old-fashioned. I want to throw everything out and paint all the walls white but he refuses. Can you help us?
Not Sentimental in Old Dime Box, Texas

Dear Not Sentimental,
The two of you clearly need to compromise. For starters, you could invite his siblings to take the items they're sentimental about. If you do the cookng, perhaps you can agree to update the kitchen to your taste. In exchange, maybe you can agree to keep elegant dining furniture but replace the wallpaper in the dining room? If you cannot compromise, hire an interior decorator who can blend your preferences.
Sophie

Cyril wore a black T-shirt. On the upper left side, a white emblem of crossed arrows was surrounded by two words: Fratres Perpetua. It was exactly the same kind of T-shirt Roscoe was wearing when he was murdered.

I had no idea what *Fratres Perpetua* was, but there was no way I was going to let Aunt Melly go anywhere alone with Cyril until I knew. "You know what? I'll go with you. There's safety in numbers. Aunt Melly? Have you got the necklace?"

"That's not necessary," said Cyril. "I'm sure you have work to do."

"I just can't wait to hear about the jewelry," I said cheerily.

"All righty then!" said Aunt Melly.

They chatted and laughed on the way to the store. I, on the other hand, was wondering if Aunt Melly had thrown the wrong man out of the house. What if Gus hadn't murdered anyone? He had taken liberties with her money and wasn't what I would call a great guy, but now I had to wonder if Cyril had some connection to Roscoe. Maybe it wasn't a coincidence that both of them came along on the trip. One of my guests was dead but hardly knew anyone in town, which strongly suggested that one of my other guests was the murderer!

While the two of them browsed around the jewelry store, I tried to surreptitiously search *Fratres Perpetua* on my phone. But I was sidetracked when a gentleman behind the display case said, "You have a very fine piece here." He raised bushy eyebrows at the necklace.

"Really?" Melly sounded incredulous. "It's not just paste?"

"Madam, may I take this in the back for a moment?"

He returned in no time. "The oval stone in the center is a sapphire of exquisite color. Very highly prized. I've never seen one this large. It's surrounded by diamonds. Excellent quality. Has it been in your family long?"

"No. My, um, husband gave it to me."

The salesman looked up at Cyril. "You have excellent taste, sir. Perhaps I could show madam sapphire earrings to wear with it?"

Cyril blushed. "I'm afraid I'm not the husband."

"Oh! I see. I think you may have a tough time competing for the affections of this charming lady given her husband's taste in gems."

Give me a break. I got to the bottom line. "What's it worth?"

"Easily six to seven thousand dollars. I'm sure you cherish it, but should you ever want to sell it, I hope you will come to me. I would be very interested in acquiring this lovely piece."

Aunt Melly's eyes met mine. I knew what all three of us were thinking. How could Gus afford jewelry like that?"

Aunt Melly tucked the necklace into her purse. We thanked the salesman and headed home.

"I can't believe it!" Aunt Melly crossed her hands over her handbag and held it tight against her body. "Where could Gus have gotten the money for this?"

"From a previous lady friend?" suggested Cyril.

"You mean he stole money from another woman and bought the necklace to give to me?"

"Something like that."

I really hated to defend Gus but I offered a less offensive theory. "Or maybe he won a lot of money gambling in Las Vegas."

Aunt Melly shot me a doubtful look. "I like that much better. But if that's the case, then he was a fool to spend it all on a necklace. I'd have preferred that he pay for our hotel room and food!"

While Aunt Melly and Cyril relayed everything to Mom

and Dad, I slipped away into my office with Daisy, Mochie, and my laptop. I didn't want Cyril to see what I was doing. I plugged it in and typed *Fratres Perpetua*.

The symbol on Roscoe's and Cyril's shirts popped up immediately. Two arrows crossed with *Fratres* curved over them and *Perpetua* curved upward underneath the arrows. I scrolled down. It appeared that it was a fraternity of sorts. The Latin words *Fratres Perpetua* meant "Brothers Forever."

That wasn't so bad. It was kind of sentimental, actually. Brotherly love. Brothers should back each other up.

I flicked through photos of the members doing good things like toy drives at the holidays, runs with homeless dogs for donations to shelters, and canoe races to raise money for children to go to camp. The fun appeared to be when they flipped over at the end.

Harmless and socially beneficial activities. I leaned back in my chair feeling relieved.

Daisy perked her ears and there was a knock on the door.

Cyril opened it and peeked inside. "Cold iced coffee?"

"Thank you! That was thoughtful."

"Credit goes to your mom. I hope I'm not interrupting."

I took a long swig. Yum! "Tell me about *Fratres Perpetua*."

"It's a national organization of brotherhood."

"You belong to it?"

"No. This T-shirt was given to me by the group at my university when I retired. Sort of an honorary thing, I guess. A good bunch of young men. I helped them with an engineering project. Why the interest?"

"Roscoe was wearing a T-shirt exactly like yours when he died."

"Interesting. Do you know which university Roscoe attended?"

I opened the door wide. "Dad? Can you come to my office for a minute?"

He showed up carrying an iced coffee.

"What university did Roscoe attend?"

"I believe it was Parcell College," said Dad.

Cyril grinned. "May I use your laptop?"

I vacated my seat, and he quickly pulled up Parcell College. "What class do you think he was in?"

We took a guess and were surprised to find the yearbook online.

Cyril scrolled through photos of students. "There's our fellow, Roscoe. Major—Parks and Recreation. And there he is again with a group of friends."

I looked closer. "Can you enlarge that photo?"

The young men in the photo were all wearing *Fratres Perpetua* shirts. And the one with his hand on Roscoe's shoulder looked an awful lot like Julian Kowalski, Dollie's neighbor.

Chapter 27

Dear Sophie,
Another domestic diva has announced that no one over the age of twelve should have a pink bedroom. I'm shattered! What do you think?
Pinkie in Blue Springs, Missouri

Dear Pinkie,
If you like pink, then go for it! There is a large assortment of pinks in different shades. In fact, blush is very much on trend right now. It adds a subtle warmth and goes beautifully with browns and other earth tones. For a light look, paint your bedroom walls the lightest blush and dress your bed in white linens.
Sophie

Hannah ambled into my office. "Sorry. Didn't mean to interrupt. I heard Natasha brought our laptops back and I thought I'd get some work done."

"What was Natasha doing with our laptops?" I asked.

"I figured the police would take computers, so when they raided your house I snuck the laptops out the back door and hustled them over to Natasha for safekeeping," said Hannah.

Dad beamed. "That's my clever girl! Join us, Hannah." Dad smiled at her, then caught her up on our discussion about the *Fratres Perpetua* connection.

I thought about the times Roscoe and Julian had been together, like at Natasha's 1920s party and on the Fourth of July dinner in my backyard. "I don't remember Roscoe and Julian chatting together at the parties, do you?"

Dad frowned. "I can't say one way or the other. I wasn't paying any attention to them. There were so many people at both of those dinners!"

"Sorry," said Cyril. "If we had known, we might have watched them. Maybe someone else remembers?"

I pointed at them. "It's your job to ask Mom and Aunt Melly if they noticed anything."

Dad tapped his fingers on the armrest of his chair. "You know, Roscoe didn't hide anything. He told us before we came to Old Town that a friend of his lived here. And he told us a couple of times that he was going to do something with his friend. It's sort of presumptuous of us to think that anything sinister was going on just because the friend in question happens to be Dollie's neighbor."

"It's true," said Cyril. "We all assumed he and Hannah were having a fling when they weren't. We jumped to the wrong conclusion."

Hannah groaned. "Hey! It's not my fault you thought I was running around with him."

Maybe Dad wouldn't say it, but I did. "If you had told us who you were with every night, we wouldn't have thought it was Roscoe. In any event, it still doesn't explain what Roscoe was doing in Dollie's basement."

Cyril leaned back against his chair. "In my opinion, there are only two possibilities. Bear with me. As an engineer, I tend to focus on what works. The first is that Roscoe went to visit Dollie. The reason is basically irrelevant—whether it's romance or friendship doesn't matter."

"Ah"—Dad interrupted—"but it does matter because a romance between the two of them is so very unlikely."

"I'll say," said Hannah. "I would be very surprised if Roscoe took an interest in Dollie."

"Perhaps in an intimate regard," said Cyril, "though it wouldn't be the first time a younger person has sought a relationship with a senior for money, and we know Roscoe was broke. But as far as his presence there goes, it's unimportant because we know for a fact that he was *in* Dollie's house. If he was invited, then Dollie must have lured him into her basement on some pretext and stabbed him."

"Eww. That would make her a very sick woman." I shuddered to imagine any such thing. "What's the second possibility?"

"If Roscoe was *not* invited to Dollie's house, then he must have gone there for a reason."

Dad took a deep breath. "Money."

Cyril nodded. "It makes much more sense to me that Roscoe went to her house looking for something."

"You mean valuables. Jewelry or money. The irony is that Dollie isn't as wealthy as she may seem. She has been steadily selling family heirlooms for quite some time. And who looks in the basement for valuables?"

Cyril's eyes met mine. "Someone who is looking for items of historic value. Basements, like attics, are where people stash old things. They can be worth a lot of money. Remember the expensive map we saw at the antiques fair?"

"That makes sense. Roscoe had a description of her house in his pocket. And a book on antiques." My phone rang just then. I was about to ignore the call when I saw that it came from Elwin. "Hello?"

"Sophie! You said to call if—" The connection terminated.

Instinctively, I shouted "Elwin?" into the phone. But there was no response.

I tried to phone him, but no one answered. "That's very weird. I'd better go check on Elwin."

Dad stood up. "Cyril and I will go with you."

We shot out of the house, crossed the street, and headed toward Elwin's home. When we got there, I banged the door knocker. The front door swung open.

"It wasn't even latched!" Dad grabbed my arm. "Don't go inside. Call nine-one-one."

While pushing the door all the way open, I made the call. We entered the foyer and listened for voices or the thud of footsteps. The house lay silent. We cautiously peeked in the downstairs rooms, but everything looked orderly.

I was glad when I heard Wong's voice at the front door. I made quick work of introductions to Dad and Cyril. "Elwin called me but the call was disconnected."

"Did he say he was home?"

"No, but the front door wasn't completely closed."

Keeping a prudent distance, I followed her upstairs. Elwin lay on the floor of his bedroom, his hand near his phone. His eyes were closed. Blood trickled down his forehead and over one of his eyelids.

Wong called for an ambulance. "Stay here. Don't move." She left the room and I could hear her in the hallway.

I knelt beside him. "Elwin? Elwin, can you hear me?"

There was no response. Not even a murmur. I checked for a pulse.

Wong returned. "All clear in the house."

"Good news. He has a pulse. But he seems unconscious."

Dad and Cyril made their way up the stairs.

"Oof. Looks like someone whopped him with that telescope," Dad observed.

I looked around. The telescope lay bent with a cracked lens.

"Don't touch anything," said Wong. "In fact, the three of you should have waited outside."

I beckoned to Dad and Cyril. "Don't touch the handrail on your way down the stairs."

Fifteen minutes later, Elwin was removed from the house on a stretcher. It seemed as if the entire neighborhood had ventured outdoors to watch. I wished Elwin could see their concern for him.

Wong came over to us. "Now explain to me why you are involved in this. Is Elwin your best friend now? You're the one he would call when he's in danger?"

"I barely know him. Bernie and I came to see him because his windows overlook Dollie's house and the alley where Tony's body was found."

"Aha. And did he see anything?" asked Wong.

"He saw Nina, Daisy, and me early one morning, so while he denied watching Dollie's house, it was obvious that he does watch what's going on."

"What were you and Nina doing?"

"Walking the dogs while it was still cool and picking up breakfast things from Big Daddy's."

"I can relate to that!"

"Bernie and I saw the telescope pretty much aimed at Dollie's house, as well as binoculars on a table nearby. I looked through them. He can see everything that goes on in Dollie's kitchen. He can probably see in the second-floor windows but those were her children's bedrooms, and they have all grown up and moved away. It's lucky that her bedroom is on the other side of the house."

"So you think he was spying on her."

"Definitely."

"Why would he call you instead of nine-one-one?"

I shrugged. "I honestly don't know. Because I live so close and he needed help?"

Wong's eyes narrowed. "Or because he wanted to tell you about something he saw."

"He knows! Wong, he knows who has been doing all this. But that person was too fast and clobbered him. Can you arrange for a police guard at the hospital?"

Wong sighed. "I'll do my best. Morales knows that Wolf and I are tight. He might refuse. Sophie, you need to be careful. It's a good thing you have a house full of company."

Unless one of them was the culprit. Though now that Gus was gone, and poor Roscoe was dead, the odds of that had decreased. "Actually, I was going to phone you. Natasha told us about someone stealing her license plate. I think that was Gus. I'd bet that he was the one who stole my car. He probably put Natasha's license plate on it. Can you put out an all-points bulletin to pull him over so I can get my car back?"

"Sure. I'll let Wolf know, too. I hear Morales is pretty unhappy with you." She grinned. "He's a jerk. Don't let him get to you."

"Wong, my dad isn't involved in this. His DNA must have gotten on Tony some other way. But Gus is turning out to be a pretty questionable guy and I saw him coming out of Dollie's yard."

Wong nodded and whispered, "Morales has it out for Wolf, so he has to tread carefully. But we're keeping an eye on you. Be careful. You hear? Morales would love nothing more than to charge you or someone in your family with murder."

"But why? I've never done anything to him. I never even heard of him before he showed up at Dollie's house."

"It's not you. It's Wolf whom he'd like to bring down. There's not much Morales wouldn't do to make Wolf look bad. And you're an easy way to do that."

"Great," I groaned. "One more thing before you go. What do you know about Julian Kowalski?"

She shot me a sly look and raised her eyebrows. "You mean besides being good-looking and a great guy for taking care of his mom?"

"Yes, besides that."

"He's been very kind to Dollie. She's so confused. I know it's wrong of me to be impatient with her. She's an old woman and heaven willing, we'll all be in her shoes one day, but I don't have the patience for her tales. Other people are having real emergencies, not being spooked by imaginary things. You heard her. You know what it's like. 'I saw a dead man but now he's not there.' Julian is much more tolerant about her fantasies than I am, and I give him a lot of credit for that."

I didn't know if Elwin had family who would be looking in on him, which worried me. But I knew from experience that I was unlikely to be able to see him until he was stable and checked into a room. "Will you be following up on Elwin?"

She nodded. "I'll keep you posted."

When Dad, Cyril, and I entered the house, Humphrey sat at the kitchen banquette with Mom, Aunt Melly, and Hannah.

Mom and Aunt Melly rose and rushed me into the foyer. Mom whispered, "Maybe you should cancel your date with Julian. Did you know that Humphrey would be here?"

"How do you know about Julian?"

"Dollie called your landline. She said to tell you to wear something alluring. We haven't told Humphrey. So don't mention it to him."

"Mom, it's not a big deal. Just a drink at Bernie's bar."

"But Humphrey came to see you," Aunt Melly protested.

"It breaks my heart that you have no interest in that

sweet Humphrey," Mom whispered. "At least put on a pretty dress. Is that blood on your arm?"

I didn't tell her it was Elwin's blood. I trudged up the stairs and washed it off. I changed into a simple lavender sheath appropriate for the heat and put my hair up in a messy bun to get it off my neck.

Mom and Aunt Melly fussed over me like I was a teenager going out on my first date. I headed out the door as fast as I could.

Julian already sat at a table in the bar when I walked in. A complete gentleman, he rose on my arrival. When I sat down, I could see Bernie behind the bar. Minutes later, Mars sauntered in. It wasn't a coincidence that he chose a seat where he could observe Julian and me. Bernie must have notified Mars when I showed up for a drink with Julian. I was more than a little bit miffed. But it was my own fault for choosing Bernie's bar. Next time I would pick a different place.

Julian wore a blue golf shirt that brought out the blue in his eyes. I had to admit that he was a very attractive man.

"Isn't that your ex-husband over there?" he asked.

"Just ignore him. Would you rather go somewhere else?"

He smiled. "It's fine. I have an ex of my own. I know what that's like. Luckily, she lives in Massachusetts. A little distance works wonders."

We placed our orders with the server.

I was itching to find out why he divorced. But how could I get him to talk about it without sounding too nosy? "Did you like being married?"

He thought for a moment. "Yes. It was great until things began to sour. I'm sure you know how it is. You work longer hours just so you don't have to go home and face the arguments again."

That didn't work. *Sour* and *arguments* could mean anything. "It was so kind of you to move in with your mom."

"That wasn't exactly the way I thought my life would be, but after my wife started seeing someone else and I was the single male dropped from our social circles, I was considering a move and a fresh start anyway. I'm still amazed by how quickly every part of my life was destroyed. She got the house and spousal support, which left me in a horrible little apartment. I'm an only child, so no one else was going to come to Mom's rescue. And I always loved visiting Old Town, so it seemed like a good fit. I thought I would buy a place of my own after Mom recovered from her surgeries, but prices are very high, and she and Dollie have come to rely on me—so here I am."

The server returned with Julian's beer and my vodka tonic.

"Sophie, one of the reasons I wanted to talk with you away from Mom and Dollie is Roscoe's death.

"I'm so sorry for your loss. I can't even imagine how you must be feeling to have lost a friend."

For a split second, I recognized surprise in his expression. "Thank you. I will miss him. Roscoe was a good guy. The thing is that his death inside Dollie's house has my mom and Dollie scared out of their wits."

I nodded. That was understandable. "How do you think he got in there? And why?"

Julian shook his head. "My theory is that he was high or stone drunk and meant to come to *my* house. Dollie must have left the door unlocked again and he somehow managed to stumble down to the basement and fall on something. That's the only thing that makes any sense."

That possibility hadn't occurred to me. It seemed like a long shot, but then sometimes strange things happened to people that looked sinister but were just bizarre accidents.

"I feel like a patrolman," said Julian. "Both of them have me scout through their houses every night before they go to bed. They're terrified that someone is lurking in the shadows."

"I can't blame them for that. I hope you're checking to be sure Dollie's doors are locked."

A grin briefly passed over his lips. "Could you reassure Dollie and Mom that no one is coming for them? Roscoe would never have hurt anyone, let alone an old lady. The guy had manners. It had to be a mistake. Roscoe was no dummy. If he had been a burglar, he would have gone upstairs, not down to the basement."

Chapter 28

Dear Natasha,
What does one serve houseguests before bedtime in the summer? Even after a big dinner, it seems like someone always wants a bedtime snack and a drink. Cocoa is a lovely treat in fall and winter, but it seems so wrong in the summer.
Clueless in Hershey, Pennsylvania

Dear Clueless,
Fruit liqueurs have long been an appropriate late-night drink. If you must serve a snack, then I recommend banana rounds with a dab of peanut butter or high-quality chocolate truffles.
Natasha

It was the same thing Cyril had said. And it made sense. It was rare that anything of value would be stashed in the basement, especially one that was unfinished and used for storage. And while I didn't know Roscoe well, he certainly hadn't said or done anything that made me think he could be a mad killer. "Sure. I'll mention it to them. But I don't know how much good it will do when they hear Elwin Martel was attacked and is in the hospital."

"What? Elwin? When did this happen?"

"A few hours ago."

"No! He always reminds me of a wizard, like his door knocker. Did you ever notice the resemblance? Who would attack *him*?"

I thought it best not to mention Elwin's hobby of spying on neighbors. "I don't know."

"Is he okay? Maybe I should bring him some dinner? I could order something to go and take it to him."

"The last I heard he was in the hospital."

"Then it's serious. Poor Elwin! Which hospital?"

I spotted Bernie striding toward us.

"Hello, Julian. I hate to interrupt but I'm told I'm supposed to deliver Sophie along with the food I promised."

"No problem. She warned me that she had obligations this evening." Julian produced his wallet.

I reached for mine, too. "If you pay our tab, I'll leave the tip for our server."

"Oh!" Julian seemed taken aback. "All right. That would be nice."

"Thanks for inviting me," I said, rising from my seat.

"We'll have to do it again when your schedule isn't quite as full."

Julian leaned over and kissed my cheek, catching me very much by surprise. Bernie, too, from the look on his face.

I followed Bernie to the kitchen and Mars fell in behind me.

"You're already kissing?" Mars wrinkled his nose.

"I must defend our fair friend. I believe she was only on the receiving end of said kiss." Bernie turned and winked at me.

"Isn't he on our list of suspects?" asked Mars. "He should be."

My phone rang as we were carrying the food out to Bernie's car. I wrestled with the packages because it was Wong and I didn't want to miss her call.

"Sophie, it's not looking good for Elwin. He has a serious brain injury and they're putting him into a medically induced coma."

My heart sank. Poor Elwin! I thanked Wong and passed the news on to Bernie and Mars. We piled into Bernie's car and were at my house in minutes.

During my absence, Mom and Aunt Melly had set the long outdoor table on my patio. Nina arrived with pitchers of sangria. Cyril returned from cocktails with Natasha and Wanda looking relieved that his visit with them was over. Humphrey brought spiced shrimp as an appetizer. Even my elderly neighbor, Francie, slipped through the gate between our yards. Her golden retriever, Duke, played with Daisy and Muppet.

Dinner was noisy and fun, full of teasing and laughter. I didn't see how it could ever get better than this moment surrounded by almost all my favorite people. My brother and his family were missing, but I would see them again in the fall.

After dinner, as the day cooled and the sun began to set, Mom, Aunt Melly, and Wanda insisted I stay put. The three of them cleaned up. Dad lit candles in the fireplace for ambiance, and Hannah delivered decaf coffee and tea as well as a selection of after-dinner drinks. I felt completely spoiled.

And that was when the conversation moved to murder.

For those who didn't know, Dad, Cyril, and I caught them up about the attack on Elwin.

"Do we know for sure that it had something to do with Roscoe's and Tony's deaths?" asked Mars.

Bernie winced. "Spying on your neighbors is dangerous business."

"We saw how his house looked. I'm just guessing here," said Dad, "but someone took his telescope and bashed him over the head with it. Telescopes aren't exactly fragile, but whoever hit him with it was strong and very angry."

Mars took a list out of his pocket and drew a line through Roscoe's name and Elwin's name. When Cyril left to make another pot of decaf coffee, Mars tapped Cyril's name with the end of his pen and looked at me.

I shook my head and whispered to him, "Cyril was with at least one of us all day. He never had a chance to whop Elwin over the head."

Mars marked Cyril off the list. "That leaves Gus and Dollie."

"Dollie couldn't have bashed Elwin like that," said Dad. "A younger, fit woman might have been able to, but not Dollie."

Bernie leaned back in his chair. "Sorry, Sophie, but what about your latest admirer? Did you notice that he was wearing thousand-dollar shoes today?"

Mars frowned. "They were nice. Good point, Bernie."

I gazed from one to the other. "You have to be kidding me."

"Are they made of gold?" asked Dad.

Bernie grinned. "If only! A lovely light brown suede with a silver horse bit across the upper. Very elegant."

"Julian and Roscoe were old friends," I said. "They belonged to a group of guys who did good things for people."

"What if it was Elwin who murdered Tony and Roscoe?" asked Humphrey. "If Julian was friends with Roscoe, he might have attacked Elwin in revenge."

Nina accepted a fresh cup of decaf coffee from Cyril. "We're not really dismissing Gus, are we? Sort of *out of sight is out of mind*. Just because we don't see him, doesn't mean he's not at the root of all this. My apologies, Melly."

"No offense taken, Nina. Gus has made his own bed and it's a mess. He deserves what he gets. But there is one other person you haven't mentioned. What about Gus's friend, Stan? He disappeared from view when I kicked out Gus."

Mom finally spoke up. "I never quite understood their friendship. Stan seemed"—she glanced at Melly—"more refined than Gus."

"How could you tell?" asked Humphrey. "Stan hardly said anything."

"Well, I know he thanked me after every meal he ate with us. Someone raised him right."

"I saw him going into an upscale hotel," I said. "Of course, that doesn't mean he's staying there, but it certainly gave me pause. If he's been there for a week, the cost would have added up by now."

"Then Gus must be staying with him! Well, now I don't feel as bad about giving Gus the heave-ho."

Mars looked up from his list of suspects. "If I had murdered someone, I would have left town. Neither Stan nor Gus lives here. Why stay? We thought Gus didn't have any money to leave, but if Stan can pay, then the least he could do would be pay for gas and the two of them could get out of Dodge."

They were right. We were giving Gus a pass. His behavior when he looked for the necklace proved that he could fly off the handle and be irrational and violent.

My guests left or went up to bed gradually. I was exhausted and ready to fall into my own bed. But I lingered in the kitchen long enough to load the dishwasher so we could start fresh in the morning.

The door in my kitchen opened, startling me.

Dollie walked into the kitchen, passed by me, and headed for the living room.

"Dollie?" Either she didn't hear me or she was ignoring me. "Dollie?"

She opened the door that led out to my covered porch, which was completely dark. Daisy and I followed her.

Dollie took a seat at the table. Only then did she turn and look up at me. "What's for breakfast? I'm starved."

I sat down opposite her. The police were right! No wonder Wong had called Dollie's daughter. I knew Wong was reliable. I should never have doubted her.

I didn't know how to respond to Dollie in this state. She had taken the time to dress and had styled her hair. I suspected the right thing to do was to play along and humor her. "Would you like some scrambled eggs?"

"That sounds wonderful! Some toast, too?"

Maybe she really was hungry. I turned on the outdoor lights, returned to the kitchen, scrambled eggs, and made coffee and toast. I brought a tray of food outside, half expecting her to be gone. But she was still there, twirling a huge ring on her finger.

I set the plate and coffee in front of her. "Would you prefer lingonberry jam or strawberry jam?"

"Lingonberry, please."

Dollie ate her breakfast as if she were ravenous, which made me feel better about making her something to eat. When she finished, she thanked me and left.

I watched her as she strode along the street in her staggeringly high heels as if it were daylight instead of two in the morning. I ran into the house to grab my phone, and Daisy's halter and leash. We soon caught up to Dollie as she strode along the sidewalk, headed for home.

At her front door, she reached for the key, still stashed where anyone could use it, over the door. She unlocked the door, returned the key, and walked inside her completely dark house. Daisy and I followed her. I locked the door behind us. "Dollie," I said softly, "do you feel all right?"

She ignored me and walked upstairs to her room. Daisy and I followed her. I could hear her brushing her teeth in the bathroom. She emerged in a nightgown. As if we weren't there, she walked past us, crawled into bed, and closed her eyes.

It was the strangest thing I had ever seen. I sat on a chair by her bed. The windows were closed but the curtains hadn't been drawn, allowing the ambient light to shine inside. The air was pleasantly cool, so I assumed the air-conditioning was running. The house lay still and quiet.

Dollie slept peacefully. Had she been sleepwalking or was that some kind of psychotic episode? Could she have been calling the police when she was in a state like that? In any event, it was dangerous for her to walk around town in that state at night. Did she watch for oncoming traffic? Would she step out in front of a car?

I took a deep breath, wondering if I dared leave her there alone. What if she did it again? I finally understood Wong and Dollie's daughter. But Wong hadn't said a thing about Dollie sleepwalking. I hated to be a nosy neighbor, but now I was worried about her. I checked the bathroom for meds she might be taking but only found over-the-counter vitamins.

Whatever was going on with her, she was sound asleep now. I tiptoed out of her room. Daisy passed me and headed down the stairs. But when we reached the foyer, I heard a scratching sound. We weren't alone in the house.

Daisy jerked her leash out of my hand and shot through the hallway to the kitchen.

Chapter 29

Dear Natasha,
My girlfriend always brings her pasta salad to outdoor gatherings. But she makes it with spaghetti! It's always a terrible mess and there's no dignified way to eat it without proper plates and utensils. I'm having a potluck and I would rather she didn't bring her cold spaghetti. How do I handle this?
I Like Pasta But . . . in Italy, Texas

Dear I Like Pasta But . . . ,
Don't invite her.
Natasha

"Daisy!" I hissed in a whisper. "Daisy!"

Nooo! This couldn't be happening. "Daisy!"

I followed her, tiptoeing toward the kitchen. The sound grew louder.

I paused and glanced around the dark kitchen. Everything seemed to be in place. Thankfully, no one was there except Daisy, who waited at the back door. I stood still, trying hard to figure out what that noise was. And then I heard a loud complaining yowl. Georgy! I relaxed when I realized that the sound I heard came from two cat paws frantically scratching at the door to get inside. I walked over to the door and opened it.

Georgy held her head and tail high and walked into the house like a feline princess who had wrongly been locked outside her castle. She jumped up on the kitchen counter and purred.

Dollie must have accidentally let her out again. I found cans of cat food in a cabinet next to the sink, opened a can, and spooned it into a bowl for her. Georgy nestled comfortably and ate her food.

I tossed the empty can into a trash bin under the sink. A plain white cup sat in the kitchen sink. I hadn't turned on any lights, but the dim lighting from streetlights and the moon enabled me to see tiny white bits of something in the bottom of it. I grabbed a plastic bag, turned it inside out, and picked up the cup.

And then it happened. I heard a voice. Dollie wasn't making up stories when she claimed she heard things at night.

It sounded like a man. I couldn't quite make out what he said. A swear word, maybe?

That alone would have scared me. But the heavy footsteps that followed scared me out of my wits. Thank heaven Daisy wasn't much of a barker.

I heard more swearing and the steps came closer. I didn't wait to identify the voice. I knew it was angry, though.

Daisy and I made a mad dash to the back door and fled across Dollie's backyard.

The gate creaked a little when I opened it, but we flew out into the alley fast. I hoped the person in the house hadn't seen us.

We ran toward the street and dodged around the corner. Daisy seemed very happy to be running. I was not.

I didn't dare stay there to watch. I pressed 911. "There's someone in Dolly Peabody's house."

The dispatcher asked me questions, but Daisy and I had to run. "Please, check it out!" I ended the call and ran like the devil was after me.

I was out of breath when I unlocked my front door. I closed it behind us, locked it, and leaned against it, breathing heavily. I didn't turn on any lights. From the kitchen window, I watched the street to see if anyone had followed us. It lay peacefully silent.

Maybe we had gotten away. Either he didn't realize we had been there, or he simply lost track of us. I preferred to believe the former was the case. But there was no way to know.

It was just past four in the morning when Daisy and I went to bed. I lay awake, unable to shake the fear. How did Dollie handle it? Did the police go to her house? Did she wake up? Did she sleep better after the police visited and pooh-poohed her? Probably. I didn't think I was brave enough to sleep in a house where I heard voices and footsteps. Had she ever actually seen the person who was entering her house?

Eventually, I drifted off to sleep.

I jerked awake just past nine. Daisy, Mochie, and Hannah were gone. I dressed in a hurry and pinned my hair up. I ran downstairs, eager to tell someone what had happened.

They were all eating breakfast outside.

"Sophie!" cried Mom. "You must have been exhausted. You needed to sleep in a little. We fed Mochie and Daisy."

Her words nearly slipped by me. I couldn't take my eyes off Dollie, who sat between Cyril and Mom, calmly eating French toast.

"Sophie?" Mom cocked her head. "Are you all right, dear?"

"Sorry. Good morning!" I poured a cup of tea and sat down. Everyone seemed so normal and chipper. I began to wonder if I had dreamed the events of the previous night. "Hannah, I hope I didn't wake you when I came in last night."

"No worries. I didn't hear a thing."

"Dollie, how do you feel today?" I asked.

"Marvelous. I'm applying to become a member of your family. I love these breakfasts!"

Did she remember anything about last night? "Did you sleep well?"

"Splendidly!"

"No voices or intruders?"

"If there were, I didn't hear them." She smiled broadly.

The cup! I excused myself and ran to the kitchen. The bag I had wrapped it in was still there, on the banquette table. I peeked inside. The white cup with some kind of tiny remnants of a powdery substance was still inside, proof that I hadn't dreamed it all. I immediately phoned Wolf.

"Good morning, Sophie."

"Hi, Wolf. I know you're not supposed to be involved in my dad's case, but I need a favor. Something strange happened last night but I can't trust Morales."

I heard him take a deep breath and sigh.

"Please? Wong thinks Dollie is out of her mind. Maybe so. But I was in her house late last night, and there was definitely a man there."

"So she had a guest—"

"No! No, she didn't. Meet me at The Laughing Hound? I'll get Bernie to give us a private room. Okay?"

"Ten thirty. Before the lunch crowd comes in."

"Okay. See you then."

I packed the cup into a tote that I often carried and stashed it in the hall closet where no one was likely to be poking around. Then I called Bernie and asked if I could reserve a small meeting room for ten thirty. A room where we wouldn't be seen. Naturally, he agreed. I returned to my houseguests and Dollie. "I'm starving!"

At ten fifteen, I entered The Laughing Hound through the back porch, where dogs were allowed and not many people would notice me. I walked through the back kitchen and upstairs to Bernie's office. He led me to a small private dining room with light green walls, a small round table big enough for four people, a gorgeous old-fashioned chandelier, and a giant gilded mirror to make the room feel larger. The sole window was actually a door that led outside to a private balcony.

"This is beautiful."

"It's popular for proposals. Who should I send up here?"

"Wolf. Um, Bernie, would you mind joining us? That way we'll have a witness."

"Sounds serious."

"I don't know if it is or not. But it might be good in case someone gets the wrong idea. I would hate for Wolf's wife to hear we had some kind of private thing and misinterpret it."

"Shall I bring lunch?"

"I don't think that's necessary."

"All right."

He returned in minutes with Wolf and three iced coffees, each of which had a scoop of vanilla ice cream floating in it.

"I've asked Bernie to join us in case anyone gets the wrong idea about this meeting."

Wolf nodded at Bernie. "Thanks."

I told them what happened the previous night. About Dollie turning up at my house like she was sleepwalking and me hearing a voice and footsteps. "I called the police and asked them to check on Dollie."

Wolf nodded. "They went to her house, but no one answered the door and no lights were on."

Well! That wasn't very helpful! I pulled out the bag with the cup in it and handed it to Wolf.

"I don't know anything about sleepwalking. But I've never seen anyone act like Dollie did last night. It was bizarre. I noticed this cup in her sink. It looks to me like it contains small granules or bits of powder. I'd like to know what was in it and if there are any fingerprints on it. I'm giving it to you for a couple of reasons. The first is that I don't trust Morales. It would disappear or come back clean. He wouldn't treat it properly. Obviously, it's not clean. It contained something. The other reason is because I know it has to go through proper channels to be used as evidence. If I take it to someone myself, it would probably be thrown out of court."

"You should have left it there to be picked up by one of us."

"I didn't know what might happen to it. Besides, I heard someone in the house right after I saw it. I grabbed it and ran!"

"You could have called me to help you," said Bernie.

"Thanks, Bernie. Initially I wasn't afraid. Everyone pooh-poohs the things Dollie claims she hears at night. Wong told me repeatedly that it was all nonsense. That when she calls about hearing voices or footsteps, there is never anyone in her house. Well, it's not her imagination. I definitely heard someone last night."

"Roscoe was in her house," Wolf pointed out.

"Why do you think I ran? The person who was in her home was anything but dead."

Wolf winced. "I suppose you've heard that Roscoe's DNA was also on your Dad's sweater."

"That's wonderful! It's exactly what we needed. That's enough to create a lot of doubt." I looked at Bernie. "Roscoe must have killed Tony!"

"Possibly." Wolf stayed calm. If he was excited about this development, he didn't show it.

I let Wolf leave first.

Bernie and I walked down to his office.

"Soph, if anything like that happens again, you can always call Mars or me. We wouldn't mind. Really."

"That's nice of you. But I had Daisy with me, and honestly, I wasn't concerned at the beginning. Thanks for the drinks. They were delicious!"

My mood wasn't quite as chipper as I walked home. Now I was worried about Dollie's welfare.

"Sophie! Sophie!" Julian waved as he jogged toward me. He panted as he caught up. "So glad I ran into you. I was talking with Natasha, who told me about your car. Actually, she told me about being stopped for driving her own car, but eventually she got around to saying your car had been stolen. If I understood her description correctly, I think I saw it this morning."

"Really? That's fantastic! Where is it?"

"Do you know where Gilded Lily Antiques is?"

It sounded familiar to me. "Yes, I think so."

"There's a little alley that—maybe it would be easier if I showed you. You probably shouldn't go alone anyway. The person who stole it might not be happy to see you."

"I'm not too worried. If it's my car, I'm planning to let the police handle it." My phone alerted me to a text. "Excuse me." The text was from Mars.

Where are you? Have info.

I texted back.

With Julian. He knows where my car is.

On second thought, I added the street intersection.

On my way.

"Sorry about that. Mars is going to join us." I smiled at Julian. "I'm really excited about my car. Thank you so much. My parents and Cyril have been driving a rental around town looking for it."

"No problem. It really was dumb luck that I noticed it at all. If Natasha hadn't mentioned it to me, I wouldn't have given it a second thought. Natasha says she helps you solve murders."

I couldn't help grinning. While it was true that she had been helpful a few times, I could imagine that she might have blown her role out of proportion. "Sometimes."

"How do you do that?"

"I don't know that there's a blueprint for it. Mostly I talk with people who might have seen something."

"Interesting. Do you have any leads on who murdered Tony or Roscoe?"

"Nothing definite yet."

"I admire you for doing that."

Mars jogged up to us, panting slightly. "Hi! Does the car look okay?"

"I think so," said Julian. "It's just down this alley and ahead on the left."

We peered to the left, but didn't see any cars until we passed Gilded Lily Antiques. As Julian had claimed, a car that looked remarkably like mine was parked in an old driveway unevenly paved with brick. Tall oaks stood to the sides of it, shielding it from view. The license plate wasn't mine, for sure. It was probably Natasha's. But I recognized a small ding on the back where a rock had kicked up and hit the car. I walked closer but Julian grabbed my elbow.

"What are you doing? What if the thief is inside?"

"I think we know who the thief is." I walked up to my car and rapped on the back window. "Gus!"

Julian froze. "I can't believe you did that!" I looked back at him. He pulled out his phone. "Uh, gotta run. Mom fell on the stairs and hurt her knee."

"Gus! Are you in there?" I shouted.

Chapter 30

Dear Sophie,
Friends are staying with me while they are on vacation. I really do love them, but I have to work and can't stay up all hours entertaining them. How do I tell them it's time to move on?

Exhausted in Ten Sleep, Wyoming

Dear Exhausted,
To avoid hurt feelings, the best way is to be clear up front. I would love to have you stay Friday and Saturday nights. But I have a busy week starting Monday. *Most people will understand that. If they don't, then give them a gentle reminder. If they still don't understand, then you no longer need to be concerned about their feelings.* I've loved having you. Where are you headed tomorrow?

Sophie

I peered in the back window of the car. What a wreck! Fast-food wrappers and chip bags cluttered the rear of my car. I could see him stretched out. I pounded the window again. "Gus! Wake up! I'm calling the police."

Gus mumbled something from inside the car.

Mars tried the handle. It wasn't locked. He jerked it open.

With a beard coming in and ratty clothes, Gus looked like a sick pirate. I almost felt sorry for him.

"What were you thinking stealing my car?"

He sat up and groaned. "I was thinkin' I needed somewhere to sleep. Will Melly take me back yet?"

"No!"

"Will she give me the necklace?"

"If you needed money, why didn't you sell her engagement ring and wedding band?"

His eyes widened. "Shoot! I forgot all about them." Gus opened the center console and rummaged through it.

"And why didn't you sleep with Stan?" asked Mars.

Gus stopped what he was doing. "Where's he staying?"

"Looks like a pretty nice hotel if you ask me," I said.

"You're pulling my leg."

I shook my head. "I was surprised, too." I wasn't one hundred percent sure he was staying there, but it was worth a shot.

"That jerk! Which hotel?"

"A fancy one on King Street."

"There they are." Gus held up the rings. "Ought to buy me enough gas to get out of this town."

"Better rethink that," said Mars. "But maybe they'll buy you a bus ticket out of town."

Gus climbed out of the car. It appeared that he had worn the same clothes since he left my house. His hair was a wild mess.

"Look in the mirror."

"Can I take a shower?" he asked.

"Not at my house. I believe you have worn out your welcome there."

"Then why are you here?"

"To get my car."

"You can't have your car unless I can take a shower."

"I'm afraid you have no cards left to play." I smiled at him.

"Wrong! I have your car keys."

"I can call the police," said Mars.

"Okay. You go over to that antique store and sell the rings for me."

I laughed. "Oh sure. Do you think we're idiots? Who did you steal them from?"

"They're not stolen. Not really."

"I don't think there's any middle ground," said Mars. "Either you stole them or you didn't."

"I got something you want." He tapped the side of his forehead. "It's up here. You wanna know what happened to your daddy's sweater?"

The man knew how to play his cards. I didn't respond.

"Go to the antique store with me to sell the rings. You don't gotta say that you know anything about them. Just go with me. And then buy me lunch and I'll tell you what I know."

He pulled a wrinkled suit jacket out of the car and brushed his hair, which already made a difference in his appearance. "Deal?"

It was worth the price of lunch. Even if he didn't smell good. "Deal," I said.

We walked to Gilded Lily Antiques. Mars and I looked around the shop but kept an eye on Gus.

He asked for the owner.

An older man came out of a back office. "How may I help you?"

Gus held out his hand to shake. "Gus Eberle. I used to own a pawnshop up north. My wife threw these in my face the other day. Looks like it's over. I can hardly bear to look at them anymore."

The owner picked up a loupe and studied them. "What are you asking for them?"

The two of them went back and forth a couple of times but finally settled on a figure. It wouldn't buy Gus a car, but it would pay for a decent hotel room for a few nights and some proper meals.

While they were wrapping up, I browsed through their merchandise. I stopped cold at a centerpiece a woman was placing in the window display. About nineteen inches high, it had handles on both sides. Elegant flowers ran around the rim and the foot. "Sterling?" I asked.

"Yes. Isn't it beautiful? We just got it in."

I glanced at the price tag. Ten thousand dollars. "Where did you get it?"

"Someone brought it in yesterday. Part of an exquisite estate."

"I'll say." It broke my heart. Dollie must have sold it to them. I was fairly certain that it was the gorgeous centerpiece that had graced her sideboard.

Now flush with cash, Gus grinned at me. "Time for lunch. I'm starved."

Mars and I took him to The Laughing Hound where I was certain of two things. If we needed help, Bernie would be there, and they wouldn't throw us out, even if our companion looked and smelled a little scuzzy.

We headed for a private table in the bar. Gus ordered a martini, a steak with fries, and a shrimp appetizer.

Mars and I ordered turkey sandwiches and iced tea. When we had our drinks, I said, "Okay, spill."

"Well, this starts back about a year or two. I had a lot of people come into my pawnshop with wild tales. There was the one fella looking at an accordion that somebody had hocked. He was pitiful. Not unlike me right now. I'd priced the thing at one hundred dollars, but he only had seventy-five. Said he could get some band gigs if he could afford to buy the accordion, but he was on his very last seventy-five bucks. He stood there admiring the thing while other customers came and went. To be honest, I didn't believe him. Who knows how to play an accordion? So, I handed it to him just to see what he'd do. By golly, he played it like he'd been born with an accordion in his hands. I could see in his eyes that he was hard-pressed. Pretty much like that guy at Gilded Lily Antiques looked at me today. I was on the verge of selling the accordion to him for seventy-five dollars, when he pulled a key out of his pocket and said, 'How about I give you this key and a story about the US Declaration of Independence that could make you rich?'

"I figured all I would get out of it was a key that didn't fit anything, but how many people were really going to want that accordion? I'd had it for two years without any interest, so I agreed. I knew I was giving it away for free. You should have seen how happy he was.

"So then he tells me this story about a doctor during the Civil War who lived in a place called Old Town, Alexandria, Virginia. Seems the good doc was very highly regarded and saved the life of a severely injured soldier who, unbeknownst to the doctor, happened to be a very prominent and wealthy man. In gratitude, the soldier's father sent him a letter of appreciation and included a copy of the Declaration of Independence, a Dunlap Broadside, to show his thanks because that boy meant the world to him. That doctor was Dollie's great-great-great-grandfather. And the broke man buying the accordion was Dollie's ex-husband. He was madder than a wet hen at her for the usual marital reasons. Said he searched all over that house but never did find the Declaration of Independence. The key he gave me was to the back door. But he warned me that Dollie regretted marrying him and swore she would never marry again, so he didn't recommend trying to sweet-talk her. I would have to find another way to get into the house. The only helpful hint he shared was that it was a corner house four stories tall if you counted the basement, painted gray cream. Couldn't remember the names of the cross streets. I laughed it all off. What was I going to do? Walk up to Dollie and ask her if I could search her house?

"But then, all these years later, I found myself as broke as he was. I didn't know how to play the accordion, though. No band gigs for me. I admit that I mooched off some ladies, but they saw the time of their lives with me. They were all like Melly. Widowed, lonely, just putzing in their gardens and remembering the good times. So I married Melly. She might hate me now, but she had a good time for a while. I was excited when I found out where you lived. It wasn't easy finding Dollie's house, though. He couldn't recall the address—said it was somewhere around King Street. Well, that's the main thoroughfare! It was no help at all. But I kept my eyes open and then one day, that bus you hired drove us right by Dollie's house."

He stopped talking to eat his steak. "Umm, best meal I think I've ever had. Junk food can't begin to compare."

"So you did marry Melly for her money. Didn't you know that she didn't have much money?" I asked.

"She had enough. I didn't plan on marrying her, but then she turned out to be a lot of fun. She didn't sour until we came to your house. Thanks a lot for that."

"And you didn't see anything wrong with living off her money?" asked Mars. "What were all those women supposed to do after you left?"

"Aww, most of them had kids. They'll sell their houses and go live with the kids."

I was thinking he should be in jail just for that. But I needed to hear what happened the day Nina and I saw him at Dollie's.

When Gus finished his steak, he munched on French fries as he spoke. "So I went over to Dollie's house really early in the morning to try the key before anyone was up. Not only did it fit, but the door was unlocked! I tiptoed inside and looked around. You know, I hadn't really believed that story her ex told me until I was in the house. She has a lot of very expensive stuff. So while I was kind of doubtful about finding the Dunlap Broadside, I figured it was worth a chance. After all, Tony told us the last one was auctioned off for four million dollars! This one might even fetch more."

We had finished our lunch and the server cleared our dishes.

"Can I bring you some dessert?"

"I'll have the triple chocolate cheesecake," said Gus.

"Should I bring two forks?" the server asked.

I tried not to shout *no*! "I'll have the lemon meringue pie, please."

Mars ordered peach pie.

I focused on Gus. "So what happened in Dollie's house?"

"I figured that if I had a Dunlap Broadside, I would keep it in a safe. Right? So I'm wandering around the first floor looking for a safe. They're not easy to spot. I'm beginning to wonder if it's upstairs in the master bedroom. But then I heard a loud thump. I thought someone was up but when I tried to run out of the house, there's Roscoe on his knees, leaning over Tony. Roscoe was wearing your father's sweater." Gus lowered his voice to a whisper. "He murdered Tony. I saw Roscoe. Roscoe saw me, and I got out of there as fast as I could."

Gus ate his cheesecake like he'd never tasted anything so good. I enjoyed the lemon meringue pie but found myself wondering how much of his story was lies. "Did you talk with Roscoe about it?"

"Are you nuts? Of course not. I told Melly we had to

get out of there and fast. She balked. Then they came to arrest your father. It was only a matter of time before they found my fingerprints somewhere in that house. I knew Melly would blab, and I couldn't take that chance so I made up a story about missing jewels. To be honest with you, I was half-glad when she threw me out. At least I didn't have to try to avoid Roscoe anymore. He knew I saw him, and I didn't want him coming after me."

"Back up for a minute. Roscoe was wearing my dad's sweater when he murdered Tony?"

"Right. Tony was bleeding bad and Roscoe was kneeling on the floor, bent over him."

"Roscoe didn't bring a car. He came with my parents, in their car. So what happened to Tony? Dollie saw him when she got up in the morning, but by the time I went over there, Tony was gone."

"Beats me. I only know I had nothing to do with it."

I studied his expression. Now sated with delicious food, he appeared relaxed and calm. But that didn't mean he wasn't a murderer. And now that Roscoe was dead, he couldn't contradict Gus's story and blame the murder on Gus. "Why did you kill Roscoe?"

"You must not listen well. I already told you that I didn't do anything to Roscoe. I never went into Dollie's house again. And I never intend to do so."

"So you weren't in her house looking for the Dunlap Broadside last night?"

He shook his head. "Sophie, I know you think I'm scum and maybe I deserve that. But I'm no killer. Somebody out there murdered Roscoe, but it wasn't me."

I paid for our lunch. "Thank you for talking with us."

"You're welcome. Thanks for the meal. I want you to know I didn't lie to you. Not a single word. That's the God's honest truth of what happened."

"Thanks. Go get your stuff out of my car. When I get home I'm calling the police to tow it."

"My DNA is all over your car!"

"You're the one who stole it, Gus. But I think they won't care about your DNA unless they find Tony's DNA in there."

When he left, Mars and I stopped by Bernie's office, closed the door, and told him what Gus had said.

"He's a liar and a thief," said Bernie.

"That he is. But one thing rang true, sort of. Roscoe had a receipt from his brewery in a pocket. On the back, he had written a description of Dollie's house."

"What are you saying?" asked Mars. "That Dollie's ex-husband ran around telling everyone there was a Dunlap Broadside in her house?"

"Something like that. Someone must have told him something. Why would he have been in her house otherwise? Tony. I bet Tony told him about it."

"And that was why he killed Tony?" asked Mars.

Bernie shrugged. "Maybe. Could be that Tony found the Dunlap Broadside."

Chapter 31

Dear Sophie,
My husband and I rented a house for our vacation. It was adorable! A little bit romantic, with lace and ruffles, a little bit rustic with lots of wood, earthy tones, and pastels. Paintings of farm animals, quilts, and throw pillows of gingham and floral prints. It's not farmhouse style, what's it called?
Gingham Girl in Baltimore, Maryland

Dear Gingham Girl,
It sounds like bits and pieces of several styles, but it's called Cottagecore. Earthy, romantic, and calming while revering the past.
Sophie

I called the police about my car from Bernie's office, and then headed for the swanky hotel where Stan was staying. Unless I missed my guess, Gus would be showing up any minute.

Mars grumbled about not getting any work done, but went along with me anyway.

We settled into chairs in the lobby where we might not be easily noticed. But when I saw my boss, Dean Coswell, stride in and greet Stan warmly, as if they knew each other well, everything changed.

Mars and I followed them into the bar where the two of them ordered drinks and had a few laughs. Dean had hired me to write my advice column about all things domestic. Originally, my column only ran in a local newspaper, but then it was syndicated. Dean was an honest and straightforward guy, so seeing him with Stan gave me some sense of comfort. What would he want with Stan?

Mars looked up the name Stan Cox on his phone. There were a lot of them. We didn't see any photos of Stan Coxes that looked like the one who was Gus's friend.

I finally sucked up some courage, insisted that Mars come with me, and the two of us sauntered by the booth where Dean and Stan sat.

"Dean!" I called. "I was going to phone you today. How fortuitous that I ran into you."

"It's always a pleasure to see you, Sophie. Sam Hersch, Sophie Winston."

Sam Hersch, not Stan Cox? That was interesting. "Yes, I believe we have met. You know Mars Winston."

"Would you care to join us?" asked Dean.

"Thanks. We would love that." We slid into the curving booth next to Dean.

"Sam is a writer. A pretty good one, too."

"Is he?" I looked Stan aka Sam right in the eyes.

"He's an undercover journalist. You know, they enter a specific environment to live the life and then report about it."

"Exactly what kind of life are you reporting on?" Mars asked.

Sam looked uneasy. "I really can't talk about it yet."

In the sweetest voice I could muster, I said, "Unless you want me to call the police right now, I think you'd better talk about it."

"Sophie! What's going on?" Dean looked to Sam. "I'm so sorry, Sam."

"I presume you have heard about the murders of Tony Fontana and Roscoe O'Brien?"

"Of course," said Dean. "Terrible stuff. I understand they haven't caught the perpetrator yet."

I met Sam's gaze. "Are you going to tell him, or should I?"

Sam winced and ordered another drink. He ran a hand over his beard. "I've been worried about this."

"You're not involved in the murders?" asked Dean.

"Not directly. I'm sorry, Sophie. You have such a nice family, and I really like your Aunt Melly. But that was the purpose of my undercover effort. I befriended Gus, which was the point of my story. He's slick and cons women out of their money. The whole point was to see how it happens. How he manages to bilk women. What kind of women fall for him. And, hopefully, as a result of what I write, women will be alert to scammers like Gus and will be smart enough to avoid them."

Dean rubbed his forehead. "So you stood by while this Gus was stealing money from Sophie's aunt?"

"It was bad enough that he allowed my aunt to be taken advantage of by this man. But now he has a bigger problem."

Sam leaned toward us. "Look, Gus is not a murderer."

I snapped back, "Gus was present in Dollie's house the night Tony Fontana was murdered. He was there and saw his corpse."

"How can you know that?" asked Sam. "He told me he didn't have a thing to do with Tony's murder."

"I caught him leaving Dollie's backyard early the next morning. And today he confessed to me that he *saw* Tony's body. He was there! He's a liar and a cheat. He may well have murdered Tony *and* Roscoe."

Dean frowned. "Sam, you have to call it off and tell the police what you know. I can't allow this to go on."

"He didn't kill anyone."

"How do you know that?" asked Dean.

Sam aka Stan glared at me. "He's a con man, not a killer."

I looked at Dean. "He also stole my car."

Sam gazed at me. "You invited him into your home."

"Because he married my aunt."

"Okay. That's enough," said Dean. "Sounds like you have plenty to base your story on. You're done, Sam."

"Really? You don't think a story about a murderer will get more attention?"

Dean sat in silence as if he was thinking.

"I don't believe you, Sam. You would risk the chance of another murder for a story? What happened to your humanity? That man crept into Dollie Peabody's house while she was sleeping. He should be put away for that alone. She's lucky that no one murdered *her*."

Mars chimed in. "What happens if she wakes and sees him when he does it again? Then Dollie will be dead. It will be your fault, on your head, on your conscience that you knew something and did not go to the police."

"He's not a killer," Sam protested. "He's a thief."

I looked at Dean.

He shook his head. "You're done, Sam. I won't be a party to this." Dean paid the check. "I'm sorry, Sophie. I'm so sorry about all of it."

Chapter 32

Dear Sophie,
My wife is into gray. The walls are gray. The carpets are gray. The furniture is gray. She says they are coordinating shades. It's like we live in a rain cloud. I want to paint the whole house white and start over, but my wife loves that gray. There has to be a way to brighten things up just a little.
Feeling Dreary in Cloud Lake, Florida

Dear Feeling Dreary,
All it takes is an item of contrast. A red chair. A sizable painting with bright yellows. Lime-green or pink throw pillows. You'll be amazed by what a difference that can make.
Sophie

Mars spun off at his house, but I walked home. The lovely scent of bananas filled my kitchen. Mom had baked banana cupcakes and was serving them to Nina, Wanda, and my remaining houseguests. I didn't mention the delicious peach pie I'd had for lunch. After all, it was afternoon, the perfect time for tea.

I filled them in on finding my car and Stan's real identity.

Aunt Melly nearly choked on her tea. "You mean he knew all along that Gus was using my money?"

"I'm afraid so."

"And he knew that Gus didn't love me? That he was taking advantage of me?"

I nodded.

"What a scum bucket!"

"Don't be hard on yourself, Melly," said Wanda. "That could have happened to any one of us."

"But it didn't. It happened to me because I'm a dolt."

"If it's any consolation, Gus said you were a lot of fun." I bit into the creamy frosting of a banana cupcake.

"When did he say that?"

"Julian found my car. Mars went with me to look at it and we found Gus living in it. He looks pretty worn out."

"He deserves it." Melly sniffed. "I'll never trust a man again. Imagine stealing my money and your car! Who does something like that?"

"The wrong man, Melly," said Dad. "The wrong man."

"Gus told us a weird story about swapping an accordion for a key to a house where there's a Dunlap Broadside copy of the Declaration on Independence. I'll give you one guess where that is."

They stared at me, silent.

"Dollie's house. Gus claims Dollie's ex-husband told him that Dollie's great-great-greatgrandfather, the doctor, saved the life of a young man during the Civil War and that the patient's father was a big shot who sent him a Dunlap Broadside as thanks."

"Wow," said Cyril. "Do you think that could possibly be true?"

I shrugged. "Unfortunately, there's a sting of truth in it

because Roscoe had a description of Dollie's house in his pocket. We'll never know where he got it, but someone must have given it to him."

"You know," said Hannah "there are websites on the regular web and the dark web where people talk about rumors and stories of gold and treasures that were known to exist but have never been found. A lot of people buried their fortunes in the old days. You'd be surprised how many there are in Virginia. Lots of legends and tales. That's exactly the kind of story you can find on some of those sites."

"Melly, that's why Gus was over at Dollie's house when Nina and I saw him leaving that morning. I know it's a small comfort, but he wasn't having an affair with Dollie."

Aunt Melly snorted. "Small comfort indeed. I shall never trust another man."

"According to Gus, Roscoe was wearing Dad's sweater. Gus says Roscoe murdered Tony, whose blood was all over him. So that's probably how Dad's DNA turned up on Tony."

"We can't let Gus leave town!" Mom's eyes widened. "He's a witness! He holds your father's future in his hands!"

"Yes, Inga," said Dad drolly, "because all jurors believe the testimony of a lying con artist."

"It could just as easily have been Gus who killed Tony," said Cyril. "Even if it was Roscoe who borrowed Paul's sweater. Maybe Roscoe was trying to help Tony. He could have been trying to stop the bleeding or something."

I nodded. "I think there's some truth in there somewhere. In any event, Dad's sweater went to Dollie's house that night, though I believe there's a good chance that Gus was the killer."

"These men have lost their minds," said Hannah. "Even if I knew for certain that someone had a Dunlap Broadside, I would never steal it. And I certainly wouldn't sneak around in their house looking for it. They were a bunch of greedy men who met up when they were being evil and were afraid someone else would find the prize. What do you bet the story is true, but that Dollie's father or grandfather sold the Dunlap Broadside decades ago? It's like the house is haunted by that story."

"The first thing I'm going to do when we get home is adopt two loud, barky dogs," Melly announced. "And then I'm installing an alarm system for my house and I'm never going out with another man unless my big brother approves of him first."

"Oh, Melly." Dad gazed at his sister. "Inga and I have been giving you a hard time about Gus. But honestly, when we first met him, we didn't think he was a con man. He was jovial and we thought he liked you. Of course, we didn't know you would run off and marry him right away."

"Dollie should stay here with us until he's arrested and in custody," said Mom. "It's dangerous for her to be there all by herself."

We were all in agreement about Dollie.

"I'll go get her," I said. "The rest of you decide what we're doing for dinner tonight."

"I'll go with you," said Nina.

Hannah caught us on the way out the door. "There's not enough room for everyone, so I'll be spending the night elsewhere. Okay?"

"Oo la la! Who's the lucky guy?" asked Nina.

Hannah blushed. "Just don't mention it to Mom and Dad, okay? They would have a cow. What they don't know won't hurt them."

"Hannah, I can sleep on a sofa in the living room. This is not a big deal."

"You can sleep wherever you want, Sophie. You're right. It's not a big deal, please don't make it into one."

Nina and I walked over to Dollie's house.

"I'm hoping she hasn't been having any bizarre sleep-walking events again. I don't trust Gus. It wouldn't surprise me if he returned to her house to snoop for the Dunlap Broadside."

"Who do you think Hannah is seeing?" Nina asked.

"Gus might murder Dollie in her sleep, and you're worried about Hannah?"

"You're her sister! Aren't you curious?"

"I just hope it's not Stan aka Sam! Aunt Melly and my parents would flip out if Hannah fell for the guy who watched Melly be conned and didn't say a thing about it. He could have stopped it, you know."

"Melly wouldn't have believed him. She thought she knew Gus. You know how it is when you're in love. You don't want to think the one you cherish could do anything wrong."

When we arrived at Dollie's front door, Julian's mom, Joanna, sat on a low gardening stool deadheading geraniums in her front yard.

"Hello, ladies." Joanna looked at us from under the brim of a sunhat.

"I'm so glad to see you up and around," I said. "Your knee must be feeling better."

"My knee? There's nothing wrong with my knees. Not since I had them replaced anyway. Modern medicine is amazing. I keep wondering which of my parts I'll have to replace next. Eventually, I'll have so many new parts that I'll look like a robot!"

We chuckled politely and I knocked on Dollie's door.

Dollie swung it open. "Girls! How nice of you to drop by."

We stepped inside.

"I hope you don't mind me calling you girls. I never know what's right and wrong anymore, but you'll always be girls to me."

"I'll take that any day!" Nina smiled at her.

"Dollie, there have been a few developments. Julian found my car. Gus has been living in it. It seems there's a story about a Dunlap Broadside being hidden in your house."

"Good heavens! Not that old tale. My two brothers turned this house upside down looking for that thing. If it were here, they would have found it. Mom always said it was sold long before she married into the family. But stories like that die hard. Even my fourth husband searched for it and talked about it all the time."

"So you knew," said Nina.

"I've heard about it since I was born but I haven't given it a single thought since I divorced. Is that why Roscoe was in my house? Good grief. If he had just asked me I would have happily told him it doesn't exist. You mean he was killed because he was looking for the Dunlap Broadside? That's so sad. Just terrible. It's just an old tale. What a shame that he died because of it. That breaks my heart."

"Dollie, when you looked at Tony's body out in the alley, you said you had never seen him before."

"Did I?"

"Yes, you did. I was there. But Gus saw Tony in your house. Tony was the dead man you saw who wasn't there when we returned to your house, wasn't he?"

Dollie's lips tightened. "My children want to put me away and lock me up. I thought it was better to deny any knowledge about the man in the alley. I had nothing to do with him. The cops would have locked me up for sure if they thought I killed him and dragged him out to the alley.

The police don't believe me anyway. If I had told the truth, it would have been very bad for me. I didn't know him. I didn't know what happened to him or how he got to the alley. I thought it best to keep my mouth shut. Wouldn't you have done the same?"

I felt sorry for her. I didn't know what I would have done had I been in her shoes. But while those men were killing each other over a document that didn't exist, Dollie's greatest fear was being removed from her house and losing her freedom.

"Dollie, the killer hasn't been caught yet. We want you to come stay at my house until this is all straightened out. We're afraid Gus might return to your house and harm you."

"Nonsense. I have Julian right next door. He looks out for me."

"That reminds me." I looked in her dining room. The beautiful centerpiece was gone. "Oh, Dollie. Did you sell your sterling centerpiece with the graceful handles and flowers?"

Dollie eyed the empty spot on her sideboard. "No. I did not. Someone must have stolen it!"

I couldn't help thinking of her sleepwalking episode. Of course, Gilded Lily Antiques probably wasn't open at night. I wondered if it was possible to sleepwalk during the day. "Are you certain? I just saw it at Gilded Lily Antiques."

"I want it back! I would never sell that. Just like my wedding portrait. There's no way I would sell those two things. They're treasures to me. The centerpiece has been in my family for generations. Those are priceless to me because they bring back happy memories of my life when I was young."

"Speaking of the centerpiece, may I see your great-great-grandfather's surgical kit?" Nina grinned at her.

"Yes, of course!"

What was Nina thinking? We had to get Dollie out of there.

She led us into the living room and lifted what appeared to be a piece of wood trim on a shelf. A door slid open to reveal the surgical kit.

"That's so cool! I love the hidden door," cried Nina.

"I stashed it in here before the police raided my house. I wasn't having them take it! I would have lost it for good."

"When did the police raid your house?" I asked.

"After your friend died in my basement."

Nina examined the surgical kit with awe. "Please let me bring my husband over to see this sometime. He would flip out."

Dollie frowned at it.

I shuddered. "I feel so sorry for all those people who lost limbs. The pain of surgery with no anesthesia must have been unbearable."

"Oh no, darlin'. My granddaddy told me that was an old tale. They used a little bit of chloroform on a cloth over their noses so they wouldn't feel it."

I shuddered again. "I hope that's accurate."

"I don't see the metacarpal saw," said Dollie. "It had little teeth along the edge."

"Like a bread knife?" asked Nina.

"Yes, sort of."

A chill ran through me. The murder weapon. "It's probably in my car. Dollie, please collect whatever you need for a few nights and let's get out of here."

She closed the hidden door.

"I'll help you," said Nina.

The two of them headed up the stairs.

I didn't really know what to do about the beautiful centerpiece. I phoned Gilded Lily Antiques and asked to speak to the owner.

"This is Sophie Winston. I was in your store earlier today and saw a beautiful centerpiece with flowers around the edge?"

"Yes. It's quite beautiful. Are you interested in buying it?"

I walked into the kitchen in the hope Dollie wouldn't overhear me. "Could you tell me who sold it to you?"

Chapter 33

Dear Natasha,
Friends of ours came for a weekend visit. We were delighted to have them until they invited friends of theirs to our house for dinner! We didn't know those people, nor were we prepared to whip together a dinner for eight extra guests. Clever hubby saved the day by recommending a local restaurant. When our friends returned, they were miffed and complained bitterly about the enormous check at the restaurant. They left the next day before breakfast and haven't spoken to us since. What should we have done?

Friends No More in Friends Station, Tennessee

Dear Friends No More,
When you are a guest in a home, it is the height of rudeness to invite other people and expect your hosts to entertain everyone. I would have thrown them out before dinner.

Natasha

"Dollie Peabody sold us the centerpiece."

"She was in your store?"

"No. She sent it over with that nice Mr. Kowalski who takes care of her."

I froze. "Did you pay by check?"

"Of course. Is there a problem?"

"Please take it out of your window display and don't sell it. I believe it may have been stolen."

"Should I stop payment on the check?"

"Yes. I think that's advisable."

"Thank you for letting us know."

I disconnected the call, hoping I wasn't wrong. It meant Julian was a thief, I reasoned. This was how he managed to buy thousand-dollar shoes. But deep down, I knew the truth. Gus was a thief. But Julian was a murderer.

Earlier in the day, I thought he was being so helpful. But now I wondered if he had been luring me to my car. When Mars showed up, Julian lied and made up an excuse about his mother needing him because of her knee. There wasn't anything wrong with her knee. I didn't know why he wanted to lure me to my car, but I now suspected that it hadn't been the helpful gesture I had thought at the time.

My phone rang, and I shrieked. It was Wolf.

"Hi, Soph. I got the results on the cup you gave me. The remains inside are zolpidem, which is a prescription-strength drug that helps people sleep. There are instructions advising against smashing the pill because it takes effect too fast and causes dangerous behavior."

"Like sleepwalking?"

"Exactly. Some people have even driven their cars and have no memory of it later on."

"Thanks, Wolf. That was exactly what I needed to know. I think someone has been giving that to Dollie. It would account for some of her odd behavior."

A scratching sound alarmed me, and I gasped.

"Everything okay, Sophie?"

I realized that it was Georgy, locked out of the house again. "Yes, it's fine. I'm just on edge. I'm at Dollie's house. She's going to stay at my place until the killer is in custody." I opened the door to let Georgy in.

"Why? Has something happened?"

Georgy hissed like a wildcat. I turned around to see what upset her. "Julian! Hi! You surprised me. My dad and Cyril are upstairs helping Dollie move a piece of furniture."

"Who are you talking to?"

"Just a friend. Are you looking for Dollie?"

"Mom said you were here. I thought you might need some help."

My mind was whirling. Why wasn't there a way to send an SOS to someone on the phone? What could I say to alert Wolf that we were in trouble? If I pressed 911 now while I was on the line with Wolf would that clue him in? I edged toward the rabbit pitcher. Maybe I could hit him with it if he lunged at me. "You could open the front door for us, Julian. That would be very helpful."

"Keep talking. We're on the way," Wolf whispered.

I moved closer to the pitcher.

Julian glared at me. I knew he was thinking that all this was somehow my fault. "Hey! Maybe you and your mom could join us for dinner tonight?" I babbled on, trying my level best not to let on that all I could think of was how I could defend myself.

"You never should have brought those people here. They had no business being in Dollie's house."

"But Dollie asked them to help."

"Not those people. The other ones. The ones who never should have snooped in Dollie's house."

"They're all gone now. You took care of Tony and Roscoe. Even Gus is leaving town. So it's all yours. I thought you and Roscoe were friends."

"We were once. I thought he could help me. But he told me I was wrong. Just like I see in your eyes. You think I'm doing something wrong."

"Did you hit Elwin with his telescope?"

"He wanted money, too. I was doing all the hard work, going through those filthy old trunks and everyone wanted a cut. Elwin said he would turn me in to the police if I didn't pay him. He'd seen me walking back and forth between Dollie's house and Mom's in the wee hours. It's a shame he's not dead yet. I can't leave a detail like that undone. But he'll be dead soon. I'll see to it."

"That's too bad. He's an interesting guy."

"Keep talking," whispered Wolf.

But it was too late for that, he was backing me behind the kitchen island where Georgy sat. I kept my eyes on Julian and reached back for the salt cellar.

He pulled out a horrid knife, the one missing from the surgical kit, I assumed. About a foot long with tiny, serrated sharklike teeth and a sharp pointed end.

I knocked the top off the salt cellar and when he moved closer, I cast the contents in his face aiming for his eyes. His scream scared Georgy, who jumped to the floor. In my haste to get away from Julian, I tripped over Georgy and fell to my knees. Grabbing her, I struggled to get up. I could hear Julian screaming curses behind me.

"Nina! Dollie! Get out of the house. Now!"

I ran toward the front door and threw it open. I yelled at Nina and Dollie. "Get out of the house! Get out of the house! Get out right now! Hurry!" I promptly fell on the grass, still clutching Georgy, who yowled like she was being tortured. "Nina! Dollie!" I tried to flip to my backside and kick away from the door and Julian.

Joanna, Julian's mother, ran over to me. "Sophie! What happened? Where's Julian?"

"Inside." My heart pounded. Where were Dollie and Nina?

Police cars screeched to a halt behind me. "Dollie and Nina are still inside," I shouted. And that was when I saw a flame. "Wolf! I think he's setting the house on fire!"

In a matter of minutes, the flame had been put out. Wolf and Wong walked Nina and Dollie outside to safety, and an emergency medical technician was treating Julian's eyes.

Wolf missed dinner at my house that night. But he was about the only one. Humphrey came. Mars and Bernie showed up, and we all speculated on exactly what had happened. Wolf arrived in time for dessert, a festive ice cream cake that Mars had brought from a local creamery.

The first thing Wolf did was clap a hand on my father's shoulder and then shake his hand. "Paul, you are free to leave Alexandria. I apologize for any inconvenience. And Sophie, you won't be seeing Detective Morales again."

"Honey, we can go home!" exclaimed Mom. "Did Julian confess?"

"Not to everything. But he's in custody. I'm sure we'll learn more in days to come. We found Gus at the hotel where Sophie suggested he might be. Gus is sticking with the story he told Sophie about Dollie's ex-husband."

Dollie thumped her hand on the table. "That man was a worm. But he sure could play the accordion. Polkas and things like that. What a jerk for telling people that I had a Dunlap Broadside. Honestly, he was almost as bad as Melly's Gus!"

"We're still not clear on Roscoe's involvement," said Wolf. "It sounds like he was trying to help Tony when he wore your sweater that night and that was when some of your DNA transferred, Paul. We're speculating that he wore it because of the chill in the air at night. He probably grabbed what he could find. Roscoe was desperate for money to save his brewery, so he went along with Julian's plan to find the Dunlap Broadside, thinking he would get some money out of it if they could find it." Wolf leaned back in his chair. "I think the Dunlap Broadside had become a quest for Julian. Like finding Noah's Ark or something. He's not rational about it as evidenced by his attack on Roscoe. Even when we tell him that it's not in Dollie's house, he insists that it's there somewhere. He's convinced that it's in one of the many trunks and storage boxes in the basement."

Dollie tsked. "I can tell you for a fact that it's not there. My two brothers were rascals and after they heard that story, they went through every square inch of the basement. My mama didn't care because it kept them out of trouble and out of her hair. All I can say is that I was right all along and all you police people wouldn't listen to me. You made my own family think I was crazy."

"My apologies, Dollie," said Wolf. "You were hearing Julian at night. He saw where you kept the keys, made a copy of the back door key, and was able to come and go as he liked. As he searched, you often heard his footsteps and probably his voice sometimes, but he always got out before the police came. He tried to make you seem like a lunatic and he succeeded. He couldn't afford to buy your house and knew you probably wouldn't sell it anyway. But he needed time to search. And that's what you heard. You weren't imagining anything."

"Well, my daughter is going to hear a thing or two from me. She wanted to lock me up! I admit that I thought his attention to me was sort of flattering. I won't be so flattered by the next man who comes along."

"What I don't understand," said Cyril, "is what happened to Tony's corpse. Julian was at dinner with us."

"Apparently, after dinner when people danced and mingled, Julian ran home to his garage where he had stashed Tony in his mother's car. He dumped Tony in the alley, then closed the garage and drove back to the party. He left his car parked near the site of the party and retrieved it a couple of days later."

"Is that what Elwin saw?" I asked.

Wolf sighed. "Oh, Elwin! From what we gather, he put two and two together because he saw Julian going over to Dollie's house late at night repeatedly. When Tony's corpse appeared and Roscoe died, Elwin thought Julian had to be involved and tried to blackmail him. They're bringing him out of the induced coma tomorrow morning. Hopefully, he'll recover."

"Will Gus be charged with anything?" asked Aunt Melly.

"We're still figuring that out. I'd like you to come down to the station tomorrow to talk about what happened to you. As for the murders, he could be charged as an accessory, or he could testify against Julian. We'll have to see how that works out."

Humphrey, who had been very quiet all evening, clinked a knife against his glass. When we quieted down and he had our attention, he stood up and said, "When I was in high school, I had a huge crush on Sophie. We were in the same homeroom class, and I thought she was the prettiest girl there was. Every day, I rode my bicycle by her house at least once. Sometimes a lot more."

Mom smiled at me, and Aunt Melly giggled.

"In spite of that, Sophie never even noticed me. When we met again as adults, she had no idea who I was!"

I could feel my face flushing and froze with embarrassment. When he pulled a ring box out of his pocket, I panicked. No! No, no, no! This couldn't be happening. Had Humphrey lost his mind?

"But then I found someone even more beautiful. Someone whom I had overlooked. A woman with the face of an angel and a heart that will never stray." Humphrey knelt on one knee in front of my sister and held up a diamond ring. "Hannah Elise Bauer, would you do me the honor of marrying me?"

Hannah was the only one of us who wasn't astonished. She smiled sweetly, and said, "Yes. Yes, I will!"

Chapter 34

Dear Sophie,
I'm going on vacation, and my neighbor will be saving my mail for me so my house won't look empty. It's very nice of her. Should I pay her?
Headed for the Mountains in Alys Beach, Florida

Dear Headed for the Mountains,
The best way to show her your appreciation is to bring her a small gift. Something typical from the place you visit, or chocolates, or a bottle of good wine.
Sophie

We all slept in the next day. Once again, I felt like I had been dropped into my own version of a *Vacation* movie. It seemed as if everyone in my house was all aflutter about something. Did Mom know where Dad's socks had gone? Did Dad know where their house keys were? Did Cyril want to drive back with Mom and Dad or with Melly?

At eleven in the morning, I had finally finished washing dishes and cleaning up the kitchen, when Mom shrieked.

"I have to go shopping. I was so upset about Paul's situation that I forgot to buy gifts for people at home!"

I thought it would relax them if we had lunch in a quaint restaurant when Melly returned from the police station. But Mom's shopping had to be done first.

We caught Natasha standing across the street from her store. The bold letters of the name were being removed. All that was left said BY NATASHA.

"Natasha honey," said Mom, "you gave up your store?"

She turned to us with a dazzling smile. "I have you to thank for that, Inga. You opened my eyes."

"You must be taking a huge loss, Natasha," Dad said, watching the *b* come down.

"Actually, it worked out okay. I found a buyer for the clothes and someone else desperately wanted to lease the store, so the owner let me out of the contract. My mom took the remaining Americana knickknacks to her store to sell there. So, it's time for me to move on. Thank you, Inga. You have a terrific business sense. We should open a store together!"

Under his breath, Dad said, "That's not going to happen."

In the evening, my parents and Aunt Melly were still packing. Daisy, Cyril, and I sat outside in the dark watching fireflies and drinking watermelon cocktails.

"You're pretty smart, Cyril," I said. "Maybe you can help me figure this out."

"Sure. An engineering question?"

"Not exactly. Aunt Melly thought Gus had left some gifts on her bed. A rose, a corsage, chocolates . . . I heard Gus yell at Dad for making him look bad by giving Aunt Melly those things. But Dad denied it. So if it wasn't Gus, and it wasn't Dad, then who could have done something like that?"

Cyril chuckled. "It's a mystery."

"Maybe it was someone who lost his true love by going too slow?"

"Melly has been through a very devastating experience. This business with Gus has made her feel terrible about herself. She can't believe she fell for his empty flattery. She's embarrassed and ashamed and needs time to recover. And I plan to be there by her side every step of the way. I guess sometimes slow is called for."

"Hmm, *Uncle Cyril*. Sounds pretty good to me. So who was the girl you didn't get? The one you lost because you were going too slow?"

"Melly. She has always had my heart."

Mom, Dad, Aunt Melly, and Cyril departed at ten o'clock the next morning. I waved to them as their cars drove away. Daisy wagged her tail when we entered the silent house.

Thankfully, the police had returned my computer. I had a ton of work to catch up on. I settled in with my usual mug of tea. Mochie lay curled up on my desk and Daisy stretched out on the floor.

For two hours, I concentrated on the Washington, DC Celebration of Art, a festival with art classes, a fantastic art show and auction, a wine tasting, lectures by famous artists, and competitions in several categories. It would be a huge weeklong event, but I knew just the hotel to accommodate it. I could only hope that Hannah and Humphrey wouldn't choose that week for their wedding! After booking the hotel and working out a schedule, my head was swimming.

Daisy snoozed comfortably, probably relieved that everyone had left. I slipped out of my office and went for a walk to clear my head. I strolled by Dollie's back yard. The gate was open and four men were in the process of removing parts of her kitchen that had been damaged by the fire.

Dollie spied me outside. "Sophie! Sophie!" She waved her arm at me. "Come see!"

I dodged the men and entered her kitchen. "It looks so much bigger!"

"Doesn't it? I'm making a few little changes." She led the way to her living room to show me a blueprint. We sat on the sofa and studied the plan.

"I never did like the location of the refrigerator," she said, "but they can move it over here, which will give me a bigger island with room for some seats."

I worried about her ability to pay for it. "Did you sell the beautiful sterling centerpiece that Julian tried to sell?"

"I would never give that up! It won't cost any more, which means insurance will pay for it. Maybe that fire was a blessing in disguise."

"How are you doing, Dollie?"

"I've been very upset with myself. I trusted Julian. Remember when I told you I got a new lock for the back door? I gave him a copy! I went to all that trouble and handed the key to the very person who was causing all the problems! I'm an old fool. From here on out, I'm not trusting anyone."

"Mrs. Peabody? Oh. Sorry to interrupt," said one of the workmen. "I didn't realize you have company. I have a quick question about the kitchen?"

"Excuse me, Sophie. I'll be right back." Dollie rose and left the living room.

I gazed around. It was a beautiful room. Rich in color, history, and classic furniture. I could almost feel the happy times Dollie and her brothers must have had in this house. It was a shame she had fallen on hard times. I studied the portrait of Dollie in her wedding gown and immediately thought of the art festival I had been planning.

Dollie bustled into the living room. “Sorry about that.”

“No problem. I was thinking about the lovely times you must have had here as a child.”

She took a deep breath. “I’ve had a lot of ups and downs in my life. Who would have thought I would be widowed so many times?”

“What hung over the fireplace before your wedding portrait?”

“A landscape. My father said it never was the right size for that spot.”

While I would never say so, the portrait was a little too large. It was beautiful but it dominated the room. A horizontal landscape might have been better. Why would he have wanted a vertical painting there? Unless . . . . “Dollie, do you think you could ask those gentlemen in the kitchen if they could take your portrait down for a minute?”

I knew I couldn’t do it. It was far too big.

“But why?”

I could see that she was taken aback.

“I had a thought. I’d like to see the back.”

“Whatever for?”

I fudged because I didn’t want to get her hopes up. “Um, sometimes famous artists leave a message on the back.”

“Really?”

I was taking a very big chance. “Did your brothers still live here when you got married?”

“Did they ever! They took my fiancé out the night before our wedding. My brothers rolled in at three in the morning and woke everyone because they got into a brawl about who would get my room! I hadn’t even moved out of it yet. They were groomsmen, of course, and those two idiots both showed up with black eyes! My parents were so embarrassed. Everything was beautiful, but all eyes were on the two of them. And at the reception and dinner afterward, that was the only thing people talked about. Can you even imagine?"

I could. "Indulge me? Let's see what's on the back."

Dollie called the men in from the kitchen and asked if they would take the portrait down. They readily agreed without asking questions.

A stretched canvas covered the back. The artist had written a few notes on the wood. Dollie's name, the date, and *on the event of her marriage*. I ran my hand over the canvas very gently. I thought I could feel the edges of something underneath it. I held my breath and debated. If I cut into the canvas, would I be damaging the painting?

"What on earth are you doing?" asked Dollie.

I took a deep breath. "Dollie, do you remember when your dad said you would never need money? You said you thought there was family money?"

Dollie frowned at me.

"I think I feel something under the canvas backing."

Dollie ran her hand over it. "I do, too."

One of the men who was holding the frame so the painting would be upright pulled a utility knife from his pocket. "You want me to cut it?"

"I think Dollie should," I said. "It should be her choice."

Dollie took the knife. "I'll just prick the canvas around that corner. Just a little so we can see if there's anything in there."

Her fingers trembled as she lightly cut a corner into the canvas backing. She pulled the little edge back. It revealed a document.

Her eyes wide, she gazed at me. "I don't understand."

"Don't cut any more. I think we need to get an expert over here so we won't damage anything." I pulled out my phone and called Chester Rutherford, who owned an art gallery in Old Town.

He agreed to come right away.

An hour later, Chester had confirmed that an original Dunlap Broadside of the Declaration of Independence had been hidden underneath the painting of Dollie.

Dollie was in shock. "So that crazy story about my great-great-great-grandfather must be true. Sophie, how did you know?"

"It was just a guess. You said that if it existed, your brothers would have found it. The one thing your father knew you would always cherish was this painting. Your brothers would never think to look under the painting of you."

Chapter 35

Dear Sophie,
My sister is furious because one of her friends failed to send her a wedding gift until six months after *the wedding! I say to quit complaining and be friends again. My sister needs to return to the real world and recognize that her wedding wasn't the biggest event of all time. What do you think?*
Annoyed Sister in Husband, Pennsylvania

Dear Annoyed Sister,
The etiquette rule of thumb is within three months before or after the wedding, preferably before. However, anytime up to a year after the wedding is still acceptable. One never knows what a person's financial or personal situation is at a given time. It was generous of her friend to send a gift, and your sister should be appropriately grateful.
Sophie

Mr. Bernard Oliver Frei
requests the honor of your presence
at half after four o'clock
at Alexandria City Hall on Market Square
on Friday, the twenty-fourth day of July, 2026.
Feasting and merriment to follow at
The Laughing Hound.

I phoned Mars immediately. "What's going on with Bernie? I just received an invitation that sounds like a wedding announcement but it doesn't show a bride's name!

"I don't know. I live with him, but I got one, too. Are you going?"

"Of course I am. If this is important enough to Bernie to send out fancy invitations, I will definitely be there. Do we dress for a wedding or what?"

"I don't know. My phone has been ringing nonstop. No one has any idea what this is about. When I asked Bernie what was up, he just smiled and said, 'I hope you'll be there.'"

"What about wedding gifts?"

"Sophie, I'm as clueless about this as you are. And I'm in a pickle. If Bernie is getting married, I need to move out! Isn't there some sort of extension date for the giving of wedding gifts?"

"Yes. You have time."

"I heard about Dollie. She'll be loaded now!"

"I'm not so sure. She's thinking about renting it out to museums for a fee so more people can see it. She'd like to keep it in the family and that way it would provide an income stream. But if she sells it, she'll split it with her brothers. She says that's only fair."

On Friday, Nina, Mars, and I dressed for an outdoor wedding. Nina and I wore sunhats that matched our sleeveless dresses. I felt for poor Mars in a suit jacket. He carried it over his shoulder, but I knew he would slide it on when the wedding began.

We arrived at Market Square. At least one hundred people filled the square, most of them dressed for an occasion. "I don't see anyone I know," I said.

"Tell me if you see the bride," whispered Nina.

"Wouldn't she make an entrance with her father?" asked Mars. "They're probably inside City Hall where it's nice and cool."

"Uh, guys, the tent outside City Hall is awfully big for a wedding. Look at all those chairs. There must be thirty or so."

"For a choir, maybe?" Nina suggested.

Someone tapped a microphone. "Testing, testing."

Bernie walked up to us looking dapper in an elegant suit. "Thanks for coming. I'll see you after the ceremony."

"Ceremony! He said *ceremony*! So it *is* a wedding!" Nina shrieked.

We walked closer to the woman at the microphone. Bernie joined assorted men and women on the chairs behind her.

At exactly four thirty, she said, "It is my pleasure to welcome you, your families, and guests to the naturalization ceremony today."

After we all recited the Pledge of Allegiance, a beautiful rendition of the national anthem was sung by a woman, then we heard moving speeches by local dignitaries. Finally, each new citizen received a packet and was welcomed to the United States of America as a citizen.

We clustered around Bernie, hugging him.

"We thought you were getting married," said Nina.

"Not today." Bernie winked at her.

"What about Britain?" asked Mars. "Do you lose your British citizenship?"

"I get the best of both worlds. Dual citizenship."

"Congratulations, Bernie." I hugged him again. "What made you decide to do this?"

He smiled at me. Wrapping one arm over my shoulders and the other over Mars's shoulders, he said, "I think I'm going to stick around here for a while."

Recipes

Krista's Favorite Potato Salad

This has pickles and pickle juice in it. I'm sure that's a matter of taste but it works for me. Leave the skin on the potatoes for some color and fiber.

5 pounds of red-skinned potatoes
6 hard-boiled eggs
1 Vidalia onion
5–6 large ribs of celery
6 sweet-and-sour pickles
⅓ cup sweet-and-sour pickle juice
⅓ cup mayonnaise
3 tablespoons mustard
Salt to taste

Cook the potatoes and cut into small pieces when cold. Peel and cut the eggs. Slice the onion, celery, and pickles (I like the pickles in little chunks). Place all in a large bowl. Add the pickle juice (if you're unsure about this, add slowly to taste), mayonnaise, mustard, and salt, and mix well.

Peach Crostata

Make this when you have the time to complete the recipe. The dough is lovely but doesn't roll out well after a few hours in the fridge. Just give it half an hour!

DOUGH:

6 tablespoons cold unsalted butter
1½ cups flour
1 tablespoon sugar
Pinch of salt
1 tablespoon vodka
Ice water* (see instructions for amount)

FILLING:

5 peaches
5 tablespoons dark brown sugar
Pinch of salt
Pinch of apple pie spice
2 tablespoons flour

ASSEMBLY:

Apricot preserves
1 egg yolk
Sugar

Cut the butter into six pieces and place it in a food processor with the dough blade. Add the flour, sugar, and salt, and pulse until combined, scraping sides as necessary. Pour the 1 tablespoon of vodka into a measuring cup and fill to ¼ cup with ice water. Add to the butter mixture. Pulse until blended and the dough will stick together when pressed. Place the dough on a sheet of waxed paper, shape into a flat round, and refrigerate for ½ hour.

Meanwhile, peel and slice the peaches. Add brown sugar, salt, apple pie spice, and flour, and mix well.

Preheat the oven to 425. Place a sheet of parchment paper on a baking tray. Roll the dough out on the parchment paper in a circle about 12 inches in diameter. Spoon the peaches and any liquid into the center of the dough and spread to about 1½ inches from the edge. Fold the dough over the edge of the fruit.

Whisk about ¼ cup of apricot preserves and spread over the fruit. Whisk the egg yolk and brush over the dough. Sprinkle two good pinches of sugar over the egg yolk wash.

Bake 45–55 minutes. Serve with whipped cream or vanilla ice cream.

Red, White, and Blue Fruit Tart

1 large egg
3 tablespoons warm water
⅓ cup sugar
1 teaspoon baking powder
½ cup flour
1 teaspoon vanilla

Preheat the oven to 350. Grease a tart pan with butter. Beat the egg with the warm water until frothy. Add the sugar and beat until thick and lemon-colored. Beat in the baking powder and the flour. Beat in the vanilla.

Pour the batter into the pan and bake 20–25 minutes. When done, cool on a cake rack. Do NOT remove it from the tart pan.

CUSTARD:

2 cups milk
4 egg yolks (from large eggs)
½ cup sugar
⅓ cup flour
1 teaspoon vanilla
1½ tablespoons unsalted butter

1. Heat the milk in a heavy-bottomed pot, but do not bring to a boil.
2. In a separate bowl beat the yolks with the sugar until thick and lemon-colored.
3. Add the flour and continue beating.
4. While beating, slowly pour in the scalding milk.
5. Mix thoroughly, then return the mixture to the pot.
6. Over medium heat, stir constantly until thick. It will

foam a bit on the top, but keep stirring until it's a nice custard-like texture.

7. Remove from heat, stir in the vanilla and the butter.
8. Pour into the tart pan over the sponge cake base. Spread to the edges.

FRUIT:

2 pounds fresh strawberries
2 pints fresh blueberries

Prepare the fruit by washing and drying it. Slice the strawberries in half lengthwise. When the custard has cooled, place the largest strawberry halves in a circle around the outer edge. Add a circle of blueberries inside the strawberries. Continue to alternate the fruit in circles until you reach the middle. If you don't like circles, feel free to make your own design with the red and blue berries.

GLAZE:

If you plan to serve it on the same day, you can skip the glaze and move on to the sweetened whipped cream if you wish.

1 jar apricot jam
2 tablespoons sugar

Put the jam through a sieve to eliminate the chunky bits. Stirring constantly, mix the rest with the sugar over medium heat. Bring to a boil. Continue to stir another minute or two. It should look clear and the sugar should be dissolved. Spoon or pour over the fruit while hot. If you need to, you can reheat any that has gelled.

Sweetened Whipped Cream

½ cup heavy cream
5 tablespoons powdered sugar
¼ teaspoon vanilla

Beat the cream until it begins to take shape. Add the powdered sugar and the vanilla and beat until it holds a peak. Fit a star tip into a decorating bag. Spoon the whipped cream into the bag. Squeeze to leave small stars on the tart.

Refrigerate the fruit tart. Before serving, push the bottom up with your hand to separate it from the rim.

Banana Cupcakes (with or without Brown Sugar Frosting)

Makes 12 cupcakes

They say a banana before bed can help you relax! These are delicious even without frosting. I'll be making them regularly. Do not make the mistake of using bananas that aren't super ripe. The recipe will not work. Use soft bananas with tiny black spots on the peel.

1 cup sugar
½ cup unsalted butter, softened (1 stick)
1½ cups flour
1 teaspoon baking soda
1 teaspoon salt
2 very ripe bananas
3 tablespoons milk
4 tablespoons plain Greek yogurt
1 large egg
1 teaspoon vanilla

Preheat the oven to 375. Place cupcake papers in a cupcake pan.

Cream the sugar and butter. In a bowl, mix the baking soda and salt into the flour. Mash the bananas and mix with milk and yogurt.

Beat the egg into the sugar and butter. Alternate adding the flour mixture and the banana mixture. Beat in the vanilla. Spoon into cupcake papers about ¾ full and bake for 25 minutes or until a cake tester comes out clean. They will look a little bit brown on the top.

Brown Sugar Frosting

1 cup unsalted butter at room temperature
½ cup light brown sugar
1 tablespoon vanilla
4 cups powdered sugar

Cream the butter with the brown sugar for at least six minutes. Beat in the vanilla. Slowly add the powdered sugar, about 1 cup at a time until it is incorporated.

Flag Cake

9x13 inch baking pan (this is ¼ the size of a full sheet pan)
2¼ cups flour + ¼ cup for berries + 1 tablespoon for greasing
1 cup strawberry pieces
1 cup blueberries
1 tablespoon baking powder
½ teaspoon salt
8 tablespoons butter (1 stick) softened + 1 tablespoon for greasing
1½ cups sugar
3 large eggs (room temperature)
½ cup milk
1 teaspoon vanilla

Preheat oven to 350. Grease and flour the baking pan. Hull the strawberries and cut into blueberry-sized pieces. Combine with the blueberries and toss with the ¼ cup flour. Set aside.

Combine 2¼ cups flour, baking powder, and salt in a bowl, and set aside. Cream the butter with the sugar. Beat in each egg. Add the flour mixture in thirds, alternating with the milk and the vanilla.

Pour just enough of the cake batter into the pan to cover the bottom. Stir the berries into the remaining batter. Pour into the cake pan. Bake 40 minutes or until a cake tester comes out clean.

Cream Cheese Frosting

8 ounces (1 stick) unsalted butter, room temperature
6 ounces cream cheese, room temperature
1 teaspoon vanilla

Pinch of salt
4 cups powdered sugar

Beat the butter with the cream cheese. Add the vanilla and the salt. Add the powdered sugar one cup at a time. When all ingredients have been added, beat for at least six minutes.

Decorating

1 pint blueberries
2 pints strawberries

Set aside 1½ cups of the cream cheese frosting. Wash the berries and dry. Spread the remaining cream cheese frosting over the cake. In the upper left corner, place two blueberries next to each other. Directly underneath them, place two blueberries next to each other. Continue doing this until the line of blueberries has crossed about ⅓ of the cake. Repeat underneath the blueberries four times.

Slice the strawberries in half. You will want a total of five strawberry stripes. One at the top, one at the bottom, and three in the middle. To create a strawberry stripe, lay each half strawberry pointing right, one after the other.

Place a decorating tip that can make a pretty stripe in a decorating bag and fill with 1 cup of the cream cheese frosting. Pipe stripes in between the strawberry stripes. Change the piping tip to one that makes small stars. Refill the piping bag and pipe a small star in the middle of each group of four blueberries in the upper left corner.

Pasta Salad

My favorite pasta shapes for salad are fusilli, which are coils, and shells, with farfalle, known as bowties, coming in as a close third. All of them have a real presence and can grab on to other chopped ingredients. But you should use whatever you like best. If you can find a mixture of fresh spinach and arugula at the store, grab it for this recipe. I think the kielbasa slices make it very special, but feel free to substitute what you like. Do not use Kalamata olives. I made that mistake! They overpower everything. Plain black olive halves or slices work much better. Caution: this recipe fills a four-liter bowl. If you are not feeding a crowd, cut this recipe in half.

1 pound of pasta
1 garlic clove
1 cup black olives cut in half or sliced
1 red or Vidalia onion, sliced thin
1 cup of cherry tomatoes, cut in half
1 red pepper, cut into small pieces or slices
½ cup thinly sliced cucumber
⅓ cup chopped parsley
2 cups of baby spinach leaves
½ cup of arugula
1 cup mini mozzarella balls (optional)
1 cup salami or kielbasa slices (optional)

Cook the pasta according to package. Peel the garlic clove and cut in half. Run the cut sides around the bowl a few times to impart the flavor. Add the cooked pasta and mix in all the other ingredients.

Dressing

½ cup extra-virgin olive oil
¼ cup white vinegar
1 teaspoon oregano
¼ teaspoon salt
⅛ teaspoon pepper

Whisk together well. While the pasta is still warm but mixed with the other ingredients, pour half of the dressing over it and toss. Pour the rest of the dressing over it and toss again before serving.

Baked Scrambled Eggs

I love these eggs. They're unbelievably fluffy. They will work with ghee instead of butter but may take a little longer to cook. If you hate garlic, simply omit it. If you open the oven to stir and it hasn't set yet, give it a few more minutes.

9x13 baking dish
½ cup butter
24 large eggs
2 teaspoons salt
2 teaspoons garlic powder
2½ cups milk
⅓ cup chopped chives (optional)

Preheat the oven to 350.

Melt the butter and pour into the baking dish.

Break the eggs into a large bowl and whisk. Add the salt, garlic powder, milk, and chives (if using) and whisk well. Pour the eggs over the butter and place in the oven to cook for 15-20 minutes. Remove from the oven and stir to fluff. Put back into the oven and bake another 15–20 minutes. Serve when the eggs are set.

Cranberry Cole Slaw

A local store occasionally makes something along these lines. This is my version. We gobbled it up!

1 small cabbage
½ of a cucumber
2 small or 1 large broccoli heads (do not include the big stem)
2 cups dried cranberries
1 cup mayonnaise
2 teaspoons apple cider vinegar
1 teaspoon salt
⅓ cup sugar
½ teaspoon celery seeds
2 teaspoons fresh lemon juice

Cut the cabbage, cucumber, and broccoli in large pieces. Using a food processor with the shredding blade, feed in the cabbage, cucumber, and broccoli. Pour it into a large bowl. Add the dried cranberries and mix. In a smaller bowl, mix together the mayonnaise, apple cider vinegar, salt, sugar, celery seeds, and lemon juice. Mix well and pour over the cabbage mixture. Mix everything well and serve!

Blueberry Buckle

This is my new favorite recipe. I hope you find it as delicious as I do!

8x8 baking pan
1½ cups flour
2 teaspoons baking powder
½ teaspoon salt
¾ cup sugar
¼ cup butter at room temperature + 1 teaspoon for greasing the pan
1 large egg
½ cup milk
2 teaspoons lemon juice
1 teaspoon vanilla
2½ cups blueberries

Topping:

4 tablespoons butter, softened
¼ cup brown sugar
2 tablespoons white sugar
½ cup flour
1 teaspoon cinnamon

Preheat the oven to 350 and grease the pan with 1 teaspoon of butter.

In a bowl, mix together the flour, baking powder, and salt. Set aside.

Cream the sugar with the ¼ cup butter. Add the egg. Alternate adding the milk and the flour mixture. Mix in the lemon juice and the vanilla. Stir in the blueberries. Pour into the prepared pan and prepare the topping.

In a medium bowl, add the butter, sugars, flour, and cinnamon. Use your fingers to mix them. Sprinkle over the batter. Bake for 40–45 minutes or until a cake tester comes out clean.

Frozen Watermelon

This is one of the most clever ideas. I had my doubts, but there are so many wonderful uses for this and it's so easy.

1 small watermelon

Caution: Baking sheets will discolor in the freezer. Use an old baking sheet that you don't care about for this. Line a baking sheet with parchment paper. Cut the watermelon into half-inch pieces (they don't have to be perfect), take out any seeds, and place the pieces on the parchment paper in a single layer. Freeze for a minimum of four hours. When frozen, they can be stored in freezer bags.

Once you have the frozen watermelon cubes, you can make a variety of drinks including margaritas and daiquiris.

Or let the frozen watermelon thaw a little bit, pop some into a blender and you have watermelon slushies for the kids! Or take out a few to enjoy just as they are on a very hot day!

Here's an example of a cocktail:

1 cup sugar
1 cup water
2 cups frozen watermelon cubes
2 ounces orange vodka
2 ounces peach schnapps

The day before you make the drinks, bring the water and the sugar to a boil and cook until the sugar is completely dissolved. Cool in the fridge overnight.

Using a high-speed blender, combine the frozen watermelon cubes, vodka, and schnapps, and add the sugar syrup to taste. More watermelon cubes will make it icier, fewer will make it more watery. Have fun!

Banana Turmeric Milk for Sleeping

Serves four. It's important to use very ripe bananas.

6 cups milk
1 teaspoon ground turmeric
½ teaspoon cinnamon
4 very ripe bananas

Place the milk, turmeric, and cinnamon in a pot and bring to a boil, stirring occasionally. Meanwhile, place the peeled bananas in a blender. As soon as the milk boils, pour it over the bananas and blend. Pour into cups and serve.

If you can't sleep and would like to make a serving for one, use the quantities below and follow the instructions above. An immersion blender works very well for one serving.

1½ cups milk
¼ teaspoon ground turmeric
Pinch of cinnamon
1 very ripe banana